The Insider

MATTHEW RICHARDSON

PENGUIN BOOKS

PENGUIN BOOKS

UK | USA | Canada | Ireland | Australia
India | New Zealand | South Africa

Penguin Books is part of the Penguin Random House group of companies
whose addresses can be found at global.penguinrandomhouse.com

First published 2021
001

Set in 12.5/15.25 pt Garamond MT Std
Typeset by Integra Software Services Pvt. Ltd, Pondicherry
Printed and bound in Great Britain by Clays Ltd, Elcograf S.p.A.

The authorized representative in the EEA is Penguin Random House Ireland,
Morrison Chambers, 32 Nassau Street, Dublin D02 YH68

A CIP catalogue record for this book is available from the British Library

ISBN: 978-1-718-18343-1

www.greenpenguin.co.uk

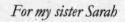

For my sister Sarah

I've scanned you with a scrutinizing gaze,
Resolved to fathom these your secret ways:
  But, sift them as I will,
  Your ways are secret still.

Christina Rossetti

Prologue

Dresden, East Germany. December 1989

The noise of the crowds was already deafening. The building seemed to shake as he hurried through the halls. Most of the staff had fled already, leaving a procession of empty desks and debris. Typewriters in the middle of being used. Rubbish bins overflowing. The faint stench of tobacco still in the air and on the walls. A half-empty bottle of vodka perched on one of the desks, its top unscrewed.

The man reached his office and locked the door behind him, the solemn words ringing in his ears again. A phone call directly from the twentieth floor of Yasenevo. The Woods, Moscow Centre itself. The instructions were clipped and urgent but recited at a whisper, intoned by the deputy head of the First Chief Directorate himself, no less.

You have one job. Find the File and destroy it. Do not – repeat, do not – let it fall into anyone else's hands.

By which he meant the crowds outside. The voices filling the air and rattling the building. The revolt which the First Chief Directorate itself had failed to spot or neutralize. It was impossible to think that this could be the end, yet what other conclusion could be reached? Moscow refusing to step in, anarchy now filling the void.

The man took care opening the safe and then reached inside. From the beginning, it was always simply the File. It never needed any other name. The information so sensitive they refused to even keep a record at Yasenevo, terrified that someone within the Centre might leak it for political or financial gain. Anarchy consuming them all.

It was, in fact, the reason he had been sent here, condemned to this curious type of exile. A trainee at the Red Banner academy, School 101. The high-flyer in the First Chief Directorate and future head of the Centre suddenly sent to Dresden, condemned to life among the second rank of KGB officers, not even fit for East Berlin itself.

All because of the File. The man opened it now and looked down at the pages again, taking care to memorize everything he could. There were no markings or official imprimatur, so far above the usual levels of bureaucratic secrecy. There was a photo and then personal details. There was a record of the initial pitch and recruitment process, followed by a comprehensive list of all contact since. Further on, there was a review of product already supplied by the asset and a note from Moscow outlining future prospects.

The man reached the end of the pages and then looked at the photo at the start again. The only photo they had. Taken on a summer's day during one of the asset's trips abroad, a break from their studying, a rare chance for handler–asset meets and debriefings. Moscow had started the asset slowly. Lecturers of interest, professors with high-level government connections, visiting speakers whom the asset could get close to, ingratiating themselves with the upper echelons of the political and diplomatic system. The next stage was already clear. Entry into public service, years spent dutifully biding their time, and then climbing up to the very pinnacle of the London establishment. The note from Moscow had already identified several key roles the asset could, one day, occupy: a senior role within the Ministry of Defence or Foreign Office, say, Cabinet Secretary in Downing Street or, even better, Chief of the Secret Intelligence Service.

All that, however, depended on surviving that long. It was said at Yasenevo that a good asset only reached full maturity and potential at the twenty-year mark. Thirty years was better; beyond that it became priceless. Most, of course, were discarded long before that moment came. This time, though, would be different.

There was another ground-shaking roar from the crowd outside. The man quickly closed the File and took out his lighter. There was a bin nearby which he picked up and emptied. He placed the bin on the desk and then, with more than a tinge of regret, lit the bottom of the File and watched as the paper was consumed. When the flames spread further, he dropped the File into the bin and carefully observed the final destruction.

The last bit to go was the photo of the asset, smiling broadly for the camera. And the name written in capitals on the top of the File. The codename chanted by the elect few within the walls of Moscow Centre and, further afield, by the highest elements of the Kremlin too.

Their greatest hope in the ongoing battle against the West. Their mole set to penetrate the very heart of the system. Their last weapon in the fight, set to rise from the ashes and fly anew. One asset, one codename.

The title the mole would be known as now and for evermore.

PHOENIX.

PART ONE

I

Chelsea, London. December 2019

The call blasted through the quiet. Shrill, noisy.

Solomon Vine pretended to sleep for one last second and then pitched to his right. Scrabbling for the mobile plugged into the socket by the bedside table. He glanced at the number, saw that it was withheld, and could already feel the rumble of dread, that ugly sensation around his stomach.

'Yes?'

The voice was quiet, almost a whisper. 'Solomon, she wants to see you.' It was always how it began. No names on their side, even on a secure line. 'Something's come up. Be here in half an hour?'

Vine knew he had no choice. Not that it stopped him imagining the alternatives, the many ways he could tell them that it was just after two o'clock in the morning and he should be allowed to sleep. But, for a professional liar, he was always curiously inept at white lies, the small ones. Anyway, the psych evaluation proved it: everyone knew he never slept. That's why they rang.

The syllables seemed to stick in Vine's throat, heavy and solid. 'Mind telling me what this is about?'

'Tricky one. Best let us walk you through it here. Not suitable for a line.'

'I thought the line was secure?'

'Not secure enough for this.'

And then, as always, the call ended. The enigma, heavy like a scent, left in the room. A faceless herald that vanished into the night as suddenly as it arrived. Vine put his mobile down and sat in the hazy darkness for another moment. Outside he could hear the soft chug of the delivery lorries passing along the King's Road. The faint murmur of early-morning workers bustling through Wellington Square. It was three years now since he had been condemned to the wilderness, earning his keep as an occasional consultant for the National Security Council. This was the tenth call of its kind. Bang in the middle of the night. No warning.

Vine got out of bed. He had become so used to staring at the ceiling of this room as he tried to lull himself to sleep that he didn't need to put the light on now. He could see in the dark. He found the bathroom, showered and then pulled out some fresh clothes from the wardrobe. The Cabinet Office was usually suits and ties, but he always tried to buck convention. Nothing too out there. Open-neck, chinos. The sort of shoes fit for an embassy. He'd never been a suit. Even in his forties, he was hardly going to start now. But he had to make some concessions.

When he finished, he headed down to the ground floor. Half hating this house. All the memories it still held. It had never felt empty when he first bought it, fresh from a spectacular bit of private enterprise betting on the markets, but now it echoed and clanged. He longed to hear the sound of other voices, and yet he didn't know whose voices. They were never distinct. An itch that wasn't loud enough to scratch. They would exist like that forever, he was starting to realize. Formless and indistinct.

He was about to try and call a cab or an Uber, when he saw the yellow glow of headlights outside. So they hadn't been joking. Whatever this was really couldn't wait. The Cabinet Office didn't like unnecessary expense. Unless it was an emergency, all precautions taken. Something must have really got them rattled.

Vine grabbed a coat, found his keys and then felt that old rush down the very back of his spine. And he knew, standing there, that he hated this life and yet loved it too. This odd, peculiar kind of torture. He took one final moment to listen to the stillness and the echo of it.

Then, when he couldn't put it off any longer, he headed out into the cold.

2

Whitehall seemed so dead at this hour. Odd, really. If any place should be alive, surely this one should. Feverish early-dawn meetings. Sleep-smudged faces scurrying through corridors with handfuls of important papers. But there was just silence. The sky was still inky, the only light the odd fuzz of colour from some of the windows lining the long procession from Downing Street all the way down towards the Strand.

The car journey had been silent. One of the buzzcut specialist protection officers who usually spent their time guarding ministers or royalty. Just a stern, humourless quiet before Vine was dropped off at the private entrance for the Cabinet Office.

Rish was waiting for him, as usual. One of the fast-trackers, he always presumed, still young enough that sleep was an optional extra. She always seemed to wear the same jacket-and-skirt combination, until Vine wondered if she had rows of them lined up in a closet somewhere. Sometimes he wondered if she ever went home at all. It was her mystery voice on the phone, somehow tinnier and less convincing in real life.

'Sorry to call,' she said. 'We thought it was going to be a quiet one.'

Vine could feel that old curiosity curl around him again.

They were making him wait, teasing him with it. 'What's happened?'

'I'll let the Lord and Master explain. But it's bad.'

They were along the main corridor now. It seemed to become more secret as they went. Less glassy and accessible. All dull browns and padded walls and decor so bad it had to be official.

They reached the office door at the end. Vine always saw the gold plaque on the outside – 'Emma Lockwood, National Security Adviser' – and wondered whether it was just ego or forgetfulness, perhaps a mix of both. Spies didn't usually like their titles being paraded for the world. Rish knocked lightly once and opened it at the sound of a loud, throaty 'Enter'.

'Good luck,' she said.

Vine nodded, their little routine. 'Thanks.'

He walked in to find Emma Lockwood sitting behind her enormous oak desk. Papers always seemed to grow out of the most unlikely places and Vine swore he could see some spattered on parts of the wall, others growing mouldy in cracks in the floor. Ever since the revelations about election hacking in America, Whitehall had gone back to a paper-only policy. Anything secret didn't go anywhere near a computer.

'Ah, Solomon. Please, take a load off.'

Lockwood had ten years on him, but it seemed more. She had that ease in high office that suggested she came with the furniture. Her CV was deliberately vague – high-flying international relations post-grad at Harvard, something at the Home Office, a hush-hush appointment at

GCHQ – which meant her failures never caught up with her. Somehow, Vine doubted they ever would.

'Urgent phone call, driver at the door, even Rish sworn to silence,' Vine said, smiling politely as he sat down. 'I guess a Cabinet Minister didn't leave his homework on a train.'

Lockwood yawned messily. 'No. Well, not recently anyway.'

Vine knew she wanted him to reach for it. A silent display of power. 'What is it?'

Lockwood still demurred, fussing with some unnecessary paperwork, the sly brush of her left hand against her ear. Those small idiosyncrasies that high office allows. Then, eventually, she said: 'How much does the name Alexander Ivanov mean to you?'

Vine felt a small uptick of surprise. 'Media tycoon. Prince of Londongrad. Russian CEO of the Jupiter Group. Owns the *Herald* and half of Knightsbridge, if I remember. Latest estimate, he had a net worth north of ten billion. Never gone public, though, so it could be much higher. Or lower.'

Lockwood nodded. 'Indeed. Close to the Kremlin, one of the pillars of Moscow high society.'

'You woke me up at this time in the morning to talk about Alexander Ivanov?'

'You don't sleep. We woke you from nothing.'

'What's Ivanov done now?' said Vine.

Lockwood sighed and yawned again. Vine wondered how long she'd been here, casting around for signs of a sleeping bag or a thermos of coffee. Though, this high up, they usually decanted straight to the Corinthia or the Royal Horseguards, tucking away the expense claim in some undiscovered part of the black budget. Lockwood reached down to her desk and picked up a manila folder, removing a single photo. She held it almost tenderly, glancing at it before reluctantly sliding it across to Vine. There was just the faintest residue from her palm still visible on the surface.

'It's not what he's done, I'm afraid,' she said. 'It's the other way round. Brace yourself.'

3

Vine stared at the photo for another moment. It showed a body lying in the middle of a room. Pricey clothes splashing against a fleecy carpet. The head was haloed in blood. The wound at the temple was visible on the right, the Glock 17 clasped clumsily in his right hand. It looked like some kind of installation piece. The vivid redness provocative against the studied blandness of the rest of the room. There was no peacefulness in death, either. Alexander Ivanov's face looked crinkled, startled even.

'We were alerted forty minutes ago,' said Emma Lockwood matter-of-factly, as if commenting on the rain. She studied her fingernails, chewed and uneven. 'One of Ivanov's staff found him.'

'This happened at Ivanov's house?'

Lockwood shook her head. 'Given his security worries, Comrade Ivanov has been keeping on the move, or so we think. He was staying in the Nelson Suite at the Savoy when the incident happened. Stupidly thought the public nature of it would deter anyone trying to get him.'

'Let me guess,' said Vine. 'You don't think it was suicide?'

'No medical problems, no history of depression. No substance abuse, as far as we know. No suicidal tendencies or previous attempts. We've sent the photo to Vauxhall

Cross and Thames House. See if their Russia desks give us anything. But nothing so far.'

Vine kept looking at the photo. 'A man like that must have had enemies,' he said. 'A Russian billionaire who shafted half the world to get to the summit. Someone had to pull him down. It's the way the game is played.'

Lockwood eyed Vine intensely. She let a momentary silence fall. 'How much do you want to be part of things, Vine? Honestly?'

Vine felt taken aback by the question. Lockwood was different now. The studied nonchalance, the calculated ennui, had given way to something else. Vine could hear the voice on the phone again and that hiccup of pressure. Unconscious, of course, but there all the same.

'How do you mean?' he said.

'If I tell you the truth about Ivanov, you won't be able to walk away, you know. The case will be yours. To investigate where you will. Down to the depths if you have to. If that doesn't thrill you, then back away now. Stay in blissful ignorance. It's entirely your choice.'

Vine could feel the prickle of nerves and dread on his skin again. The hint and taste of something forbidden. The very thing that had lured him into this world to begin with.

Vine heard the words leave his mouth before he could stop them. 'What aren't you telling me?'

Lockwood recovered her composure. 'You really want to know? We can really trust you? No second thoughts, no scurrying off to safety.'

Vine was getting restless now, impatience biting at him. 'I'm in,' he said. 'What don't I know?'

Lockwood smiled mournfully. 'In this case?' she said. 'Everything.'

4

'What I'm about to tell you is known to only five people in the world,' continued Lockwood. 'You're about to become the sixth.'

Vine shuffled slightly in his seat. Usually he was allergic to grandiose pronouncements like that. Still able to see the comic inflection, the fumbled reach for profundity. But now he watched the seriousness in Lockwood's eyes.

'Who are the other five?' he said.

'I'm one. Two, the Cabinet Secretary. Three, the Chief of the Defence Staff. Four, the Permanent Under-Secretary at the Foreign Office. And, finally, number five, the Chief of the Secret Intelligence Service.'

Silence again. Vine ran through those names. The praetorian guards of the British secret world. Usually to be found in an undignified wrestle over budgets, personnel and operational fiefdoms. Now united in the shared knowledge of one secret. Vine carefully noted the lack of political grandees among that list. No PM, Foreign Secretary or Home Secretary. Which made it even more special. No politicos or placemen.

'Something about Ivanov, I take it?'

Lockwood looked down, giving herself one final moment before she did it. Once spoken, it could never be clawed back. At last, she said: 'Over a decade ago, the wiser among us foresaw that the true threat no longer lay with the Islamists, but somewhere else. The sound and fury over Afghan, Iraq, all of it was a helpful smokescreen for an older foe. The enemy that dare not speak its name, still treasured as a possible democratic ally. Smothered with all kinds of love by the Obama White House and the object of secret detente plans by our own side. Mother Russia.'

'I remember it well. Others in Whitehall didn't agree.'

'And so the wiser heads decided to take action before it was too late. A pre-emptive intelligence strike, if you will. Find the ultimate source. Recruit an agent-in-place who could become our gold mine when the Russian bear turned on the West again. A source so secret it wouldn't even have a codename. The most prized asset of British intelligence who could penetrate the very highest levels of Kremlin decision-making and provide us with the best treasure in the business.'

'Enabling us to get back in the good books of the Cousins?'

'Precisely. Just when the White House was going cold on us, we could walk in with product from our new source and repair the damage. Spooks riding to the rescue of the politicians, as ever.' Lockwood held up the crime-scene photo again. 'Tonight, that golden source was taken out. Wet work of the cleanest kind.'

Vine looked at the photo again. The rehearsed calmness of it. The work of seconds, no doubt. Russian wet work was immaculate, its practitioners trained to move without being heard, exist without being seen. Ghosts in every way. 'Was Ivanov's name ever stored anywhere?' he said. 'Six, Five, National Security Council? Is there any way the Russians could have hacked their way in and bided their time before striking?'

Lockwood shook her head. 'Hardly. No, the distribution list was tight. Immaculate, in fact. Ivanov's name, even the product itself, was never shared at Vauxhall Cross or Thames House. Nowhere near the NSC and kept firmly from the PM's red box or any of the spads or wannabes around him. Ironically, we went full Moscow Rules on the tradecraft front. There's no way the Russians could have got this digitally.'

Vine considered the next option. 'Five Eyes, then. A leak from the Cousins. Australia, New Zealand, Canada. Someone talking out of turn.'

Another shake of the head from Lockwood. Like a teacher getting frustrated with a pupil. 'No Five Eyes, either.'

Vine tried to hide his surprise. He was trained to be sceptical of claims that any intelligence secret was really golden. Spooks were terminal prima donnas, making up in private hyperbole what they lacked in public recognition. No source was ever complete without being known as the most secret source ever. But not sharing this product with Five Eyes put it in a different order entirely.

Lockwood resumed. 'And that's not all. A week ago, I received a message from Alexander Ivanov via the usual protocol to arrange a meeting. He claimed that British intelligence was compromised and that his life could be in danger.'

Vine hadn't uttered the words for so long. Just the single syllable seemed heavy in his mouth. Painful against his lungs. 'A mole?'

'Don't get me wrong. Ivanov was getting paranoid, the usual toll paid by any long-term agent-in-place. The early excitement had gone and now all he saw was the danger. We'd become used to his more hysterical pronouncements. Every time he received a dirty look from someone he was convinced that the Special Actions Department were about to manhandle him back to the Lubyanka.'

'*Vyshaya mera*,' said Vine.

'You've been brushing up on your Russian.'

'Roughly translates as the highest or ultimate measure.'

'Shot like some kind of common traitor. As you can imagine, not his thing at all.' Lockwood paused, as if summoning the conversation with Ivanov again. Her eyes still flicking across to the crime-scene photo. The fear and the subsequent reality. 'Put it this way. We'd all learned to take his warnings with an industrial quantity of table salt.'

'But you thought this time was different?'

'In hindsight, I wish I had done. But the distribution list was so tight. He looked tired. He was facing problems with his business. I thought the weight of the world was on him and some po-faced diplomat from the Russian embassy had simply given him the cold shoulder. Nothing to fret about.'

'You bandaged him back together and sent him out again?'

'Something like that. Now, of course, it appears that he was right and I was wrong. Somehow, somewhere, there has been a terrible breach in the system. The Russians have managed to take out our most valued asset. In intelligence terms, I'm afraid this is a declaration of all-out war.'

Vine waited for it. The slow unravelling of everything that had happened tonight. The call. The government car waiting outside. The surprise indoctrination into the secret. All of it, every last piece, had been building up to this single moment.

'You say only four others knew about the Ivanov operation?' said Vine, at last.

Lockwood nodded. 'If Ivanov's theory was right, if there has been a breach, then there is only one viable conclusion. The breach must be someone who had direct access to the Ivanov product. Given the restricted circle of indoctrination, there are only four people who could be responsible for the breach.'

'Someone at the very top of the state.'

'General Sir Max Rashford, Chief of the Defence Staff. Dame Claire Sutherland, Chief of MI6. Dame Olivia Pope, the Cabinet Secretary. Or Sir James Norris, Permanent Under-Secretary at the Foreign Office.'

The logic sounded even worse when said out loud. Lockwood had just recited the four most important and powerful figures in Whitehall. The four people who controlled everything. People with armies at their command.

Vine let his thoughts settle, and then said: 'Why me? Of all the people you could have chosen, why ring my number?'

'Because no one else can be trusted. Not to carry out

this mission, at least. You're outside it all, free from influence, the best mole-hunter that Whitehall has ever had. Not afraid to ruffle feathers and step on toes. I need someone untainted by recent events. Apart from odd jobs for us, you've been in retirement for three long years, enough time to clear your head. Almost a clean skin, if you like. Only you can do this.'

'And what exactly is it you want me to do?'

'Go down to the crime scene and find whatever you can before it's too contaminated. I need anything which connects back to Ivanov's intelligence work and any clues he may have left behind.'

'You said it yourself. I've been out of the game for three years. I have no official authorization or legitimacy. Why would the police let me have access to a crime scene?'

'I've pulled some strings. You'll be issued with a Section 9 pass for the duration of the assignment. Issued only by the National Security Council, signed personally by the Prime Minister. It gives you automatic precedence over law enforcement or intelligence personnel. Top dog status all round.'

Vine had long heard rumours about the fabled Section 9 powers. He was intrigued and somewhat amused to hear they were true. 'You know how much the boys in blue love to see an old spook like me.'

'I called the Commissioner as soon as this came through. Made sure the Met put their best from murder squad on it.'

'Do I know them?'

'Gender-neutral pronoun. Very civil service. But I

doubt it. DCI Kate Calman. She helped us out with a ton of stuff when working counter-terror.'

'If she's that good, then surely she won't want my help. Spies are best kept in the shadows.'

'If it emerges that we've let another Russian illegal on our soil, and allowed them to kill right under our noses, we'll be a bloody laughing stock.' Lockwood seemed to tire of him now. It was sudden, almost unexpected. Her attention danced between varying points around the room. 'On your way out, we'll kit you up with a clean mobile and everything else you need. Just try and play nicely. For my sake.'

That was the thing: it was always so brief with Lockwood. Vine could remember a time when those in charge at least tried to sweet-talk you. Drinks tray, one of the finer bottles. Lockwood, by contrast, was all business.

Vine got up and headed towards the door. He opened it and was almost back in the hall when he turned, feeling the last echo of sleep die away somewhere behind him.

'One more thing,' said Lockwood. 'Stick to the secure phone. No burners. And, above all, no private enterprise. I'm trusting you with the crown jewels of British intelligence. Find the breach. Gather the evidence. Stop anyone else being killed. Don't let me or the government down. Are we clear?'

Vine paused, debating his final question. 'And if I find the truth,' he said, 'what then?'

Lockwood paused, exhaustion invading her face. 'I'm afraid that depends,' she said. 'On what that truth happens to be.'

5

Vine met Rish back at the entrance and was handed everything he needed. The Section 9 pass to allow him access to the crime scene and a clean mobile, battered slightly around the rim so it didn't look too new. The driver was offered again, but Vine waved it away, trying to reassure himself that he wasn't geriatric yet. It was only a matter of minutes to walk from the Cabinet Office to the Savoy. He might have been out of active service for three years, but he could still manage that.

It was perishing outside and the gloom showed no sign of ever lifting. It was that unfortunate spell in December when it seemed as if summer had always been an illusion. Vine nestled his hands deep into his coat pockets, an old habit to help him think, and walked slowly along Whitehall, watching the leftover brightness twinkle ahead of him. Billboards, garish tourist windows. He glanced over at the Houses of Parliament behind him, the place still draped in sheeting. He shook distant thoughts from his mind and crossed the road, following the street as it curved towards the Strand. There was the distant wash of car headlights passing him and now the first patter of rain. Cold and intrusive. He flicked his coat collar further up and increased his speed, trying to duck the worst of it.

As he neared the entrance to the Savoy, he saw the first

signs of police activity. Two or three IRVs and a forensics van. The entrance was a funny horseshoe shape, usually filled with endless glittering cars that cost a small fortune. Now he saw uniformed officers loitering round it, arguments between a suited hotel manager and an officer trying to erect an outer cordon. The inner cordon would be nearer the hotel itself, preserving everything they could, the glamour of the place overrun by uniforms.

Vine showed his Section 9 pass and saw the PC in question talk into his airwave radio. He could already see scores of CSIs in full forensic suits. Glad, again, that he chose the secret world rather than the revealed one. Any uniform was torture — school, funerals, work — but the forensic suits even more so. Seeing the scene made him long for the old days again. The Fort, the field. Initiation into the secret service was like a defence against the clammy hand of bureaucracy and rules. A barrier against being just another foot soldier.

Soon enough he saw one figure waiting in the middle, barking orders to a CSI who was being more than usually clumsy. The woman had a teacherly look about her, as if the rest of the world was guilty until proved innocent. She spotted Vine now and walked up to him.

'So,' she said. 'I can see you're not one of ours. Only spooks look that uncomfortable at a crime scene.' Her voice was low, as if each syllable had been tested before coming out of her mouth. 'DCI Kate Calman. And this is police only.'

Vine wasn't used to being so obvious. He wondered if it was the early morning, his age, or a combination of the two. Vine handed over the Section 9 pass again. He waited while Calman glanced at it, immediately recognizing the significance.

'Is this some kind of joke?'

Vine was getting irritated again now. He didn't like to be kept waiting. 'I've been sent by the National Security Council. I have full rights to the scene.'

Calman kept hold of the pass. 'Unbelievable. Which one are you, then? Five or Six?'

Vine was struggling to keep his composure. He could see the CSIs and other uniforms turning towards them now. He didn't have time for this. 'You know I can't answer that.'

'Then you know I can't give you access to my crime scene.'

'It's not your crime scene,' said Vine. He reached forward and took the Section 9 pass back. Then, without invitation, he ducked under the outer cordon and began making his way through. 'Check with the Commissioner's office. Make as many irate phone calls as you want. But that pass means it's my scene until I say so.'

'At least give me a name.'

Vine turned and smiled as placatingly as he could. 'Sorry,' he said. 'That's classified.'

6

It was bizarre seeing a hotel transformed into a crime scene. Vine had been in and out of this place over the years and enjoyed the golden shimmer of it all, that hidden sense of discretion and luxury. Now it felt as though the whole thing had been stormed. Even the lift was filled with discarded scene tape and a spare set of shoe-coverings which someone had forgotten to pick up. He entered the lift and the doors were about to close when DCI Calman shuffled in beside him.

'Perhaps you didn't hear me,' said Vine.

The lift doors pinged shut and the lift began whirring upwards. 'You're not wearing a forensic suit,' said Calman, handing one over. 'Spies don't get to contaminate crime scenes. No matter what sort of authorization you have.'

Vine reluctantly took the forensic suit, praying for the lift to reach the floor faster. 'I need the scene cleared. I'll tell you when I'm done.'

'And what business do spies have at crime scenes? Or, let me guess, that's classified as well?'

'You're catching on fast.' Vine could feel a mix of curiosity and annoyance brew inside him. 'Look, I'm not here to tell you how to do your job.'

'You have no idea what my job is. None of you spooks do. Fly in, fly out. Let everyone else clean up your mess.'

He didn't answer. They kept whirring upwards and Vine began to feel mildly claustrophobic, the narrowness of the shiny, metallic walls pressing against him. For the first time, he could almost imagine the warmth of his bed again, and wondered why he'd ever agreed to get back into the game this way. He could have spent the rest of his days with his laptop and his trading account, playing the markets and watching the money stack up. Blissful solitude.

The lift reached the floor and, after a second, the doors opened with a bright ping. They were immediately greeted by the inner cordon. If downstairs was chaos, this was worse. Vine could barely move for the number of CSIs buzzing around the place. In the middle was a series of stepping stones. Vine could feel his mental powers whir again, the subconscious spitting out a name: the common approach pathway, ensuring evidence wasn't disturbed. In theory, no one was supposed to approach the principal scene without using it; in reality, no one seemed to give a damn.

Marshalling the operation up ahead was a lean beanpole of a figure, with a gangly spread of arms and maladjusted joints. He immediately looked up as he saw Calman and Vine step out of the lift, giving a small nervous blink and struggling across towards them.

Calman led the way forward. 'Meet Andrew Holt. My Crime Scene Manager.'

Vine said, 'I need these people gone. If you have any questions, call the switch at Downing Street. They'll be happy to remind you what Section 9 powers mean.'

Calman stared at him. 'One of us to monitor, at the very least.'

'I work alone.'

'Put the bloody suit on. That's non-negotiable.'

'Everyone in this floor needs to be out within the next two minutes. Cooperate, and you'll have your scene back in half an hour. Get in my way, and you'll be in uniform before the night's over. Which is it?'

Calman looked around at her team, all of them waiting. Finally, she sighed. 'Half an hour,' she said. 'No more.'

7

By the time the last of the CSIs had cleared out, the floor seemed as though it would never recover. Vine tried to imagine the usual look of it. Gloss and finery, everything immaculately in place. He was always amazed at how thin the divide was between order and chaos. Even the ritziest places turned into building sites within minutes. Vine chucked the forensic suit away. He was a spy, not a member of CID. He couldn't think zipped up in something like that. They would have to eliminate his prints later.

He made his way down the last bit of corridor until he reached the door for the suite. The Nelson Suite was the most expensive on offer from the hotel, hidden away on the website. The stories about what happened inside were routinely whispered about by the hotter-headed members of the diplomatic corps. And yet now, up close, the door looked surprisingly drab, like any other room. The scratchy gold plaque with the name of the suite etched out in the middle, the silver room card buzzer by the handle, a disappointing dent in the middle of the paintwork.

Vine walked on and saw things begin to change. For one thing, the space seemed to balloon out, bloating to almost limitless heights. The first room was the large reception room, decked out in palatial reds and golds and cream, that fin-de-siècle gloom, twilit and romantic. It looked more like a state room than a hotel suite. The sort of place to negotiate a treaty or declare war from, a place fit for counts and dukes and princes. Until a few seconds ago, it had been an unholy mess of people and tawdry camera flashes. Vine continued walking, trespasser in a sacred space. Until, finally, he saw the body.

He went nearer now, still somehow unable to take his eyes away. He had seen enough of death to cope with the reality of it. Like seeing a dead animal reduced to nothing more than skin and bone. But, even so, this was different. The other bodies he'd witnessed during his career – one dead Chinese diplomat, a former MI6 head of station who'd committed suicide in his kitchen, a GCHQ cryptographer who'd been killed in a car crash – had been unknown to him. Simply cogs in the wheels of the state, walking secret-keepers who needed to be vetted, even in death. Alexander Ivanov wasn't like that. He had been in the headlines for the last twenty years, almost as long as Vine could remember. Those broad, square Russian shoulders. The meaty, silent face, brutish and shy at the same time.

Vine stared at the bullet wound in the side of Ivanov's head. This close, it looked even more hideous. Bodies were ugly when alive, but in death they seemed to take on a new texture. Lumpy mounds of matter and far too much skin. The blood redder, the flesh more scarred. No, the photos hadn't done it justice. In person it was more violent than any camera could capture. Vine tried to imagine the moment and the way in which the assassin would have aimed the weapon, how close they must have got.

He heard all those dark boasts again, echoing down the years: the tales from the career MSS and FSB officers and the careless goading of the IRGC or the Stasi. The moral vacuum of wet work.

Vine stared at the body for another minute or so. Silently storing all the vital details. No matter how many years passed he could never unlearn the lessons of the Fort. Cops and civil servants had their paperwork. Spies lived in their heads. Every detail, every nugget quietly stored in a mental drawer, able to be opened at any time. Take the Glock 17 in Ivanov's hand, for instance. It was staged, naturally. The shattering force of the bullet at his temple. Then the tidying up, the way the hand had been positioned round the weapon, the body arranged so it took on the appearance of suicide. The smaller details too: the faint, citric tang of aftershave; the fleck of mud still clinging to the right-hand trouser leg; the shadow of stubble, complementing the outdoorsy, alpha image.

Vine finished memorizing the details until he had them locked. Then he began searching through the rest of the hotel room. He had done so many of these that he could detect things on instinct. To the amateur eye everything appeared ordered and neat. But there was a subtle clumsiness to it. The drawers left minutely ajar. The cupboard with a gash of blue fabric clenched between the two doors. No, Vine was sure these rooms had been searched. Taken apart by whoever pulled the trigger.

Vine began inspecting more closely now. Seeing clothes mussed up in drawers and tiny marks showing that items had recently been moved on the desk. Nothing

ostentatious; it never was. But the killer had already followed standard protocol, gutting the place of any trace.
The artful minimalism of the search was a matter of
design. First up, all digital items appeared to have been
taken. No laptop, phone or anything else tech-related. No
digital exhaust that Vine could follow. He started searching under every surface, wardrobe, door and space in the
main room. But there was nothing.

Next he went into the en-suite bathroom. Unlike the
bedroom, with its lingering scent of CSIs and the army
of police, the bathroom was still pristine and intact. The
whiteness of the tiles so dazzling in the light that Vine
took a second to get accustomed to it. Every fitting was
new. The place looked like a display unit. The grand roll
top bath, the roomy shower, towels of every size in abundance. It felt almost wrong to upset the perfection of it,
but there was no other choice. Vine got to work here too.
First, the usual places – the cistern on the toilet, underneath the sink. Then the more unusual, the places only
spies ever usually looked. Vine walked into the shower
and unscrewed the shower head, reaching in behind. But,
as with the bedroom, still drew a blank. If Ivanov had left
anything here, he was drawing on all his reserves. Beyond
the imagination of even the most determined adversary.

Finally, Vine walked over to the sink. There was the
usual array of items. The squeezy handwash with added
moisturizer. The can of deodorant, shaving foam. The
tube of toothpaste and the electric toothbrush still charg-
ing. Vine looked at the small blinking light at the bottom
of the toothbrush and suddenly felt the reality of the dead

body in the room. Just beyond this wall. Only hours ago, Alexander Ivanov had been standing in front of this mirror brushing his teeth. Now he was staining the bedroom floor. An object for all of them to crowd round. Debate, discuss, analyse.

Vine looked in the mirror. He tried to focus but was surprised by his own reflection. His skin was sallower than before, dirty-grey bags drooping ominously from both eyes. He was at an age when people claimed to be morphing into their fathers. Except Vine never knew exactly what that meant, the orphan only able to tease it out in partial form from the physical evidence in front of him. Is this what his father would have looked like? The brush of brown hair, the pinched face, the intensity of the eyes. The otherness of the entire aspect. Not hearty or jolly or friendly, even. But forgettable and distinct simultaneously. The face of the perfect spy.

It was then that Vine saw it. Or, rather, that he saw it again. It had seemed too ordinary the first time round. Sitting there with its dull silver-black coating and its cylindrical shape. But the more Vine considered the deodorant canister, the more perfect it looked. Where better for Alexander Ivanov to hide something in case the worst should happen? The drawers, the desk, the cistern, the shower head – all were the first places trained eyes would look. But the deodorant canister required a certain degree of guile.

Vine picked up the canister and felt the curious lightness of it, even for deodorant. A nothingness. He reached underneath and with some careful fingerwork realized that it had a detachable base. Click, click. The silvery disc underneath sliding off in his hand. Now for the necessary precautions. Vine double-checked he was safe, scanning the ceiling for cameras, and then finally turned the canister upside down. He looked down through the opening and saw the canister was completely hollow inside. Designed like that. Except for one thing. A piece of paper lodged neatly right at the very top, folded so precisely it was matchstick thin.

Vine carefully reached inside the canister and tweezered out the document. Now was not the time to open it. Never at the scene, always later. He had a small bag with him and tucked the document inside a zipped pouch, checking it didn't bulk out the sides. Then he conducted one final check around the room. Every crevice and corner, ensuring there was nothing he'd missed.

Finally, he stepped back into the bedroom. He took one last look at the body of Ivanov, restless now at the prospect of what he'd just discovered. Feeling the tug of that old adrenaline. Of what life had once been like in the field.

Already Vine could hear the noise of distant conversation in the hallway. Calman and her police team were back, despite their promises. Vine checked his cargo and then walked towards the suite door. Already, he knew one thing.

Alexander Ivanov had left a trail behind.

8

Calman didn't looked impressed as Vine emerged into the corridor. She looked him up and down with that same teacherly scowl. 'Still no forensic suit?'

He smiled and switched into diplomatic mode, eking out whatever charm he had left. 'What can I say. The colour didn't suit me.'

'You spooks really are something else.'

'We try to be.'

'Find anything good?'

'No,' he said. The lie was fluent, just like the old days. Barely a pause or hesitation. 'The room's all yours. What about the man who found the body?'

'Ivanov's assistant. Sebastian Quinn.'

'Where can I find him?'

Calman didn't answer immediately. Then, with no other option, she reluctantly said: 'The conference room on the second floor. Try not to contaminate him too.'

Vine didn't let the smile dim. 'I'll do my best.'

He stepped back over the common approach pathway until he was at the lift again and tried to imagine the drama at the hotel manager's office. The knowledge that the great and the good would wake up tomorrow and find their central London oasis transformed into a crime scene. Vine wondered, too, how the rich and entitled of the world would cope being bossed around by uniformed cops. He would almost pay to see that. A spectator sport.

The lift finally whirred up, the doors sliding apart with another metallic ping. Vine stepped inside, the lift smaller than it seemed before, shrinking while he viewed the body. He pressed and waited.

When he arrived, Vine saw the second floor had been transformed into makeshift office space; almost as many people were scurrying around as had been upstairs at the main scene. There were corporate meeting rooms branching off the corridor and Vine could see a variety of DCs carefully going through boxes. The golden hour – either a literal sixty minutes, or more usually the first few hours of a case – was the vital time for any murder investigation. Already the team would be hoovering up as much passive data as they could from phones, laptops and CCTV cameras. Anything which could help reconstruct the scene, narrowing down a list of people to trace and eliminate. Vine didn't envy them.

There was a DC at the door to the conference room. Vine held up his Section 9 pass again. After a quick radio exchange with Calman, the DC nodded him through.

Vine pocketed the pass and tried not to show his annoyance. 'Thank you.'

Inside, the conference room was bland and corporate. The sort of place lined with bottles of still water, baskets of box-fresh croissants and, on a usual day, enough suits to fill a department store. Vine wondered how many meetings would have to be cancelled today and how impossible this would be to contain. The Savoy was too central. The smallest indiscretion would grow into front-page head-lines within hours.

In the middle of the room was a forty-something man in smart casual dress, a pair of cream chinos with a pale blue shirt and a jumper over the top. Tawny hair that was usually swept back in a parting now flopping slightly over his brow. He was pacing distractedly, unable to work out what to do with his hands, dragging them through his hair, his pockets, scratching at his palms.

'Mr Quinn,' said Vine. He debated which alias to use, deciding it was better to avoid a name altogether. 'I'm from the National Security Council, liaising on behalf of the security services. I wondered if I could have a word?'

Quinn nodded, a disapproving smile. 'Right.' A rich, mellow voice. 'National Security Council. That sounds ominous. If not entirely surprising, bearing in mind who Alex was.'

Vine tried not to give anything away, his expression neutral. 'It's standard procedure in the case of any high-profile foreign national with intelligence links. We just need to make sure we're not overlooking anything.'

'Sure.'

There were two chairs at the top of the meeting table and Vine indicated towards them now. 'Shall we?'

Both of them took a seat. Still Quinn didn't seem to know where to rest his hands. 'They took my phone from me,' he said, trying to soften the comment with an uncon-vincing laugh. 'Swear that thing hasn't left my hands in about ten years. I'm not quite sure what to do without it.'

Vine didn't bother with a pen and paper. Total

concentration was always more effective and unnerving for an interviewee. 'At this stage, we're just trying to establish a basic timeline,' he said. 'If we can get an overview on your and the victim's movements, that would be very helpful.'

Quinn nodded. 'Of course.'

'When did Mr Ivanov take up residence at the hotel?'

'We only arrived here yesterday. Checked in around midday.'

'Where had Mr Ivanov been staying before that?'

Quinn grew more pensive now. 'Mainly Mulberry Hall, his place in the country. Nice long drive and security teams on the gates. Alex always felt that gave him all the protection he needed.'

'Why did he change?'

Quinn composed himself. 'He became anxious about something. Wouldn't tell me what, no matter how many times I asked. He'd been getting more like that recently. Always on about his security. He thought being here, around people, would make it harder for anyone to move against him.'

Vine continued watching Quinn. Wondering whether to believe him. 'Walk me through what happened from the time you booked Mr Ivanov into the Savoy.'

Quinn looked as if he was groping for the memory through the fog of the last few hours. 'Let's see. I called and managed to get the Nelson Suite. Not an easy task, mind you, at that short notice. I arranged for Alex's stuff to be carted round here by midday, usual routine. Multiple cars. Two decoys, one real. Just as a precaution.'

'Ivanov was really that worried about his security?'

'When you're worth over ten billion, you're always worried about your security, yes. Alex kept going through bodyguards too, convinced that one of them was on an enemy payroll. Ended up firing them all and just keeping me. He even had an old phrase from his GRU days here in London. Moscow Rules. The highest level of tradecraft on everything.'

'What did Mr Ivanov do when he arrived at the Savoy?'

'Meetings, I imagine. I usually arrange everything. But Alex, for all his virtues, has – *had*, I should say – a woefully short attention span. He was always randomly booking appointments on his own, forgetting to tell me so I couldn't update the diary. That day was slightly different.'

'How so?'

'We'd had a bit of a falling out over his paranoia and the demands he was making on the staff. I said something about my life being in danger too. By his side, you know, first one to take a bullet if someone else started shooting. I banged on about his responsibilities as an employer. But I should have known, I guess. Appealing to Alex's better instincts as an employer was hardly a message that ever went down too well with him.'

Vine considered for a moment. 'So what were you doing while Mr Ivanov was having these meetings?'

'Taking some time off, if you must know. I'd been working without a break for the last four weeks straight. So I caught up on some personal admin and did some shopping. Never strayed too far, of course. Alex's moods were always changeable, that was the only constant thing about him. You were in Siberia one minute, back in his good books the next. Sooner or later I was sure he would call me. So I sat and waited until, sure enough, he did.'

'And you'll be able to give us a full account of your movements in the twelve hours or so before Mr Ivanov's death?'

'Full as you like, yes.'

'When did Mr Ivanov message you?'

'Just after midnight. My job is a live-in post, I should say, so I don't have a permanent address any more, put it up for rent years ago. I was planning to try and find a Travelodge or somewhere. Then I got a message saying he needed my help urgently. Alex did his usual conjuring trick and wanted me at the Savoy as soon as humanly possible.'

'Did he say why?'

Quinn smiled. Rueful, almost sad. 'When you're worth as much as Alex is – sorry, again, *was* – your relationships with other people become different, you see. For a start, manners tend to go out of the window. So do most, if not all, of the common courtesies. Alex hadn't explained or justified himself for about thirty years. He never bothered to say why. You were just expected to turn up.'

'What did you do when you got the message?'

'I called off the search for a Travelodge and hightailed it back to the Savoy. Sounds pathetic, I know. Surely anyone with dignity should have just quit and reclaimed their pride. Believe me, it's not as if I hadn't thought about it. Dark night of the soul many times. But, in the end, I didn't.'

'So you reached the Savoy when?'

'After fifteen minutes or so. I came on foot. I was here by about half past.'

'You went straight up to the suite?'

'Yes.'

'What happened then?'

Again there was the pause that Vine had noticed before. Quinn looked down, ran a hand through his hair, stayed still, as if trying to steady himself. Vine had sat through endless interrogations and watched as suspects revealed all manner of secrets simply through inadvertent tics in their body language. There was still something too frenetic about Quinn's movements. Small, edge-of-the-seat impulses.

'I reached the floor,' said Quinn. 'And, well . . .'

'You didn't see anyone else?'

'No.'

'And next?'

'I knocked on the door but got no reply. I tried again but the same thing happened. Eventually, I had to ring downstairs and someone got access.'

'You didn't have a keycard?'

'No. It was part of the security requirements.'

'And, once you entered the room, what did you find?'

Quinn breathed deeply. 'Alex was just lying there. It was like someone had reached inside my head and turned my worst fear into reality.'

'What were your first thoughts when you saw the gun in his hand?'

Quinn brushed aside the question. 'I knew it wasn't

suicide, if that's what you're asking. Alex was never the type. But then I had a difficult time believing it was murder either.'

'Why?'

Quinn paused, wrestling away a variety of emotions. 'Look, we booked two suites in the hotel. One under Alex's name, one under a false name. Alex always stayed in the one with the false name. We took every precaution possible. Even if someone external had reached the floor, the difficulties of getting access to the room would have been considerable. Alex was the only one with the key and he would never have let anyone external – anyone unvetted – in.'

Vine focused again on Sebastian Quinn. Waiting to see the spasm of reaction to his next question. 'You think Alex opened the door to his killer?'

Quinn spoke more quietly now in a hushed, almost reverent tone. 'Yes,' he said. 'I think whoever killed Alex must have been someone he already knew.'

9

Quinn's words rang inside Vine's head as he made the rest of his inquiries. First up was a general recce of the hotel premises. Checking fire exits, doors, trying to get a mental map of the place. Details that the casual tourist would never notice, but which were ingrained in Vine's training. The routine of the front desk, the rituals of the porters, the blind spots from CCTV, how this place operated after dark.

Once he'd absorbed all he needed, Vine visited the hotel's operations centre and got the details on cameras. The security guard was jumpy. Vine saw the usual debris: the ketchup-stained takeaway carton, a creased copy of the *Sun*, a set of headphones plugged into an iPad, the red Netflix logo partially visible. Security guards usually didn't survive such egregious breaches. The man seemed to know it; there was a despondent edge to his replies. Measuring out his life with coffee spoons.

'The system was attacked two nights ago. Full on cyber,' the guard said. He pointed to the bank of screens, the bald, colourless reflection. He held up his radio instead. 'We had to make do with these. All the porters and guards called in updates every half hour.'

'So there have been no functioning cameras for forty-eight hours?'

'The tech people were meant to be visiting tomorrow. Trying to get it back up and running.'

Vine looked at the guard again. The distance between his experiences and those of others always struck him. An ashy, haunted look was creeping round the side of the guard's face. He began fiddling unconsciously with the pen jar on his desk.

'They'll say this was me, you know,' he said. 'I'll be the scapegoat. It was my duty to protect the hotel.'

Vine had no salvation to offer and no lies either. Instead, he gave the guard the number for his secure phone. 'If you find anything else,' he said, 'make sure to call me.'

The guard nodded. 'What was the name again?'

Vine smiled. 'I'm with the National Security Council.'

He left and took one final walk through the place, checking for anything he'd missed. A cyberattack hours before the hit was further evidence for Lockwood's mole theory. It suggested premeditation, a smooth elegance to the planning. Not just another organized crime saga or a business dispute settled in blood. The feeling was gathering in him now, as it had done so many times before. Those endless counter-espionage trips. The hidden, unspoken sense of what had gone on here.

Plans like this were only dusted off *in extremis*. The ripples were designed to be seen by the intelligence community. A boast and a warning. Don't betray us, it said, or pay the price. See your brains splattered all over the floor. Moscow Centre didn't act with such flair unless it had to.

Vine left the Savoy by the main entrance and navigated a path through the uniforms and the papery-suited CSIs.

He stood on the Strand and smelt the early morning air. Thinking of Ivanov, the mole, the fear of a breach and those four suspects.

All of it suddenly sounding real.

Like all worlds, the secret universe had its own jargon. A dialect in which only the initiated could converse. Vine remembered hating it at first, the obsession with acronyms. But the instructors at the Fort had done their job well enough. No matter how much Vine tried he could never unlearn it all. Fluent in a code that had almost become part of him, stitched into his very being.

After leaving the hotel, he'd walked from the Strand to Pimlico, following the earlier instructions. And now he looked up at the building ahead. The OCP. Known in the MI6 handbook as the Operational Clandestine Premises. It was designed to appear anonymous. Yet another Pimlico townhouse with the obligatory pillars and the sense of Regency grandeur gone to seed. There was a plaque at the front, noticeable only to those curious enough to peer closely, that read: 'Office of Trading Standards'. Anyone combing through the records would find the paperwork in order. To the outside world, this was a minor outpost of a minor government agency. It was routinely swept for bugs and the top floor was heaving with encrypted equipment. The passcode had been part of the briefing package at the Cabinet Office. This was to be Vine's base for clandestine meetings and debriefs. Wellington Square would serve as the centre for analysis and reflection.

He opened the door of the townhouse, becalmed the alarm system and then familiarized himself. The house was on four floors. A small kitchen downstairs just off the hall. A sitting area on the first, a bedroom on the second. Then nestled into the old top floor was the small, cramped operations room. A scattering of desks and enough encrypted PCs to please a skeleton covert team. It felt palatial to have this all to himself. Strange, too. He had become used to the clatter and hum of embassies, or the shiny newness of Vauxhall Cross. This felt like a return to his youth, the overhang of the Cold War. Every MI6 operation was conducted in a variant of this place. The same mousy walls and forgettable furnishings, all of it designed to be both present and invisible.

He looked around and felt tiredness ache within him. The lack of sleep was almost part of his existence now, there for as long as Vine could remember. It sharpened him in some ways, dulled him in others, but there seemed to be few ways to banish it entirely. It had been his trademark ever since Cambridge. Like a secret he wanted to protect from others unless they caught up. The nights were still precious. Everyone else dozed and wallowed in their beds but Vine could get ahead of them, glimpse things they never would.

He splashed some water on his face in the bathroom and then inspected what remains had been left in the fridge on the ground floor. There were the usual government issue rations. A carton of milk, still mercifully within date. Some ham, a loaf of bread, coffee, tea. A box of corn-flakes. All the OCPs were serviced constantly. Cleaned, restocked, all in case of moments like this. An urgent assignment, say, or a sudden defection. The mother of all debriefings. The spartan nature of it reminded Vine of his childhood and that old puritan grimness, an echo of all the institutions he would pass through: Trinity, the Secret Intelligence Service, exile. The same loveless routine.

After fixing himself a cup of coffee – black, as always – Vine walked back up to the top floor. He sat down and ignored the blank PC screens and the strict laminated instructions Blu-Tacked to the wall about usage. Instead, Vine reached into his pocket and removed the document he'd found in Alexander Ivanov's hotel bathroom. Slowly straightening it out and laying it flat in his palm. A message from beyond the grave.

Vine had resisted a glance until now and looked at the contents for the first time. Some small, ever-naive part of him hoping for text. A bracing clarity to the secret message Ivanov had left behind. A breadcrumb trail leading directly back to his killer.

Instead, there was just a long number on it, bordered by a clutch of letters. Vine stared at it for as long as he could, until each digit and letter were firmly lodged in his consciousness. Remaining there through wake or sleep.

0089035TFSLL

Meaningless on a surface level. Literally, numerically, cryptographically. And so, as ever, the true work began. The process looked like nothing. Vine had seen others do it on visits to the Doughnut at GCHQ, the curious blankness to the face, the unremarkable sag in the eyes. And yet the neurons were cranked up and firing, crunching through all mathematical possibilities. The silent art of the codebreaker. Not that Vine was the certified sort, at least not according to the Cheltenham brigade. A weekend amateur, a mathematical sleuth. Resurrecting the lessons of his youth.

Vine preferred to work without any additional help. There was no pad of paper sitting emptily beside him and no pencil chewed and rechewed. Just his mind. The mental emptiness that would slowly be filled by form and structure, the answer hinting its way through the layers until it stood vividly before him.

Was it an easy substitution cipher? Yes, then no, then maybe. What about part of a phone number? The same hope followed by the doubt then the question. That solution evaporated as well.

Think. What was Alexander Ivanov trying to tell him now?

Vine spent the next few hours in his usual routine. He walked the house, tried to focus his mind on other things, drugged himself with extra strong caffeine, repeated the pattern once and then again. Still nothing.

He spent several more hours trying to decode the numbers and letters. Then – when he was about to give up entirely – some synaptic flicker occurred, and he peered at the hidden piece of paper again. His eyes now drawn to those two letters at the end: 'LL'. Every variant had been worked through and the repetition didn't seem to fit any standard encryption code. Added to that, the mix of letters and numbers seemed almost incidental cipher-wise.

And, as he hoped, the minutes and hours of solitary thinking began to congeal, until the various fragments made up something. What if it was a basic category error? What if this wasn't a code at all? Not impossible, simply different.

Now Vine felt his mind stir. He moved the chair forward and held the paper from the deodorant canister and saw it take on a different shape. Alexander Ivanov had left behind a clue. Logically, it had to lead to another location. The only thread of connection had to stem from the letters at the end. An acronym.

'TFSLL'.

Digital methods were only used as a last resort, but Vine switched on the PC in front of him, inputting the necessary passcodes and usernames to sidle through the computer's security questions. He opened up the secure browser and typed in 'TFSLL'. A blizzard of obscure references flashed up, but nothing usable. Then he tried searching for just the numbers: '0089035'. Another flurry of results without yielding any gold.

Now, finally, he turned back to the piece of paper. What if you separated the 'TFS' from the 'LL' and pondered each part in turn? Vine spent the next half-hour searching for any locations that could be related to 'TFS', then tried the same with just 'LL'. Anywhere that Alexander Ivanov could have visited. Somewhere in central London, a place someone like Ivanov could have passed unnoticed. A dead-letter box of some variety.

The second location after his hotel room.

Thirteen minutes later, Vine saw one hit throb at him from the screen. A page that included a reference code buttressed at the end by 'LL' like the one in front of him. Vine clicked on the page and looked at the square logo on the top of the website. The photo below had shelves overflowing with old, jacketless books. He checked the address.

14 St James's Square.

Vine shut down the PC and grabbed his coat, checking he had the keys. He folded up the piece of paper and made his way down the rickety staircase towards the ground floor.

He couldn't be sure. But he thought he knew where Ivanov was leading him.

II

The London Library was hidden away in the corner of St James's Square, a private lending establishment founded in 1841. Vine always marvelled at these pockets of silence within the clatter of the city with their blue plaques on the walls and the sense of history seeping through the place. He stopped before the entrance and tried to imagine Alexander Ivanov here. Perhaps it was the only time of the day when the disguises could be dropped. Tycoon, power player, traitor. It was a chance for Ivanov to lay the path in case the worst should happen. Yes, Vine could taste that feverish mix of paranoia and adrenaline, so deliciously Russian.

He walked through the entrance into the London Library and showed his members' card. He tried to remember the last time he'd been in the building. At one point it had been a haunt of his, if a library could ever be worthy of that name. It was like a safe house of sorts, one of the nooks that he enjoyed nesting in during those spare weekends back from active service overseas when longing for that heady blast of England again. The serried rows of shelving were a reminder of Cambridge, still unmuddied by the secret world and what was to come next. He had a functional library at Wellington Square but had spent hours here nonetheless.

Vine took the folded piece of paper out of his pocket now and looked at Ivanov's code again.

0089035TFSLL

He took in the immediate surroundings too: the sprinkling of people all buried in books of some kind and the librarians restacking shelves. Any one of them, Vine knew, could be a watcher swaddled in hoodies and hats, distorting their features with glasses, changing everything from gait to height. If spying was anything, he'd come to realize, it was an addiction to the dressing-up box. The thrill of imagination met reality until something new was born. Had Ivanov been tracked here? Was someone waiting for Vine to service the dead-letter box? There was always the chance of walking straight into a trap and Vine took his usual precautions. He clocked each of these people, remembering positions, checking sightlines. In the end, though, all you had was instinct. It was the only constant guide.

When he was satisfied, Vine began looking through the various stacks. If 'LL' stood for the London Library, 'TFS' was for something within it. He was searching for anything which corresponded with those three letters. He proceeded carefully, never letting that watchful sense of danger desert him. Vine never thought of himself as a field man. But then the idea of being a desk officer similarly appalled him. A career in counter-espionage had always been an odd mix of the two. Perhaps, in the end, that was his skill. He was able to sense danger while also being able to think his way out of it. Field men always seemed to have short shelf lives, anyway. One mishap and you were gone. The desk jockeys inhabited the corner offices and went on to rule the world.

After ten minutes of searching, Vine found the first crumb. He looked at 'TFS' on the note and then at the sign in front of him: 'Translated Fiction Stacks'. This was a sparsely populated bit of the library. Vine allowed himself a small smile. No doubt that's why Ivanov had chosen it, a neat bit of tradecraft. Any London Library member worth their membership card would read in the original language, or at least pretend to. Lugging round a translation didn't bolster the bookish image. Vine checked either side of him, but the space was free and uninhabited. No one had a direct view of him here. So far, he was alone.

Vine worked his way along the shelves, making sure he didn't miss anything and checked the piece of paper one more time. Now for the numbers: '0089035'. He moved along until he saw the numbers begin to correspond. Nearly, nearly. And then the number was right in front of him and hidden on a laminated label attached to the spine of a book. It was a slim volume – more a novella than a novel – with a plain light-blue covering. Vine checked around him, scanning the ceiling for cameras, then gently tilted the book towards him. He inched it out slowly in case anything dropped. It was the one thing others always forgot. Ivanov wasn't just the media tycoon and C-suite power player. He'd once been a certified hood in the GRU, Russian military intelligence. For him, the little details were everything.

Vine held the book in his hands, once again intrigued by the slimness of it. He glanced at the spine and saw the title and author in small gold letters. *Notes from Underground*. Fyodor Dostoevsky. It was a solid Russian classic, if not the obvious choice. *Crime and Punishment* too famous, *The Brothers Karamazov* too thick. The slimness was deliberate, as Vine began to sense all things with a man like Ivanov would be. It was placed between two fatter books and hiding in plain sight. Vine still had no idea where it might lead him. But this curious, makeshift code was the only trail left. Ivanov's last gift to the world.

His training was too built in to open the book then and there. Instead, he stepped away from the Translated Fiction Stacks and allowed himself another quick glance around the place. Each dot of a person was still in the same place. No matter how hard a watcher tried they would give themselves away eventually. The key was knowing what to look for. The instructors used to call them the wrinkles: actorly tropes and manners and a thousand other nameless indiscretions.

Vine looked, but there was still nothing. He didn't know whether he really was safe here or just out of form, the years of exile blunting his reactions. He shuffled along now, letting the book slip into his bag. He walked down to the main floor again and began happily browsing a random selection of other books, allowing anyone else to reveal themselves. When he was sure there was no suspicious movement, Vine found himself a quiet desk, shaded slightly from any prying eyes. He checked the ceiling for cameras and the ever present wink of a phone. But he was clear, again.

Then, finally, Vine picked out the slim book and placed it on the table in front of him. He eased open the cover and flicked through. The type was crabbed and faded in places. Words were packed together and elbowing their way off the page. The middle or the front would be the natural place to hide something. But Ivanov was fluent in the small mental biases and all such amateur tics. Vine kept flicking through the book until he almost reached the end. Then he saw a flicker of colour against the yellowy paleness of the old paper. He didn't dive for it immediately, but slowly teased it out. Small, rectangular. Two items, in fact.

The first item was a card with an embossed logo on the front. But, apart from that, minimal and bare. The second item was another folded-up piece of paper. It was almost a replica of the clue Vine had found in the deodorant bottle in Ivanov's hotel room.

He turned to the piece of paper first, flattening it out on the desk with the base of his palm. There were no letters on this one, unlike the first piece that led him here, but just a series of digits. Vine scanned the numbers and juggled them in his head, trying to spot any obvious pattern within them. But he was sure there was nothing.

Next he turned to the card. He flipped it round and got used to the glossier feel of it. There was no writing on the card apart from a crest at the top. Vine knew these sorts of cards, or had once upon a time. They weren't designed for public consumption; rather, they were a private boast. The equivalent of a secret handshake. He turned the card over and looked at the crest again and let his mind work.

He'd seen it before. Once – twice maybe. Yes, definitely before. A private members' club.

He tucked the card and the piece of paper back in the book. Then slipped the book into his bag again and got up. Someone like Ivanov would have had an exit route planned ever since he set foot in London. Modified, perhaps, but never overhauled. The bit-part hood could get away with public hiding places like lockers, storage facilities, the everyday things. But Comrade Ivanov needed the next level. Not just fortified, but non-existent. A bolthole no one else could see.

Vine was down near the exit now and pushing his way back out into daylight. He counted the seconds and waited for another pair of footsteps, the rap-tap-tap of a tail, always keeping that impossible line between distance and proximity. But there was just the gaping sound of silence. Either a watcher team had eyes out here or Vine's precautions had served him well.

He walked quickly through St James's Square and down on to Pall Mall with clubland lining the view. The flags fluttered and the elaborate fluted entranceways stood proudly, as they had for centuries. Near, but not near enough. There was only one place the crest on the card could be pointing to. It was the ultimate private members' club, far more exclusive than any establishment here. Reserved only for the invisible people of the security world. Hereford, Poole, Her Majesty's embassies.

Alexander Ivanov had hidden his next clue in a destination so exclusive few knew it even existed.

The next part of the trail could only lead to one place.

12

The Special Forces Club was located in Knightsbridge, hidden behind a suitably anonymous front door. From the outside it looked like the home of a dubious finance shop, the sort of pinstriped outfit that quietly funnelled money into unknown corners of the globe. The very people Vine had made his fortune betting against. The trickle of pedestrians walking past here, day or night, could comfortably ignore it, which was just as intended.

Vine waited across the street and observed the door for a while checking entry and exit. It was quieter now and there was only the odd suited figure deposited outside, quickly disappearing inside a cab. For a minute Vine worried about a chance encounter. There were any number of former counter-espionage colleagues who could be inside. Some soldiers, too. He prepared a cover story should he have to use one, something about an old contact he was meeting, the usual meaningless patter about how life was going and holidays, weather and sport. The club catered to a very odd cabal. The membership list consisted of serving spooks and operators, as well as those who'd long since moved on or moved up, the sort who were civil servants now or the politer type of mercenary. All of them with too much history and too many stories.

As Vine crossed the street and wrapped his coat tighter

against the winter chill, he could feel that old fluency coming back. The lies and invention massed in his head until he could slip into a whole new life as if on command. The book from the London Library was tucked securely out of view. He monitored the scene around him until he could memorize everything. Spot, repeat. Like a magic trick.

He decided to make his move, walking up the flight of steps and pushing open the anonymous door and walking in like a regular. The place had undergone a revamp since Vine's last visit. There was nothing crassly modern, but it was all cleaner and more functional. The lights were brighter and the walls bolder, as if a coat of polish had been applied over everything, noticeable in the winking shine of it all. Vine saw two others up ahead by the front desk and he loitered, taking in the geography of the place again. There was the long arc of stairs leading up to the first floor and the shaggy thickness of the new carpet and the pleasing silence. There was no restaurant jazz or café playlist. It was a by-product of age, Vine knew, this general friction with the world around you. But silence was an old virtue and an underrated one. Thankfully, this place was as quiet as the grave.

The other members ahead of him had their queries answered. Both then disappeared up the long staircase, quietly lost in the cavernous spread of rooms on the first floor. Each of them, of course, had their deliberately misleading names. The Coffee Room. The Smoking Room. The Library, at least, did what it said. He began walking up to the front desk. The staff here, Vine reminded himself, were constitutionally unable to smile. Their emotional range began and ended with the smallest flicker at the corner of the lip. Most were former military and there were no loud greetings or factory-setting friendliness.

'Can I help you, sir?'

Before, Vine had always been here as a guest. He was usually wafted up into the upper glories of the place without pausing at reception. He felt a fractional doubt, again, as if some ritual or code had to pass between them first. But it was too late for that now. The distant glint of CCTV was already on him. It was unavoidable, if not ideal. Vine reached into his bag and carefully withdrew the ticket from the book. He placed it on the reception desk, as if this were the most normal thing in the world, maintaining that compulsory insouciance.

The staff member didn't blink. Playing the game. He scooped up the card and gave it a cursory glance. And then replaced it on the counter. 'Do you have the number, sir?'

Vine waited, ticking off all possibilities. What could Ivanov have left for him here? Some kind of safety-deposit box, perhaps. Papers, an encrypted device, hopefully bounty worth the effort. The number from the second piece of paper in the library must be the next passcode. Vine decided to chance it, sure he hadn't missed anything. He could still feel the eyes of the security cameras pressing in on him. Lights, camera, action.

Vine didn't reach down to the book again. The number had already been lodged in his memory from the first reading. It was eidetic, technically, another party piece from the Fort. 'Yes,' he said. 'The number is 1475683.'

The staff member nodded. 'One minute, sir. I'll just go and check.'

'Thank you.'

This was always the moment. The surface politeness, the ensuing silence, and then curtains. The distant sound of shoe leather on the hard floor, a tug of hands, the cold feel of the cuffs, and then marched off without a word and forced to accept whatever came your way. It was the living nightmare of every counter-espionage officer. The prospect was always made so much worse by the haunting vagueness of it.

Vine tried to shake off such thoughts. But perhaps that was the price of so long in this profession. Dreams like that were indelible. No matter how many other memories you conjured, they could never be replaced.

There was a sound to Vine's right. Two suited men began the long descent down the stairs, ignoring Vine as they clattered back on to the tiled floor. They looked military, with the physical, Tarzan swagger that was anathema to the spookier types. Compact, too, as so many of the operators were, all barrel chests, necks squashed into the head, bodies strained beyond reason. The old intelligence hands were beanpoles or bellies, never in-between; they were crushingly ordinary, in the way all spies had to be, proudly featureless.

The two men left and there was the faint squawk of noise from the street outside, rushing through the entrance and then disintegrating as quickly as it arrived. The staff member was back now. He was carrying something, too. It looked smaller than Vine had been hoping for. Woody-brown, crinkled, wrapped. A package of some kind. The sort that couldn't be safely delivered in the post. The staff member seemed to be cradling it, ferrying the package across in his palms rather than his fingertips.

The staff member reached the front desk and paused for effect. Was this some final test? Vine tried to keep his features blank. He imagined the CCTV camera above him angling down now and trapping any guilt or tension on his cheekbones. He could remember those old counter-surveillance exercises, dodging Fort hands as you sneaked round Gosport town centre, calculating how many watchers you spotted and the sense of ever-present eyes.

The staff member finally finished his deliberations. He looked up and glowered slightly. 'I believe this is it, sir.'

Vine looked at the package. The first thing he noticed was the heaviness. It was more than he'd been expecting, with a thud-like bulk. Paper, then. Documents of some kind. Whatever it was would have to wait.

'Of course,' continued the staff member, 'we *will* need the final security number.'

Vine stopped and felt a familiar lurch deep in his stomach. He had been naive – too long spent out of the field – to genuinely believe it would be that easy. Vine assessed his options and tried to buy time. He fussed and checked his pockets. The staff member had retreated back into silent, non-existent mode. The package was resolutely withheld and the cameras still trained. Security ready to move.

Vine desperately tried to think back to the contents of the book in the London Library. Was there another code? But he was sure there wasn't. It was one of the messy realities of the espionage business – so different in reality to the glossy smoothness of fantasy – that errors occurred and mistakes slipped through. Ivanov had been fearing for his life, hurrying, scrambling to put this trail in place. One small detail, one small error. Vine didn't have the security code. He would have to improvise. He looked up and held the staff member's gaze and wondered how much the staff member knew. Had word already leaked back here that Alexander Ivanov was dead? Was there a silent chain of understanding from the Savoy onwards? Another name struck from the club records.

'I'm sorry,' he said. It would have to do. He looked suddenly unwell, a stoic wince. It was basic, yes, but the only way to ensure a diversion. 'Where can I find the . . . er—'

'Down the corridor on the right.'

Vine nodded. 'Of course. Thank you.'

He moved away quickly, walking faster than usual, until he reached the suitably bedecked entrance to the ground-floor gents and found a cubicle. There were no cameras in here, as expected. As he flushed, Vine reached inside his jacket pocket and took out a lighter. He had a cigarette packet in his other pocket, kept just for these situations, and teased a cigarette out now, lighting it and then carefully propping it up on the top of the toilet so the smoke began arcing its way up towards the detector.

Finally, Vine left the cubicle, dousing his hands for effect and emerging from the bathroom. Five seconds later, the fire alarm began sounding throughout the ground floor of the club. The single sound seemed to build until the entire place was alive with the thin, unbearable echo. Other uniformed staff members were busy now, dashing round, debating whether to follow protocol and evacuate the club premises. Vine proceeded across the foyer slowly and waited until the main staff member behind reception was distracted. The alarm continued and the chaos increased.

Vine reached the reception desk and saw the staff member's back turned momentarily. The package was still sitting there. Vine calculated the exact camera angles for a final time, judging his body movements to try and obscure any direct front-on view of his face, and then moved. Sudden, almost invisible. He reached forward and scooped the package up from the reception desk and buried it in the give of his jacket, folding his arms across to disguise the bulk. By the time the staff member had turned around Vine was already pelting towards the entrance, ducking through the throng of other guests and staffers distracted by the noise. He could hear the commotion behind him. The staff member trying to give chase.

'Lock the doors! Lock the doors!'

Vine could see the moment of indecision on one of the staffer's faces; the split second was all he needed as he rammed his way through and out into the open air. He transferred the package from his jacket into his bag and continued sprinting, disappearing into the side-streets and calculating the safest way back to Wellington Square. The Tube was too unpredictable. There was always the chance of some watcher forcing their way past and escaping with the bag. A taxi would be better. But it left a trace. Too obvious, too showy.

After the theatrics at the club, Vine decided to complete

the journey on foot. The OCP would be dangerous now. No, it would have to be an alternate location. He ran until he was sure he'd left enough distance between him and the club, the sudden burst of energy crackling through his body. Then he slowed to a brisk walk and paused every ten minutes. Looking in a shop window and searching for a reflection; bending down to tie a shoelace and seeing the choreography blend and alter; turning back suddenly, a purposeful act of indecision; the loops and cul-de-sacs and childish game-playing. Everything to usher a tail into the light. Someone on him from the club or from an embassy. The escape had been louder than he would have liked, breaking cover, drawing attention. He continued mulling over the suspects around him on the street. A woman with a buggy, heedless of her charge; two men in casual clothes, their front-of-house banter too staged. One old lady who appeared too young, her movements lithe and agile. Any of them could be candidates. Possibly all, possibly none.

He reached Chelsea and turned into Wellington Square and could feel the weight of the package in his bag. The scene at the club had been close. Vine saw Ivanov's body again in his mind. He felt a sudden lurch at the reality behind the make-believe and the bloody simplicity of it. One bullet. Brains splashed across the floor. Just another lump of meat.

Vine reached his front door and checked around him one final time. Then, when he was sure, he went inside and shut the door.

Finally, he was home.

13

It was hard to register time. Wellington Square was hushed. The King's Road was similarly quiet. Vine sat in his library at the familiar perch on the first floor with the curtains closed and a single lamp to guide him, positioned as far from the window as possible. After the sterile uniformity of the OCP, this was a land of civilization. His kingdom, his fortress.

The parcel had been prised open carefully. The contents now sat on the desk. Vine's earlier guess had been right and the pile of paper looked older than he expected and was curled around the edges. Though 'pile' was, strictly, the wrong word to use. It was a sheaf, both weighty enough to feel it, but coherent enough to be a single entity.

Alexander Ivanov's last message to the world.

Vine had read the contents once, then again. The first time just to take in the basic format and ingredients, the second to start isolating details. Ivanov had left behind thirty pages in all. From the dates, they ranged from 1987 through to 1990. The elaborate headings soon made clear they were old intelligence reports, ferried back from the SVR's London station to Moscow Centre in the final years of the Cold War. Genuine, authentic KGB files. Vine's Russian was unpractised, but he could grasp enough.

Each document – eleven in all – was a report on a new protocol being set up by the KGB for a box-fresh asset.

The first document in the file concerned the asset's codename. It was agreed that this asset should take on a new moniker, helping Mother Russia begin again – PHOENIX. The next four documents concerned logistics, namely how to service this new asset. It included the fact that the PHOENIX asset worked in Whitehall, right at the heart of the establishment. Ideas were mentioned about routes, cameras, cafés, possible dead-letter boxes. The next six documents were all about distribution. Who within the Centre was allowed access to the PHOENIX product. How would it be chopped, plated and served. Instructions were issued that the PHOENIX product should be kept only for those at the very top of the Centre and, for greater operational security, any information about the asset would be stored outside the UK. Plus, there were to be no careless leaks to the GRU or attempts to curry favour with the Kremlin. Such was the high value nature of the operation that PHOENIX was kept as secret as could be.

Vine read through the old KGB file for a fourth time now and felt the scale of it seize him again. This file represented Alexander Ivanov's trail back to his killer. The faded typewriter letters. The functional, bureaucratic Russian stretching across the pages. He imagined the KGB analysts stuck alone in the boxier corners of London station, wreathed in cigarette smoke, hurriedly bashing the keys. These pages represented one thing: at the end of the Cold War it appeared that Moscow Centre believed they had recruited a high value agent-in-place codenamed PHOENIX who worked at the heart of Whitehall. Someone stitched into the fabric of government who could help Russia in the new post-Cold War world. A sleeper waiting to be activated at the right moment. The full weight of it sat on Vine, heavy and awe-inspiring. He felt energized and intimidated. This wasn't just turning someone at the top of the tree. This was a traitor built and nurtured, growing into the role, able to leak out information in drips even before they reached the peak of their powers. Vine tried to calculate the volume of secrets that could already have been soiled and ruined. The final count was almost numberless.

When he was done with the file, Vine turned to the last items from the pack Emma Lockwood had given him at the Cabinet Office. Not a sheaf of physical paper this time, but documents on an encrypted, air-gapped tablet device. Small, square, somewhere between a Kindle and an iPad. Government issue and government designed, dreamed up by the best of GCHQ in Cheltenham.

It contained the four vetting briefings on the key people indoctrinated into the Ivanov operation. The only people who knew that Alexander Ivanov was a double and who had the chance to read his reports as customers. First, General Sir Max Rashford, Chief of the Defence Staff. Second, Dame Claire Sutherland, Chief of the Secret Intelligence Service, more commonly known as MI6. Third, Sir James Norris, Permanent Under-Secretary at the Foreign and Commonwealth Office. And, fourth, Dame Olivia Pope, the overlord of Whitehall and Cabinet Secretary at 10 Downing Street.

Each of them had been vetted numerous times through-out their careers. Background, relationships, finances, property, holidays, contacts. Anything and everything which could jeopardize the security of the United Kingdom. As Vine read carefully through each file, the entire thing seemed both magnificent and almost delightfully absurd. Sitting here in Wellington Square, alone, exiled, a hired gun woken up in the middle of the night and handed an off-the-books mission. Stringing together the posthumous trail of one of the richest and most influential figures in the world. Now looking at four people who could have betrayed him, each of them occupying the most powerful offices in the land.

Chief of the Defence Staff. Chief of the Secret Intelligence Service. Head of the Foreign Office. And Cabinet Secretary at 10 Downing Street. All four schooled and familiar with the product. All indoctrinated into the greatest secret of British intelligence. And yet each now with a lethal question mark hanging over them.

Vine picked up the KGB file again and compared it with the vetting files, the two linked by the passage of thirty years. If the KGB London station reports were to be believed, one of these four was the agent-in-place known by Moscow Centre as PHOENIX. Vine flicked through each photo in the vetting files once, twice, three times. He knew these faces so well, the epitome of authority and success. Each one of them was supposedly a loyal subject to the government and the Crown and garlanded with every honour their positions afforded.

Rashford. Sutherland. Pope. Norris.

Four suspects. One mole.

Vine picked up his secure phone and typed out a new message.

There was a final place he needed to visit.

14

He tried to get some sleep, managing a fitful few hours and rising again before dawn, his body still pumped and on alert after the club escape. He exercised, showered, then checked the encrypted government mobile. The reply was waiting, just as he hoped. It had the typically enigmatic sign-off from a lifetime versed in the doublespeak of the intelligence world: *Smoke signal received and understood. Armour awaits you. SB.*

There was one last calling point before the investigation could go any further. It was a favourite detour for MI6 types looking for a day's respite from the job and had acquired a mythical status within the secret world, one of the last outposts kept quiet from the general public. So far there had been no exposés, memoirs or documentaries which stripped away the mystique. Hanslope Park was surrounded by the tightest possible security and remained officially deniable. Vine hoped it always would be.

Driving was out of the question so he dusted down one of his old alias bank accounts and bought a variety of train tickets using a fake name. Even if the Russians had managed to penetrate through his pseudonyms, Vine knew the flurry of possible destinations would confuse them long enough to get him there securely. One particular weak spot was luxury. For the Centre, intelligence work had always been a fast track to a higher standard of living. First-class travel, forbidden food, queue-jumping on an institutional and epic scale. Vine always made sure to book numerous different first-class tickets, sure that any SVR watcher would immediately try there first. No Russian spook would dream of slumming it in standard class. In such details lay the secret of clean operational work.

Vine checked himself thoroughly on the journey down to Buckinghamshire, changing his appearance in the on-board toilet, swapping carriages, even at one point swapping trains. He'd decided against pre-booking a taxi, instead ensuring he had enough cash to find a cab at the final station exit. Asking for Hanslope Park directly would set off too many alarm bells, local cabbies warned that Hanslope was something under the radar with the MoD. Instead, Vine asked for a destination within a fifteen-minute walk and then carefully picked his way along the rest of the route.

The 'SB' of the encrypted message was a former Vauxhall Cross hand, now all-round fixer and Whitehall liaison at Hanslope Park called Dr Sienna Brokenshire. The person in charge of shaking more cash from the Treasury and buffing up the Park's mythic status at the Joint Intelligence Committee. Once upon a time she had been Vine's preferred successor as head of counter-espionage at MI6. She was still one of the best analytical brains he had ever come across outside the hallowed walls of academia.

Vine reached the edge of the Hanslope estate and saw the whorls of barbed wire alongside the unmissable MoD signs, ensuring no visitor or trespasser got anywhere near.

There were a selection of guards patrolling the perimeter and Vine spotted a single entry point to his right with a small hut and a barrier beside it. One fidgety security guard monitored the place from his computer.

Vine had deliberately dressed more smartly than usual in a shirt, jacket and chinos. Nothing too corporate, but tidy enough to be allowed through. Perhaps that was corporate now, come to think of it, everywhere embracing the tie-less culture. Smart enough, anyway, to convince a bored security guard that he wasn't another fantasist with theories about James Bond and Q Branch wanting to get photos of park staff on his phone.

Vine presented himself at the security gate and discreetly showed the Section 9 pass. There was the same sceptical reaction as before, the guard double-checking. Then the change in demeanour as surliness blended into a smile. It was five-star treatment from then on. The guard phoned through to the main building itself and then opened the gates and issued final instructions. Vine declined the offer of a guide and walked through. He was now penetrating the inner sanctum.

Hanslope Park looked as grand as he remembered with the large house, the crunch of gravel underfoot and broccoli-green acres spreading out in every direction. He had often wondered what it must have been like during the war when Blenheim and the other great country estates had been converted into intelligence centres. Perhaps that's where the secret world had gone wrong now. Everything was open plan. Vauxhall Cross, Thames House, the Doughnut in Cheltenham – they had the atmosphere of a call centre, all of them. There was no sense of history breathing through the walls.

He could see her before he even made it to the steps. Sienna Brokenshire was standing at the front door, surveying the grounds, as if all this was her estate, which wasn't far off the mark. Vine had never quite bottomed it out, but the Brokenshire clan had an impeccable pedigree. There was a country pile here, a townhouse there, the obligatory retreat north of the border. Vauxhall Cross was a modernist monstrosity on the wrong side of the river. No wonder she'd taken the chance to decamp to this place. Permanently, if rumour was to be believed.

'Well,' said Sienna, smiling as she saw him approach. 'At last the exile returns.'

15

It was only in company that Vine appreciated how long he'd spent on his own. Solitude was such a seductive force. It enveloped you gently at first and then voraciously until any alternative seemed noisy and formless. Solitude gave you control. Now, as he watched Sienna walk and talk and emote, Vine could feel that absence rise again. The pain and glory of it.

'A mystery message in the middle of the night announcing an emergency visit,' said Sienna. 'You're really back then?'

'It would appear so,' said Vine. With company came the terror of indiscretion, that lovelorn pressure familiar to all spies, always on the verge of some innocuous comment or slip that gave the entire game away. 'Let's just say it's official but not through the usual channels.'

'And I'm not supposed to ask more?'

'You can ask. I'm just not allowed to answer.'

Sienna raised her eyebrows. 'My security status has been upgraded, I'll have you know. I have eyes on everything now.'

'Trust me. This is way beyond strap four.'

'I see. I'm just meant to service the asset and keep schtum then?'

'Usually the easiest way. Anyway, that's the first time I've been called an asset.'

Sienna smiled again. The pretence dropping. 'It's good to see you, Sol. You know that. Sometimes I miss the old days.'

'Then you can't be remembering them correctly,' said Vine. 'Prowling the shadier corners of the secret world trying to find the crooks and the traitors. There wasn't much to miss.'

'Wasn't so much the people we were hunting, it was the group of us hunters. Do you still keep up with any of the team?'

Vine tried to think back to all those who had worked for him when he ran counter-espionage from Vauxhall Cross. His mind was almost incapable of forgetting. The names, details, personal quirks and current career destinations were embedded in his head. But he hadn't spoken to any of them for years. Such extra-curricular activities would have breached his oath to the Service. Not that the Service had ever given much back.

Vine continued staring round the place and the opaqueness of it. 'I can't say I have.'

'You never were the chattiest boss.'

'A good thing or a bad thing?'

'For a spy, definitely a good thing.'

Sienna turned a corner and led them through a double door. Inside was a small room, more drably office-like than Vine had imagined. His last visit here had been for a briefing before heading overseas. Now, though, he was seeing inside the park complex for the first time. He'd expected shiny gadgetry and tech-style decor, something like the government version of a secretive tech company, the surroundings meant to silently intimidate a visitor. But this was the threadbare side of the public sector with its faded carpets and peeling walls.

'I had some difficulty processing these for you,' said Sienna, busying herself with a box on the other side of the room. 'But, I must say, the Section 9 thing did help smooth matters along. Once upon a time I thought it was just an urban myth.'

'Until I got one, so did I. Cabinet Office issue. From the National Security Adviser herself.'

'You really must be working on the crown jewels. Tell me they're allowing you to keep it at least?'

'I wish. I'm Section 9 until the end of the mission, then back on civvy street. No questions allowed.'

'Shame.'

Sienna picked up the first item from the box. 'First, a new passport,' she said, handing it over. 'I chose the name myself. William Thomas Harding. Thought it suited you. Will for short. I added a few years to your age as well.'

Vine looked down at the photo and then the fake name. He saw the altered birth date. 'Couldn't you have taken some years off?'

Sienna looked at him. 'Hate to be the one to break the news, but those lines on your forehead aren't getting any better. You frown too much. Going down wasn't an option.'

'I see. Brutally honest as ever.'

'Why I never made much of a spy.' Sienna removed

another item from the box. 'Second in the goody drawer, some new passes. MoD, Home Office, Palace of Westminster and Foreign Office. All in the name of Will Harding, Esquire. Civil servant and all-round Mr Forgettable. They should see you through any of the security barriers. Free access to the departments and on their systems too, in case any pesky security guards decide to have a nose around.'

Vine took the four different passes, each a different garish colour. The photo had been modified for each. Vine's face looked evermore conventional with no trace of the field man or spy. Not fast-track, not top-drawer, but the sort of lifer who went unnoticed in the corridors of Whitehall.

'Last up,' said Sienna, removing a much smaller item from the box. 'My team had a bit of fun with these. Nothing too tacky, I assure you. We thought you might need a new pair of earbuds.' Sienna held up two wireless earbuds, like knock-off Apple versions. 'They work normally, of course. You can Spotify the hell out of them.'

'More of a Radio 4 man.'

'You really haven't changed.' Sienna passed over one and kept the other for herself, demonstrating as she spoke. 'Keep them in your pocket. But one tap and they record everything. Long distance too, so no need to worry.'

Vine examined the earbud. It was impossible to tell the difference from any store-bought version. 'And the other thing?'

'How long since you last smoked?'

'So you *have* been spying on me?'

Sienna took out the last item. 'Vaping device. Not a bad sort, either. Big hit with all the new MI6 embassy types. Totally usable and works as a mini-camera too. Point, tap, the rest is history. You can even build up a decent photo album.'

Vine took the vaping device and the other earbud, glancing at them momentarily and then storing them in his bag. 'Easily damaged?'

'Not a chance. Put them underwater, throw them against a brick wall. You name it. Solid as steel.'

'What about security scanners?'

'Our variety or abroad?'

'Both.'

'They shouldn't be a problem, certainly not on our patch. It's impossible to be totally sure elsewhere, of course, but I'd risk it. They'd have to be better than us to find anything.'

'And you still don't think anywhere is better than you?'

'I don't think, Sol,' she said. 'I know. That's my job.'

Vine closed his bag and imagined someone searching it and seeing the ragtag objects inside, so flimsy and vital. There was that old spasm of worry again. Soldiers had armour; politicians had conventions. What protection did spies have? Only household objects manipulated into something other than themselves.

Sienna was packing away the box. Vine watched her, not yet wanting to leave. He had been too harsh before about the old days. He often wished he could go back, if just for a second. All of them had still been young and on the cusp of something. The world had seemed more pliant then, not the jagged and capricious thing it did now.

'You don't have to flee just yet, do you?' said Sienna. 'You haven't had the full tour.'

Vine knew he should head back, but he wanted to pay his dues too. The turnaround on this had been faultless. 'Of course,' he said.

For the next thirty minutes, Sienna showed him round the rest of Hanslope Park. The decor, the style, the very smell of it was all like the main house, either moth-eaten or blandly austere. There was a small canteen and they sat over lukewarm machine-poured coffees and talked about everything but the reason he was here. And, for a moment, Vine could imagine another life for himself like the one Sienna had created. Away from London, the Service, the clank and sweat of it all. He could have a small flat to return to each day, the geometric surety, no moles and no paranoia.

It was over as quickly as it began. Sienna was called back for something, her mobile buzzing with an incoming call. Vine was ushered out by a nameless colleague and set back on to the gravel as an outsider again. He felt the presence of his new weapons in his bag, like myths from his childhood.

Passport, e-cig, departmental IDs. They weren't magic. But they were weapons. And, this time, the monsters seemed very real indeed.

16

After another fitful night of rest at Wellington Square, Vine woke early, if that was even the right word. Woke implied sleep and he'd had none. The rest of the square was still quiet at this time and there was only the occasional sound of cleaners treading home after a night shift. He made coffee and digested the news headlines, preparing himself for what lay ahead. Emma Lockwood had secured the first of his major interviews, so very different from the secret rhythms of Hanslope Park. That had been round one in the hunt to find the PHOENIX mole. Today would be altogether grander. Vine braced himself, half wishing the day was already done.

He dressed awkwardly and fitted into his one good suit. It was the last one he ever hoped to own with its irritating prickle and the throat-strangling effect of the tie. He packed the earbuds in his trouser pocket and the e-cig in his jacket pocket and both disappeared easily. He would soon see whether Sienna had been exaggerating or not. One bleep during the security scan and this entire operation would be over.

He made the familiar journey to Vauxhall Cross and, as he arrived, wondered again whether the architecture had been a joke of some kind. It was known as Legoland, the sheer visual head-turning quality making it the most improbable secret intelligence headquarters imaginable. The Security Service, at least, hid behind forgettable grey walls, batched together with the drearier outposts of Whitehall. The average passer-by could comfortably miss it. Even the way the two buildings faced each other seemed faintly ironic. MI5 stood on one side, MI6 on the other. A duel of some kind played out across the Thames.

Vine knew the protocol and reached the necessary entrance. He uttered a silent prayer before he stepped inside and then double-checked the earbuds and e-cig. For a moment, he considered ditching them both, imagining a former head of counter-espionage caught red-handed with illicit equipment and the total, whole-body humiliation.

He decided against it in the end, submitting instead to the full circus of the security check. This place was like an airport without the busyness. Figures in shirt-sleeves wanded him down and processed the plastic box with items from his pocket, the earbuds and e-cig rattling through the scanner. Vine waited for the full bleep and the army of security officers to crowd round. But he was waved through and the plastic tray bumped to a finish. Vine collected all the items and replaced them in his pockets. Hanslope Park 1, Vauxhall Cross 0. The magic weapons hadn't been detected.

Coming back here was like returning to an old dream. It was the same but different. Furniture had been moved, colours changed, the small details twisted into new ones. Part of him had almost been hoping to run into someone. He wanted a glance of recognition or a nod of approval, some hint of welcome from brothers or sisters in arms. But time had moved on. There was no legacy in the secret world. He was no more than a number here now, stuck in old payroll records. Worse still, he was a cautionary tale, youthful brilliance slipping into rebellious middle age.

Vine fought an urge to leave, forcing himself to see it through. There were four suspects to interview and all of them were well versed in the details of Ivanov's murder. The newsflash would have blitzed its way through the shadier corners of Whitehall. But, officially at least, Vine was merely tidying up the pieces. This was a review, an audit, a dusty report of some kind for the National Security Adviser. One interview and then he'd be gone.

An aide from the sixth floor came down to meet him, just like the Cabinet Office private secretaries with that peculiar sing-song formality. Vine could still remember the older functionaries here and at Century House. The Cold War had lingered with an old-school habit for prefixes and titles. There was none of that now, merely a brassy 'Solomon' and the imperious nod to follow, as if he'd come to fix the lights or debug the computer system. They took a lift and ascended upwards, spiralling through the various layers of the place, before being pinged out on the sixth floor. At least one thing hadn't changed. Every other floor had a hustling urgency to it. The sixth floor – the holy of holies – was more chapel than street corner. Nearing the orbit of true power.

They reached an office and Vine took a seat in the waiting room. Eventually, the phone went and the figure behind the desk ummed and ahhed and nodded for him to go through. Vine checked his watch. Fourteen and a half minutes. They were softening him up with a classic counter-espionage mind game before the interrogation began. There was no mercy, even for a former comrade.

He opened the door and walked into a vast office. It looked ministerial, almost, though the woman in front of him had never been elected to any office. There was a glassy desk on the left and a sitting area on the right. Art graced the walls and elsewhere was a smattering of personal photos. There was no hint of the real work that went on here or the true identity of the woman advancing on him now. She was medium height with a sensible crop of biscuity hair and a floodlit smile. All angles and primary colours. Dame Claire Sutherland. Chief of the Secret Intelligence Service. 'C' herself.

'Solomon,' she said. There were no air kisses and no handshake; somehow her voice was both warm and cold at once. 'Why don't we take a seat?'

17

Here, now, it seemed almost impossible to imagine that the person in front of him could be a double. The setting was too official. Importance oozed from the room. This was the nerve centre of it all. Case officers, agents, sub-agents, NOCs, freelancers, fellow travellers – all of them were controlled from here. One word from Claire Sutherland and lives could be saved or lost, assets offered safe passage or left to the fates. Few continued to have power of life and death. But the person in front of him did.

The secretary from outside shuffled in moments later with a tray. Coffee for Vine, a bastardized smoothie for Sutherland. Vine could remember when the sixth floor ran on alcohol, no meeting – no matter the hour – complete without that initial clink of glasses, the slurring sound of liquid being poured into a tumbler. He could feel the earbuds in his jacket pocket now too. Before entering the room, he'd gently tapped the side of both, as per the instructions. One tap to record. Three to turn off. This entire interview would be set down and listened to later. It was a small, but important, act of subterfuge.

Sutherland sipped and let the silence linger. It was crucial, Vine knew, to wrest control of these meetings from the start. There had been decades for the four suspects in this case to finesse their acts. They had total mastery of

Whitehall mannerisms, office politics, how to control the ebb and flow of a meeting. Sutherland, in particular, was known as the chameleon, able to shape-shift at will. Like all intelligence officers, she had spent a lifetime coaxing information out of assets, an almost invisible power. She was analytical, unobtrusive and, usually, deadly.

Vine poured his coffee and collected himself. Then he said: 'I take it Emma Lockwood told you why she's sent me here,' he said.

'Yes,' said Sutherland, glancing down at her smoothie and the congealed texture of it. 'Someone has to mop up the crumbs from the Ivanov case. Between us, I'm glad it's someone who's been house-trained. For a minute I thought she might bring in a Security Service foot soldier. Or, heaven help us, some external consultant.'

Sutherland was good. Of course she was. No one ascended to this office without that extra something. But Vine had forgotten how adept she was at the emotional side of this business. Other Chiefs were fine minds but woeful people managers. Claire Sutherland had made her name turning the fiercest enemies into the most unlikely assets. The flattery was already on show.

Time to fight back. 'I want to start at the beginning,' Vine said. 'How did the operation begin? How did a Russian media tycoon like Alexander Ivanov become Britain's number one agent-in-place?'

Sutherland smiled again. It was wintrier this time and flecked with a certain scepticism, her own tactics rumbled. She sat back in her chair and said: 'You have to remember what it was like back then. 2010 came along. A new decade and a new government. The National Security Council was set up and all of us spooks got the chance to crowd round the Cabinet table on a regular basis and collectively make our case to the PM. Thankfully, we still had your talents to call on. As you know, there was a lot of chatter about the so-called Litvinenko dilemma.'

Yet more personal references. It was the spy's version of flirting, Vine knew, the compliments and the asides, warming up an asset and making them feel special. The oldest trick and still the greatest. 'Did you get on with the politicians?'

'Some of them were half decent. Both of us have been in the game long enough to know how to play them. I'd been on the hawkish side of the Russia debate for a while. Downing Street was still trying to pump as much Chinese and Russian money into the system. But they also realized that Moscow was never going to be our friend. We needed to fight back.'

'That's the official version,' said Vine. 'I'm here for the unofficial version.'

'Ah, the famous Vine stubbornness,' said Sutherland. 'I'm glad to see you haven't mellowed with age.'

'Perish the thought.'

'So that's why Emma Lockwood picked you for the task. You were the only one not afraid to piss off your elders and betters.'

'Something like that.'

'Beholden to no one.'

'Come on,' said Vine, increasing the pressure now. 'You could have picked up some third-rate cultural attaché at the Russian embassy and slowly manoeuvred them into a position of power. Why take the gamble of going after one of the richest media tycoons in the world? Why *Ivanov*?'

Sutherland looked at Vine. The spy was being edged out by the diplomatic side of her, shape-shifting again. Hands folded; reasonableness incarnate. Damping down the story before it could consume her. 'I told you to remember the time we're talking about.'

'Don't worry, I was.'

'The new force of social media rocking the world. Leaks left right and centre. Total paranoia in Whitehall about the possibility of everything we did being published online for all the world to see. Going down the usual recruitment route seemed like a recipe for trouble. We needed our own exclusive and top-secret distribution list for this operation.'

'A conspiracy of the elite. How very democratic of you.'

'Needs must, I'm afraid. Someone, I forget who, nicknamed it the Elders' Committee. The top brass from the key Whitehall power centres.'

Rashford, Sutherland, Pope, Norris. The four suspects, yes. *The Elders.*

Vine said: 'So you took yourself away from any form of accountability. You wanted to go back to the old days? The wise men and women sitting behind closed doors.'

'If we did it all ourselves then we reduced any prospect of a leak. It would be like no secret operation conducted on these shores since before the Second World War. Four of the most senior figures in the land running their own spy off the books. Deniable, unofficial, potentially radio-active. And, you know what, I'm not ashamed of it either.'

'You're avoiding my question,' said Vine. 'You still haven't told me why Ivanov in particular.'

Sutherland continued. She was enjoying the games-manship of it, as she always did. Shameless, in that way, as all top spies had to be. She said: 'You have a decent brain, Vine, try using it.'

'I'm retired. What about a helping hand?'

She smiled. 'Very well. The recruitment pool wasn't exactly large. First, and most obviously, the new asset had to be a Russian national. Second, just as obviously, the asset had to have access to the very top levels of the Krem-lin. Not just visiting rights but bragging rights. A *name*. Third, and less obviously, the asset would preferably have some kind of intelligence past. Fourth, this asset should ideally be someone completely outside the usual list of MI6 assets. The surprise factor. Put all four together and Alexander Ivanov almost picked himself.'

'It all sounds very dubious,' said Vine. 'No daylight. No civil servants. No ministers. To an impartial observer it seems like you went rogue.'

Sutherland looked away. 'I must be missing the cam-eras. Which gallery are you playing to exactly?'

'I bet you wrote nothing down either.'

'Get off your high horse, please. It really doesn't suit you. Look, OK, we didn't want some clunky inquiry being splashed across the front page of the *Sun*. We took sensible precautions, just as you would have done in my position. Moscow already seemed to have its claws in every area of British life. Few areas – only the blockbuster secrets – were still ours. We wanted to keep it that way.'

The sly dig again, reminding Vine of his failures. He said: 'The voters may disagree.'

'This is espionage, not *Question Time*. I don't answer to the voters, thank goodness.'

'How were the spoils divided?'

'Logically, I suppose. The Cabinet Secretary would handle the political side. The Foreign Office Permanent Under-Secretary the foreign affairs material, Chief of the Defence Staff the military and GRU-related product, and anything relating to the SVR would be my domain. It would be the perfect operation.'

Vine nodded. 'Until the asset in question ended up with his brains blown out on the floor of the Savoy Hotel.'

Sutherland looked mournful now and haunted too. The reality of all the games she played. 'Yes. Until that.'

Vine waited, letting the blow land, before saying: 'Of course, there's one key figure in all this you're missing out.' He looked at her, watching the first crease of doubt on her face. 'Why don't we talk about your husband?'

18

No matter how much he tried, Vine could feel his studied detachment soften now. Nothing else could quite compare to this. No other stimulant repeated the sheer excitement and the pull of something forbidden. Interrogation was the one part of the counter-espionage job he had most savoured, whittling away the lies and exposing the raw, messy truth. The battle between competitors with both of them trying to outdo the other.

He breathed slowly and pinched his skin and thought of all those old techniques from the Fort. Then he concentrated on Sutherland again. He couldn't let her win. She sat back a fraction now and tensed up unconsciously, flutters of movement with her hands.

'I never put you down for a sexist, Solomon,' she said. 'But we all have hidden depths, I suppose.'

The personal attack was pre-prepared, he could tell. Like all great case officers, Sutherland had aimed it well, adapted the insult to the asset. Vine wasn't married. There was no partner or kids running wild at home. It was a good smear to fling and try to frighten him off the question, scuttling back to safety.

'My question isn't sexist.'

'Would you be asking a man in my position about his wife?'

'If his wife was a fund manager with substantial investments in Moscow and Beijing, I would, yes.'

Sutherland didn't respond. Instead, she folded her arms, a classic defensive posture; she was seemingly bored and irritated by Vine's ongoing presence here, which was just the way he wanted it. The first rule of interrogation was never to let the interviewee feel comfortable.

Sutherland sighed and said: 'Look, China will soon become the world's largest economy.'

'Yes. Having served in over twenty countries around the world, I was, surprisingly, aware of that fact.'

'My husband also invests in oil and gas. Russia happens to be one of the world's top exporters.'

'You shock me.'

'I see you've added sarcasm to your repertoire.'

'One of the joys of retirement.'

Sutherland kept glancing to the side of the room, pausing over the decorative features on the walls. Vine wondered again if the room was bugged. Microphones turned on at the Chief's nod to be listened to later. She said: 'What exactly is it that you're accusing me of?'

'I don't remember accusing you of anything. Unless there's something I *should* be accusing you of?'

'I've been vetted to within an inch of my life, Solomon. The government knows every song I listen to, every holiday I've ever been on, my credit-card history and my favourite supermarket. It knows more about my husband's business investments than he probably does.'

Vine nodded and considered, working up to his next question. 'What about 2009?'

Sutherland rubbed at her eyes. 'You clearly have more time on your hands than I do. How on earth is that relevant to the death of Alex Ivanov?'

'In 2009, right after the financial crash, your husband's company was on the brink. They'd been wiped out in the subprime crisis and were days away from going bust. Six months later, the firm was back in rude health and had switched its focus. No more subprime nonsense. It went on a hiring spree, opened up offices around the world. Just at the time you returned from a spell at the Joint Intelligence Committee and came back here as Deputy Director of the Service.'

'My husband is a very resourceful man,' she said. 'He adapted to circumstances and saw off the threat. That's why I married him.'

'Either a very lucky man, yes, or Lazarus himself,' said Vine. 'It appears he'd been saved by a mysterious investor – or group of investors – who plugged the gap and tided him over. We know the account number, sure, but the ultimate beneficial owner of the account remains hidden.'

'That's routine,' she said. 'You know the financial world as well as anyone. We're the shell company capital of the world for a reason.'

'I suppose it's just a coincidence then?'

'Like so much of life.'

'Your husband gets a mysterious new investor and then pivots his fund to focus almost exclusively on energy with substantial interests in Russia.'

'You *are* accusing me of something?'

Vine had analysed how to frame it ever since doing

the research. With a civilian interviewee he would have approached it more gingerly, tried to gull them into an indiscretion. But Claire Sutherland knew too much and was versed in the same tricks of the trade. 'Back then, perhaps it seemed innocent. We know the Russians have bought their way into every legitimate sphere of society. Mansions in Belgravia, peerages in the House of Lords, front-row seats at the donor dinners with the PM on one side and the Home Secretary on the other.'

'Solomon Vine the conspiracy theorist. What an unlikely departure.'

'You're a Crown servant. This job doesn't pay the bills. If your husband's fund had gone under, you'd have lost everything. His reputation would have been eviscerated for good, and you'd have been forced to leave the job you loved to sing for your supper in the private sector. Kids out of their prep schools, house on the market, debts up to your eyeballs. That mystery investor was like Mary Poppins and Santa Claus all at once.'

'I see. So what's your theory? I pop down with my official driver and pass brown envelopes to dodgy men in raincoats, do I? My way of saying thank you.'

This was the moment, Vine knew, the climactic surge at the end of every interrogation when voices were raised and the room became smaller, constricting the interviewee and forcing them into a mistake.

He leaned forward and his voice dropped to a whisper. 'No,' he said. 'You do nothing. That's the beauty of it. They do nothing. You continue with your job and rise to the very top and all is well with the world. And then – just once, when the moment comes – you're allowed one indiscretion. No papers, no microfilm, no secret cameras or things hidden in diplomatic bags. Merely a name whispered in the right ear at a dinner party. A nod or a look when someone is mentioned. And then, somewhere else, a deed is done. No one else ever knows. No one else ever will. But *you* do.'

'You're accusing me of helping take out Alexander Ivanov?'

'Did you?'

'I was the architect of the Elders, for heaven's sake. Ivanov was *my* joe. Why on earth would I give him away?'

'Because there's more to life than this job,' said Vine. 'It takes a lot and gives very little back. You had to protect yourself for a change. No one else ever would. You were simply looking after number one.'

And now, as he heard activity build outside, Vine knew his time was nearly up. Sutherland didn't say anything immediately. The silence was sharper than before.

'I had nothing to do with the death of Ivanov,' she said again, as if the statement made it so. 'I didn't even make the initial approach to him.'

Vine held her gaze, slowly taking it in. 'No? Who did?'

'Max,' she said. 'It was always Max.'

And, just like that, the moment was gone. Sutherland recovering, Vine sitting back. He saw the intensity had flustered his opponent, revealing an early weakness. The man who'd recommended Ivanov become an agent-in-place, who started the process which saw that agent lying dead in a London hotel room, was the Chief of the Defence Staff himself. General Sir Max Rashford.

Suspect number two.

The next interview.

19

Vine left Vauxhall Cross and walked back to Whitehall. The sensitivity of the Ivanov operation meant it had to be measured in hours rather than days and the interviews had been arranged to quickly follow each other. Finding the truth was like trying to trap water: one missed second and it was gone.

As he reached Whitehall and entered the Ministry of Defence building, Vine ran through mentally what he'd read about Max Rashford. There were the many recycled tales about heroics in the first Gulf War, putting his name on the map for the first time, and the stellar ascent ever since in Afghan, Iraq and Libya. Whitehall had categorized him as a charmer, the sort of military top brass who could be presentable with the political and mandarin classes. Spooks were always easier to read, despite their training. The military types were more stubbornly difficult. They were open and closed, always strategizing.

Vine was shown up to the office and endured the familiar wait. Finally, the office door opened and Rashford himself emerged. A general, Vine reminded himself, though Rashford was only a decade older than he was. Vine had that sinking feeling again, unable to slow time down. Generals and police officers, the whole world in fact, were getting younger. Rashford sent another visitor on their way with an effusive handshake and then turned to Vine. His voice, like the man himself, was loud and confident with a peacocky showmanship about it.

'Mr Vine, of course,' he said. 'Such a bore keeping you waiting. Please, please, come on in.'

The handshake was of a piece, a bearish, bone-shattering squeeze, the back of the hand lightly furred with jet-black hair. Rashford was dressed in shirtsleeves. Vine followed through into the Chief of Staff's office and noted the contrast with this morning. There were gold-framed paintings on the walls and framed photos propped on the desk and a sense of order and military neatness everywhere. There was a triumphant swagger to it as well, a lingering and suppressed violence always near the surface.

Heat was pounding from radiators and they took their seats in front of the unlit fireplace. Vine declined the option of more drinks. The vista from the office, looking across the Thames and the South Bank, gave any visitor a curious aura of power, as if this place controlled and protected it all. Which, Vine supposed, once upon a time it did.

In person Rashford was even more imposing than his photo suggested. He was more finessed too, with a clear and slightly distracting attention to personal grooming. His thatch of darkish hair was swept back and silvering at the edges. His cheeks were dotted with designer stubble expertly trimmed and camera-ready. The gym-toned torso was clearly visible underneath the shirt.

'Solomon Vine,' said Rashford. 'Sol . . . right?'

There it was from the start. That barrack-room mateyness, as if they were both sharing an afternoon pint down at the Red Lion. The accent was triangulated, halfway between Sandhurst posh and estuary twang, straining for normality.

'Solomon,' said Vine. 'Do you prefer General, Sir Max or Rashford?'

'I'm easy,' said Rashford, flashing those pearly-white teeth again. 'Sounds silly being in the army and all that, but the whole protocol thing bores the pants off me. Sometimes think I should have been in your world. No ranks, no salutes, no morning parades freezing your backside off. The full 007. Don't worry, I won't do the licence-to-kill joke.'

'For the record, I don't,' said Vine.

Rashford laughed, the smile still in evidence. 'For the record, I do,' he said. 'Though, between us, who knows what the hell else will go now. The woke warriors rule the universe. Soon I'll be telling the troops to head into battle with a bunch of avocados. Engaging the enemy will be called out as a micro-aggression. We'll have to send the SAS for re-education.'

It was the great paradox of the army high command, Vine knew. To the world they had to be socially fluent, right-on, in step with the people they were meant to defend. Behind closed doors, however, they were trained to kill. The jokes were deliberately taboo-busting. Rashford was tempting him, trying to get a reaction and forge some kind of subversive bond. Like two kids smoking behind the bike sheds.

Vine dropped the first question almost casually. 'I want to start with the approach to Alexander Ivanov,' he said. 'Why do you think you were chosen to make the pitch?'

Rashford's eyes widened at the suddenness of the question. No warm up, straight to it. 'I see. Right in the deep end then, Sol. Easy does it.'

He was nervous, Vine could tell. The nickname thing was a proxy for trying to impose himself on the situation. The jokes, too. Anything to dilute the seriousness of this.

'Not rock, paper, scissors then?' said Vine.

'Might as bloody well have been.'

'Where did the initial recruitment take place?'

'Davos,' said Rashford. 'I'd been ordered off to drum up interest in British arms contractors and mingle with the banking classes. Put away the uniform and show that the British military could do the whole plutocrat scene. Ivanov was also at Davos and it seemed the best moment.'

'Had you met before the pitch at Davos?'

'No.'

'What happened at the conference?'

Now the details seemed to come more easily for Rashford. The initial hesitancy was replaced by a fireside voice. No spook or soldier could ever resist narrating a history of their own triumphs. He said: 'I arrived and glimpsed Ivanov a few times, got a sense of his schedule. Alex was there to participate in a panel on the media. My mission was to flutter my eyelashes and do the business.'

Vine didn't want to let Rashford wriggle out. Bland generalities were the last refuge of the guilty interviewee.

He pressed harder. 'So you made your approach on the second night?'

Rashford nodded. 'Ivanov's panel was over. He'd been like a monk and drunk nothing the previous evening. But I knew he wouldn't be able to resist that second night. Never get between a Russian and a decent bottle of vino.'

'How was Ivanov when you first spoke to him?'

Rashford tilted his head back. He sighed. Then he said: 'You know, that was the first sign for me. The whole incredible idea of it – what became the Elders' operation – might actually bloody work. We began talking like old friends. Not stupid stuff, either. He seemed interested in stories he'd read about the British military – weapons, special forces, the changing nature of warfare. We were multiple martinis in by that point. He was weakening, I could tell. So I began feeding him the first morsel from the Elders to see if the bloke would bite.'

'This was improvising or all worked out beforehand?'

'Seat of my pants the entire way,' he said. 'Only method that works for me. I looked Ivanov in the eye and told him plainly that people in high places in the British establishment were looking to make further connections with Moscow. Someone who had clout with the Kremlin. And if that certain someone maintained access and influence, the British establishment could guarantee safe passage when – *if* – the vital moment came. The full Gordievsky, including for his extended family.'

Vine imagined Alexander Ivanov – former hood, now shiny and newly minted billionaire – in the snow-covered retreat at Davos, several drinks in, hearing this for the first time. Recognizing the pitch, interpreting the spy dialect. Words he had expected, perhaps even longed, to hear. It was the decision all spies – no matter how long retired – were eventually forced to make. Loyalty or betrayal. Peril or safety. Which compromise was acceptable and which one was not.

'That night was your first encounter with Russian intelligence?'

Rashford smiled. 'As I far as I know, yes.'

'Any first-night nerves?'

'Trembling like a leaf,' said Rashford, smiling again and teasing at his knuckles, producing an audible click. He looked up and away, burrowing down even further into his memory. 'I tried to shut up after that and get his tongue wagging. My grand conclusion was that he would have to agree to pass the British side key information about the Kremlin's future plans, both military and political.'

Vine pictured the scene again now as the memories of his own experience returned to him. The first pitch, the silence that followed, those awful few seconds when any number of horrors were still possible. It was one of the rituals of any decent intelligence officer. So close to romance with the fear of rejection or, worse, of total apathy.

'That sounds painfully direct.'

'I was being careful. And, of course, Alex responded like an old pro,' he said. 'He was trained. Only amateurs reveal themselves and I never expected any flood of emotion. He had the best poker face I'd seen for a very long time. He took a final sip of his Martini and said he would have to sleep on it. Roll it around. He was a businessman. He never committed himself in the meeting.'

'It was really that easy?'

'Or I'm really that good, yes. That night, in my room, I used the secure protocol to contact the Elders and update them. In the worst-case scenario, we'd blown our chance and Ivanov fled. Best case, we got a thumbs up the next morning.'

'You really thought nothing in his reaction was suspicious?'

Rashford flashed that mercurial smile again; it was like a trademark. 'I had no reason to,' he said. 'Sure enough, the next morning the world changed forever. The magic had worked and the Ivanov operation was officially born.'

Vine waited. 'I see.'

Rashford was annoyed now, rattled by Vine's tone. 'You sound suspicious of me,' he said. 'I feel like the naughty kid at the back of the class. What have I done wrong this time?'

'I've been reading your vetting file,' said Vine. 'And I'm curious.'

'About what?'

Vine looked at him without flinching. 'I'm curious about why you're lying to me.'

20

Vine let a moment of silence fall. Outside he could hear the faint chug of traffic, largely muffled by the glass. The swirl of Westminster was all around them, with New Scotland Yard, Portcullis House, the Palace of Westminster and the Abbey. Vine was struck again by the sheer audacity of the entire enterprise. To sit here, ensconced within the beating heart of the British establishment, while pledging allegiance to a foreign power. That took a certain type of person. Not someone who enjoyed fear, but someone who needed it. Someone who craved adrenaline like a drug.

Vine turned back to Rashford. He looked scratchier now, not used to having his authority or position questioned. He was always the one who dished out orders and expected total obedience in return. There was a wounded swagger about him.

'I'm not sure I like what that's implying,' said Rashford at last.

Vine kept his voice low, even, emotionless. 'I didn't ask what you liked. I asked why you lied. The Ivanov pitch wasn't your first encounter with Russian intelligence. Far from it.'

Rashford leaned forward in his chair now, elbows on his knees. There was that switch again, anger replaced by bargaining and a determination not to lose his cool.

'Listen, Sol, go easy on a fellow compatriot, OK? I feel like I'm on bloody *Mastermind* here. I thought this was a friendly confab, not two rounds with the grand inquisitor.'

It was a trait, Vine saw now. Whenever Rashford felt cornered, he tried to turn on the charm. Anger was too obvious. The matey patter was more subtle.

'Tell me what happened in East Berlin?'

'For a spy, you know, you're very absolute. I thought you MI6 types were meant to be all smarm and grease. Butter me up and send me into the great beyond.'

Vine pressed on, knowing he was rattling Rashford now. 'Do you want to tell me the truth about East Berlin or should I give you a refresher?'

'You've clearly been swatting up.'

Firmer now. 'There seems to be one thing your official biographies miss out. It's quite a large gap, as it turns out. There was one point in your career when you were considered more a liability than a hero?'

'No, please, not that rubbish about the papers again.'

'In 1988, while part of the Defence Intelligence Staff, you took out top-secret documents from the East Berlin embassy against all protocol. Some of the papers were later found in a restaurant toilet and were about to be published by a Reuters journalist who was eating at the same restaurant. The top-secret documents related to highly sensitive intelligence about troop movements.'

'That whole saga was cock-up not conspiracy, trust me, Sol. A simple, if regrettable, human error.'

'You were court-martialled.'

'It was a shedload more complicated than you're claiming.'

'Of course, if the story had been published with Reuters you would have been thrown out of the army. Instead, you got a slap on the wrist and the lightest possible punishment. Quite a comeback, considering.'

'Which, my friend, tells you all you need to know. There is no story here.'

'Unless something else really happened that night,' said Vine.

Rashford sat back, yawning for effect. 'Don't tell me, I'm meant to guess now, am I?'

'We know GRU officers tailed all defence attachés round East Berlin,' said Vine. 'Either you were planning to shop the papers to a contact, or you were careless and the GRU stepped in to save your blushes.'

'I see. Now we're going into science fiction. Next there'll be spaceships ready to beam me up to Mars.'

'You still haven't answered my first question. Why lie to me?'

'OK, OK. You've clearly got a bee in your bonnet on this. Let's get things straight, Sol. "Lie" is a very misleading word. The documents were slightly on the sensitive side, yes, but not the nuclear codes, right? Technically I should have stayed and trawled through them at the office. Bad Max. But the office was a hole and we were pretty sure the Stasi had rigged the place from top to bottom anyway. So heading out with some weekend reading was standard procedure, even if no one had officially updated the damn manual. Yes, I mucked up royally on leaving my bag at the restaurant. The Reuters journo couldn't understand the acronyms anyway, so the risk was always minimal. He realized his patriotic duty was to hand the docs back. I made one small error and it nearly cost me everything. But that's all it was. An *error.*'

'It was really the Reuters journalist discovering his better side?' said Vine. 'It wasn't the GRU pressuring him and saving your skin?'

'You've read too many spy stories,' said Rashford.

'Perhaps the Reuters journalist was merely cover. A GRU man trailing you around town and waiting for an error. They have the documents; they hand them back in. They helped you and now you have to help them. Quid pro quo.'

Rashford looked melancholy for a moment, staring down at his shoes. 'You know what? Damn it, you're right. Funny, I always knew this day would come. I've been dreading it for thirty years. They've promised me an apartment near Red Square and a chestful of medals when I defect. The only thing I'll miss is the cricket and my favourite type of marmalade. Kids, too, probably. But don't tell them that.'

'You think this is a joke?'

'Sol, Solomon, Mr Vine . . . I generously agreed to be interviewed to help find the truth about Alex's death. You seem to have taken that as an excuse to revive your career as a counter-espionage kingpin. I'm afraid to say your skills have gone decidedly rusty in your retirement, just as I'd been warned.'

'I appreciate the feedback.'

'Going around Whitehall accusing the top brass of selling their souls to Mother Russia won't make you the most popular guy in school. Take my advice and stick to your brief next time.'

'Tell me the truth next time and I will.'

There was a knock on the door. Rashford looked relieved. 'My next meeting.'

Vine nodded and started packing away his things now, getting ready to leave. 'Out of curiosity, you joked earlier that you did have a licence to kill. How many times have you pulled the trigger before now?'

'You don't quit, do you? I have a terrier who's more placid.'

'I've been called worse.'

'I hope so.' Rashford was up as well now, walking Vine to the door. He paused, looking back at Vine with a more solemn expression. 'I fought wars. I served my country. If that meant taking out our enemies, then so be it. That isn't murder. That's service. I like to think I know the difference.'

Vine nodded and took one last glance at Rashford. 'Of course,' he said. 'I'm sure you do.'

It was the curious thing about Whitehall. Everything was so close. As Vine left the Ministry of Defence he looked across and saw the gated entrance to Number 10, the uniformed Met officers from Parliamentary and Diplomatic Protection bustling outside with their radios flaring and the occasional flutter of excitement, as if the prime ministerial Jaguar was about to scythe through the crowds. The Treasury stood at the side of Number 10 and the Palace of Westminster and Big Ben rose like colossi across the road. All of them were nestled snugly here together.

Vine walked slowly, inhaling it all and rolling over the Rashford interview again. Memory had always been his curse. The job of any decent counter-penetration spook was to avoid letting personal emotions creep in. And yet, now, Vine found himself helpless with the rush of adrenaline and that vaporous, all-night sensation. He imagined Rashford back in the plush confines of his Davos hotel room sending the signal up to the other Elders. The feverish pacing and the fear that Alexander Ivanov could that moment be sending up a similar flare to the Centre. The operation, the entire gamble, made redundant in one fell move.

And then the morning after. The fumbled excuses, the rheumy eyes, both parties meeting again over croissants and coffee. The telltale flicker in Ivanov's face and a granite hardness in his voice. Rashford listening as he heard Ivanov's acceptance. January 2010. It felt longer than a decade ago somehow. The Ivanov operation – the star of the British intelligence firmament and the most prominent Russian play from Whitehall since Gordievsky – had been set in motion that morning. Vine could feel all those old emotions rise inside him. The wish – the craving, almost – to be part of it and once more indoctrinated into the very highest levels.

Vine crossed to the other side of Whitehall and reached the door to the Cabinet Office for his debrief appointment with Emma Lockwood. There was the habitual silent procession towards the inner sanctum, the space-age minimalism of the surroundings. Vine could remember a time when everywhere in Whitehall seemed unable to shed its imperial coating, decked out with wood panels, threadbare carpets and faded grandeur. An unbroken line of succession back through the Cold War, all the way to figures like Philby and Churchill. One continuous story written into the fabric of these buildings. Somewhere along the way that had been shed, never to be replaced.

Emma Lockwood was waiting for him in her office. There was the customary lack of greetings or finesse. Vine took a seat opposite the desk. Lockwood was the new managerial generation, he kept reminding himself. There was no rolling the pitch first.

'So,' she said. 'Have you found them yet? Do you have a name, at least, I can give to the PM? Tell me you have *something*.'

Vine looked at her and knew, or hoped, that she was joking. This was the problem of putting civilians and politicians in charge of intelligence operations. They treated the secret world like an offshoot of a government department. Levers pulled, answers extracted. The intelligence world had a logic and timing of its own.

'I've made progress, if that's what you mean?' Vine said.

Lockwood smiled. 'Not quite, and I think you know it. Progress doesn't get me into the good books of the people upstairs. But if progress is all you have, so be it. What have you found?'

Vine had spent the walk over trying to condense all the various bits of data floating around his head. He explained about the room and the trail and then led up to the PHOENIX mole. 'The documents all concerned the recruitment and servicing of a new agent-in-place. An asset the KGB turned in the dying days of the Cold War.'

'And did this asset have a codename?'

'Catchy, if unimaginative. They decided to codename the agent-in-place PHOENIX. A system hoping for resurrection.'

'So it seems Ivanov was telling the truth after all,' said Lockwood, taking a deep breath. 'The breach was real. And you're sure these documents are genuine? We're not looking at a paper trail mocked up and left for our amusement by the pranksters in Moscow Centre?'

Vine could hear again all those stories from his early years in the Service about Department 2, Directorate S. The legendary KGB unit whose sole purpose was to produce props of the first order and build legends through fake passports, driving licences, degree certificates and medical records.

'I did the usual checks,' he said, 'on the paper and typography. As far as I can tell, the documents are genuine, yes. My guess? Our friends in Department 2 haven't been at work here.'

'Then you know what this means?'

Vine nodded. 'We're looking for a double, on our own side this time. A penetration agent, thirty years in the making. Someone right at the heart of everything. By this stage, they'll have risen to the very top of Whitehall, just as intended. If Ivanov is proved right, of course, we're looking at an internal breach even more serious than the Cambridge Five.'

'Sir James Norris. General Max Rashford. Dame Claire Sutherland. Or Dame Olivia Pope. What did you get from Sutherland and Rashford?'

'Both certainly fit the PHOENIX mole profile. Both have served thirty years in and around the centre of power. Both have reached the very top of the greasy pole. Both, of course, were fully indoctrinated into the Ivanov operation. Part of the famed Elders' Committee. On the current evidence – circumstantial evidence – Max Rashford is the most likely candidate for the PHOENIX mole. He was in Davos and made the initial pitch. He also had previous form when operating out of the East Berlin embassy in the eighties as part of Defence Intelligence.'

'The Chief of the Defence Staff working for Moscow. You seriously don't think that's enough for me to take to the Prime Minister right now? Even the hint that it might be true? The man who has direct access to our country's special forces, troop movements and nuclear football?'

'Not if it doesn't turn out to be Rashford, no. It's impossible to draw many conclusions without gathering the evidence first.'

'Tell me you haven't lost your touch.'

'I haven't.' Vine had debated how to describe it. The logical gymnastics of this case. Then he said: 'It's one of the oldest tricks in the spy playbook. The pitch, the approach, the covenant between asset and handler. It all depends on perspective. The skilled spy plays on that and frames the optics as they wish. Able to recount the moment in its full glory without giving away what they don't want to.'

Lockwood frowned. 'Now you really have lost me. In civilian speak?'

Vine saw the intricacy of it again, like a philosophical conundrum. The answer depended on how you viewed it. 'It all goes back to the hall of mirrors. Max Rashford and Alexander Ivanov both had spells in military intelligence at the start of their careers. Decades later, both men meet in Davos. Supposedly one is the asset and one is the handler.' Vine paused, waiting before saying it. 'The key question of this case is which way round was the Rashford–Ivanov relationship? Was Max Rashford recruiting Alexander Ivanov, or was Ivanov actually checking up on Rashford?'

Lockwood tilted her head back and rubbed at her eyes. 'Wait, you think Alexander Ivanov could have been Max *Rashford's* handler?'

'I think anything's possible,' said Vine. 'I discount nothing until I have the evidence for and against.'

'In which case Ivanov was never working for us at all?' continued Lockwood. 'Rashford saw his chance when the Elders' Committee was set up and recommended Ivanov. In reality, it would have been a way to make it easier for Rashford to meet a GRU handler in plain sight. The mole–case officer relationship inverted.'

'That's the beauty of it. Exactly.'

'In that theory, then, the Elders would have effectively given the PHOENIX mole official cover without realizing it.'

'Yes,' said Vine. He yawned suddenly, unable to catch it, the tiredness spreading across his face and body. 'The true spymasters arrange situations so it's impossible to give them one definition or shape. Everything is double and has multiple meanings. For the PHOENIX mole to have spent thirty years rising to the very top of Whitehall, they are better than good. The best. The greatest double this country has ever seen. Able to cover their tracks and divert suspicion, never putting a foot wrong. Whoever they are, they will be almost impossible to catch. They can think round corners in a way few of us can ever comprehend.'

'So your job's impossible? Or is this a roundabout way of saying you want a raise?'

Vine smiled. 'In previous mole-hunts, both Langley and MI6 have almost destroyed themselves by pointing the finger of suspicion at everyone. Suspicion grows exponentially. The real PHOENIX asset will have designed things so a similar pattern emerges here. We chase our tails and they continue to hide the evidence. Rushing to judgement is the amateur move.'

And then, just like before, things were over. Lockwood got up and looked towards the door. 'I'll hold off troubling the PM. That should give you more time.'

'Thank you.'

'Do the rest of the interviews,' she said. 'But, if it is Rashford, I have to be the first to know. We must be clear on that.'

'Yes,' said Vine, longing for open air again, a taste of freedom. 'We're perfectly clear.'

22

Vine was annoyed with himself at the yawn. Sleepless-ness was his private flaw, buried away with all the others and never to be displayed in public. He was a functioning insomniac, or so he liked to think. Perhaps it was age that was doing this. He wondered what other vices might soon expose themselves and then banished the thought, hap-pier not to wonder.

The OCP in Pimlico was for clandestine meets and changing up the routine, the last bolthole should he need it. Wellington Square was still home, filling up again after the day-long lull. Vine ignored the children freed from school and the parents briefly liberated from their offices. The house seemed cold now and unloved. Exile had seen him take up almost permanent residence here. There were no more sudden trips abroad and no escaping troubles of the past or the present. Wellington Square had become lived-in, graced with a constant presence, acquiring that tatty but familiar look.

Vine headed straight upstairs. He showered, then decided to try and see if he could force himself to sleep with the usual embarrassment of techniques. Counting sheep, counting fences, counting anything possible. Soothing thoughts and calming music. This time, though, sleep did seem to steal up on him. Vine saw the faces and names of the four suspects again: James Norris, Claire Sutherland, Olivia Pope and Max Rashford. All had their establishment smiles and a corridor-of-power strut. And yet one of them – one of those faces – harboured a secret so all-consuming it had resulted in the death of Alexander Ivanov in that suite at the Savoy and blood puddling over the floor.

The thoughtless half-sleep went on until another noise sounded. It was distinct and tuneless, a hard, ugly rattle that refused to die and go away. Vine ignored it at first, and then his ears began picking up the singular rhythm. He tipped out of his semi-sleep, looking across and seeing his official Cabinet Office phone on charge and vibrating.

The rest of reality crept in now. The restricted number and the advanced hour. Vine looked at the bedside alarm clock and saw he had been asleep longer than he thought. It was already after midnight. He reached across and pawed the phone towards him and saw the number was withheld. He fumbled with the screen now, trying to clear the gravel from his mouth, the elastic of his jaw sticking.

'Hello?'

'Mr Vine . . . *Sol*.'

Vine sat up and quickly groped for the lamp switch. He was grateful for the press of it between his thumb and finger, the sudden gush of orangey light that filled the dark room. The filmy, sleep-drenched quality vanished now. He knew the voice. 'General?'

'Yes. I thought I was right to call you. That you'd understand.' The voice of Max Rashford sounded different now. The laddishness gone completely. The acoustics were definitely that of the man Vine had seen only hours ago, but the tone was impossible to connect. Skipping through registers.

'Is there something wrong?'

A pause, then the voice dimmed. It was more whispery, as if betraying a confidence. 'The plant by my office. I wasn't sure whether you saw it when you arrived. I meant to explain. It's quite a specimen.'

Vine endured another pause. Then he said: 'General – Max – what's going on? Is there something wrong?'

A laugh now. Humourless and strangled. Despairing, even. Then the voice said again: 'I'm breaking all protocol, I know. In fact, I'm calling from home on my private line. But I was thinking more about our conversation today. Ever since you left, actually.'

Vine waited. He had that instinct again, honed and sharpened over decades in the field, of knowing when an asset, a sub-agent, even a hand-me-down source was going to confess. The pressure points of a human being. The key was staying silent, letting them get there on their own.

And then it came: 'I think I could be in danger. There's, well, there's something I didn't tell you during our interview. Something which I believe could be of vital importance in discovering Alex Ivanov's killer.'

Now Vine was free to speak again. Priest, counsellor, friend. 'What is it, Max? What do you want to tell me?'

A further pause. A throat-clearing, the cogs still whirring. Then Rashford said: 'The last asset–handler meeting between me and Ivanov. We observed the usual protocol, just as it always had been. But Alex, you see. Well, he gave me something. More than something, in fact. He wanted me to keep a document safe. A vitally important document.'

Vine felt his insides curl again and the tension exist solely in his stomach. He was close, now, so close. The mystery of this case – the revelation, as the tutors at the Fort had always called it – was almost within reach.

'What sort of document?' said Vine. His voice unemotional.

'Alex told me it was a document that might prove essential to national security. That's all he said.'

'Just the one copy? Or were there more?'

'No. Just the one,' said Rashford. 'Alex was clear on that. One copy with no digital backup. Strictly within my possession. Safekeeping, he called it. He said I was under strict orders. The document could never be shared with anyone without his approval. He was giving it to me for safekeeping.'

Vine increased the volume in his voice a fraction, sliding up the dial. 'And did he say anything else? Can you remember, Max? Anything else at all?'

Silence, then: 'Yes. Yes, he did. Something important. Vitally important. I didn't believe it at first. I thought he was mad. But then Alex told me—'

And, like that, the line went dead.

PART TWO

PART TWO

23

He checked everything – the electrics, the connection, all the basics. But Vine's gut told him it was none of those things. It was the inner sense of all spooks with decades behind them. No longer the click on the end of a line or the sound of heavy breathing but the suspicion, the ache, that other ears were listening. That the words being exchanged were no longer your own. Co-opted and stolen by an invisible enemy.

The air was already flashing blue by the time Vine approached Max Rashford's house. Vine had paid in cash for the cab and then made the rest of his way on foot. Rashford had a nice four-bedroom in Warwick Gardens, Kensington. Old family money and whatever he'd saved from his army work. As Vine walked by the house, he began memorizing everything he saw. The approach, the front gate, the two police cars parked either side, one with the lights still going.

Two uniforms were conferring outside the property. A cordon was already being established by another, securing the scene. A common approach pathway was being laid out. Forensics would arrive soon, then the SIO would emerge to walk the scene. Vine didn't need to see inside to know what had happened. He had known it ever since that last syllable was silenced on the phone line. The same fate that had befallen Alexander Ivanov in the plusher setting of the Nelson Suite. A single bullet in the head that was clean and immaculate. The sort of invisible technique and efficiency of the best wet workers, those ghosts of the secret world.

Vine still had the Section 9 pass in his pocket. He considered using it again, barging his way into the scene and seeing the evidence for himself. But he was warier now and cursing his earlier clumsiness. Pitching up at the first scene had exposed him. Traipsing through another would only make matters worse. Taking out a media tycoon and a Chief of the Defence Staff within days of each other was a desperate act, an escalation only sanctioned if the asset being protected – the PHOENIX mole – was worth its weight in gold. If the Centre was willing to go after Ivanov and Rashford, Vine would be easy prey. A retired spook disowned by the government and the powers that be. From now on, Vine would have to deploy full Moscow Rules. No chances, no shortcuts, no fly-bys.

Another police van pulled up and a variety of forensic officers piled out. The suiting-up was beginning. Vine watched from a distance for another ten minutes, then quietly slipped away. He hugged the black spots, making sure he wasn't picked up on any of the CCTV cameras. He found another cab fifteen minutes later and navigated a winding detour, watching the area around him closely. There were no follow cars, at least not yet. The darkness was at its most intense, with only the speckled yellow of street lamps and the occasional lighted window to relieve it. Vine could hear Rashford's voice on the phone again and he pieced together the final words. The answer Rashford was about to give before the line had been cut off.

Yes. Yes, he did. Something important. Vitally important. I didn't believe it at first. I thought he was mad. But then Alex told me . . .

What? Vine had rolled over every possible completion to the sentence. Another document which Ivanov had given to Rashford for safekeeping perhaps? The next piece of the treasure hunt. Or another breadcrumb laid down by Ivanov before he died. It was like the spook's form of insurance, with each piece of information hidden so no one could easily destroy the whole. Everything came down to that training again, as ingrained in Alexander Ivanov as it was in Vine. Once known, never forgotten.

As he sat in the back of the cab, Vine closed his eyes and tried to reach back and see all the assorted bits of data. The noise, the fuzziness and the emotion mixed in with everything else. Ivanov was trained, but so was Max Rashford with his time in Defence Intelligence. He had the smarts and aptitude to leapfrog his way to the top. It was why Rashford had called so unexpectedly. Not a last phone call to distant friends or family. But to Vine. It was operational, then. Rashford, like anyone trained in this world, knew to put the most important information first. Tabloid, as they called it at the Fort. First line, first para, first word.

It all came down to the call. Vine went back to the start.

Yes. I thought I was right to call you. That you'd understand.

Confirmation of intent. Rashford indicating his reasons.

The call to Vine wasn't a fat-fingered mistake. It was for a purpose. An operational purpose. Next, then.

The plant by my office. I wasn't sure whether you saw it when you arrived. I meant to explain. It's quite a specimen.

Bizarre on an initial read. The small talk of the condemned man? Rashford was afraid, not knowing what was coming out of his mouth. Perhaps. But, logically, no. Rashford wasn't a civilian asset or some perspiring functionary in his polyester shirt and stifling government office, betraying his country and seeing danger round every corner. He was a soldier with frontline experience. Death wasn't something abstract and terrifying for him, but familiar. Something he'd inflicted on others. No, the strangeness of it wasn't that.

The plant in my office. I wasn't sure whether you saw it.

His home office? Again, unlikely. The point of the call would be to direct Vine to the next dead-letter box. The place where the document in question was stored. His MoD office then, surely. The decorative plant, like the deodorant canister, hidden but useful when the right moment came. That had to be it. What had come after that? Think, now.

I'm breaking all protocol, I know. In fact, I'm calling from home on my private line. But I was thinking more about our conversation today. Ever since you left, actually.

Rashford had switched to seriousness from then on. The plant section was the only one where he deviated at all. Vine went back over the entire conversation one final time. But, by now, he was sure. Or as sure as he ever could be. Rashford had called to send the message about the plant pot, a last desperate attempt to ensure that someone knew the backup protocols in case the worst happened. Vine had been entrusted to continue following the trail. The deodorant canister, the library book, the Special Forces Club – one piece at a time. Until, at some point, all the various pieces would make a new kind of sense.

Vine moved forward in the back seat and tapped on the glass separating him from the cabbie. He gave the name of a street five minutes' walk from the OCP in Pimlico. And then he sat back and watched the city wash by outside the window.

He knew what he had to do next.

24

Vine changed his clothes at the OCP and then took another cab back to Whitehall. He made the approach to the Ministry of Defence building through Whitehall Court, passing the National Liberal Club on his left and retracing his steps from earlier. Half wishing he could call this whole thing off and escape for an early-morning nightcap. Scotch on the rocks, a good book, watch the dawn rise and this place emerge into a new day.

There was something eerie about conducting operations on home turf. Abroad was easier, like a holiday of sorts, the mistakes and errors able to be wiped away. Here was different. There was no room for error. One tiny slip and Vine knew his face would be plastered across every front page. One arm of the British state caught spying on another. The spirit of democracy, the chorus of accountability, would ensure that there would be no brushing under the carpet this time. The old days of cover-up were long gone now. This was total success or total failure.

Vine stopped at the end of Whitehall Court. He looked up at the Ministry of Defence building and did one final check. He ran through his cover story and glanced at his alias – 'Will Harding, Senior Policy Analyst, Ministry of Defence'. He saw the plastic casing and the doctored photo, wondering now whether it would all hold and if the technicians at Hanslope could be completely trusted. Then, at last, he put away the nerves and moved fully into character and the bored insouciance of the civil service lifer arriving for work. Someone so familiar with the surroundings that they were almost furniture. It was the part of spying to which so few seemed to give credence: the actorly flourish, inhabiting another person's life as if it were your own, every successful spy a brew of analyst, dreamer and thespian.

Vine didn't nod to either of the armed police officers at the main entrance. It would be too conspicuous. He was Will Harding now, not Solomon Vine. An official with Harding's length of service at the MoD wouldn't gawp at armed police officers. They would have learned that the patronizing nod or greeting got a hostile response too. Much better to keep the head down, walk on, let the officers do their job uninterrupted by the fuss of over-polite civilians.

He was through into the main area now. There was the familiar security apparatus, common across every major Whitehall department, the see-through pods with scanners swishing open on either side. It was slightly sci-fi, made more so by the futuristic beeps and whooshing sounds, as if the pod could enclose you permanently, suddenly plunging downwards into some forgotten lair beneath the ground.

Vine tried to put such disaster scenarios out of his mind as he walked up to the pod directly in front of him, the doctored security pass from Hanslope clutched moistly in his right palm. Cameras were all around him now, that was for certain. For the first time, Vine began to feel mentally unfit, so long out of the field that he was thinking his way through this. He tried to calm his thought process and get back in his body and do this on instinct. The easiest tells of any asset or sleeper were always the unconscious ones. Experienced field operatives learned how to use their natural instinct. A bit like method acting, crossing the line between fact and fiction.

Vine loosened his grip on the security pass and casually placed it on the scanner. Then he walked straight ahead. He didn't wait for the dot to beep green. According to his legend, Will Harding had worked in this building for twenty-three years. His pass always beeped green. The answer was never in doubt.

Vine walked through into the pod now, seeing the array of security officers standing on the other side. The one major disadvantage he had was timing. There was no other movement, no crowd of staff tumbling in after their morning commute. Vine was the only one trying to get into the building this early and the rest of the world still in bed. All eyes were trained on him.

The wait in the pod seemed an eternity. Vine resisted the urge to look ahead of him, knowing that the camera would spot it. He looked bored, instead. Impatient to get on with things. He checked his watch, as if deciding how soon he could be out of here and get home. This was an errand, after all. A pick-up job. If anyone asked, that was why Mr Harding was back in the office. Collecting and returning briefing papers. Nothing more.

Finally, the second pod door swished open. Vine didn't

rush, but stepped out calmly, still looking at his watch and adding in an annoyed shake of the head for good measure. He strode purposely forward now towards the bank of lifts up ahead, making sure the security pass was hung round his neck and displayed prominently on his chest. He didn't glance towards the other armed guards inside. But he could hear them, sensing their lingering presence.

Vine reached the bank of lifts. He'd spent the journey over here from the OCP going back through the early stages of the Rashford meeting. Summoning every detail. First up, the floor number. Vine was sure the aide who met him had pressed for the eighth floor. Sure, but not certain. The technical details hadn't had his full attention. Vine pressed for the lift, waiting forever as the numbers ticked down. The urge to glance sideways, get a read on the armed guards to his right, was almost irresistible. Finally, the lift doors opened and Vine stepped inside, producing another irritable, middle-manager sigh.

The memory of the earlier visit wasn't perfect but the best he had. So Vine pressed now for the eighth floor. The lifts doors closed and he felt that almost invisible movement upwards. The next bit would be the hardest. Everything depended on precision here. This was the part of the memory he'd worked on most. During the Rashford visit, he could remember the lift stopping at the correct floor. The doors opening and the aide taking a right. The eighth floor was reserved for the very top brass. The Secretary of State occupied a giant office on the left. The Chief of the Defence Staff bookended it with an equally grand office on the right. The collection of junior ministers were squashed into smaller offices in between. According to Vine's recollections, there had been no obvious security before the CDS's office. No uniformed guards or weapon-wielding plainclothes.

As the lift continued whirring upwards, Vine rehearsed his cover story once more. The Chief of the Defence Staff had asked him to drop some briefing papers off before an important call with the Pentagon. Mr Harding, in haste, had left the wrong briefing papers behind. This was merely an errand to retrieve the wrong papers and replace them with the right ones. A simple administrative fix.

The lift stopped now. Number eight appearing on the small display screen. Vine took a deep breath and readied himself. The only certainty on any operation was the unexpected, those small twigs to trip over. A cleaner on the early shift who alerted security downstairs, or a military aide unmasking the cover story. Vine prepared for all eventualities and then, as casually as he could, walked out on to the eighth floor feeling the dawn hush of the empty building all around him.

The first thing was the lights. All of them were still on. Not a subdued glow, like some offices, but the full wattage. It was easier in some ways, allowing Vine to navigate the corridor, but more difficult in others. There was no escaping now. Everything would be captured in high definition.

The golden rule of all covert entries was demeanour. Vine proceeded at a leisurely pace, deciding to head right, trusting his memory now. The floors were all carpeted and Vine's shoes made only the softest sound, audible against the total quiet elsewhere. As he passed each door he glanced inside, expecting to see someone, to nod briskly to them. But each ministerial office was empty with their tired collection of chipped desks and squeaking office chairs. The odd photo or two propped up near computer screens and any papers cleared away, as per regulations. The MoD, like other select Whitehall enclaves – Thames House, Vauxhall Cross and the twitchier parts of the Cabinet Office – employed full need-to-know protocols throughout the building. Desks were cleared, documents signed for, safety measures strictly adhered to.

Finally, Vine reached the end of the corridor. The earlier visit to interview Rashford came back to him again now. For the fallback to work, Vine knew that the dead-letter box had to be placed outside Rashford's office. He reached forward and gently tried the handle to the outer office, feeling it give and wondering whether the action had already triggered a tripwire somewhere. Red lights flashing in the control room hidden in the bowels of this place. Sure enough, he spotted a sensor above the door leading directly into Rashford's office. Once triggered, it would give him minutes at most. Whatever happened, he would have to be quick.

Vine walked into the outer office. As expected, this area had been cleared too. The reception desk was tidied of all papers, just the magazines and yesterday's newspapers still perched on the side-table by the sofas. He looked round, repeating Rashford's exact words again. The only clue he had to follow.

The plant by my office. I wasn't sure whether you saw it when you arrived. I meant to explain. It's quite a specimen.

Vine carefully took in everything he could, silently noting the geography of the room. A plant of some sort. There was nothing by the waiting area or the desk. There was nothing by the door into Rashford's inner office. Vine could feel the sweat gathering around his collar and hear the seconds ticking by in his head. He imagined steps accumulating by the lift door, uniformed security heading straight this way. He stopped and tried to still his breathing and listened to see if there were any other noises around him. But, as before, there was nothing.

Vine began walking through the room, slowing his thought process down. And, suddenly, he saw it. There was a small flowerpot on a shelf near the window, adjacent to Rashford's office, with a slightly limp piece of greenery sprouting inside. Vine did one more check of the rest of the office, in case he'd missed anything, then walked up to the flowerpot. He angled his body away from the camera sightlines. If someone was watching, they wouldn't be able to catch the next part. Merely the image of his back to the camera shielding everything else.

Vine looked down at the flowerpot. The soil was smoothed and covered over. Newish, too. Claw-lines were inscribed in the middle. Rashford must have deposited the fallback recently, half suspecting that it might be needed. Perhaps even the previous afternoon, Vine's earlier visit triggering the sequence of events.

Vine quickly checked the door behind him and paused again, alert for any other sounds. Finally, he began scrabbling around with his right hand. He felt the soil embed itself under his nails. Rashford was meticulous, an army man through and through. Anything here would be hidden at the bottom. Nothing obvious enough to be run into by a secretary or cleaner.

Vine continued searching for several more seconds. Then, at last, he felt something solid and metallic. He got a grip of it with his thumb and forefinger at the second time of asking. Making sure it didn't drop. Slowly he lifted it out of the soil until his hand was clear and he felt the jagged teeth of it brush against the tip of his index finger. He looked at it now, slowly shaking some of the soil off, making sure it didn't litter the carpet.

A key.

Once the key was clean, Vine walked over to the main door connecting to Rashford's inner office. He checked first that there wasn't any obvious sign of an alarm or keycode that had to be entered. Nothing stood out, but it was impossible to know for sure until he was inside. When he'd checked everything, Vine took the key from the flowerpot, braced himself to trip the sensor and inserted the key into the lock. He heard the satisfying clunk as it fit and the door opened up to the large office Vine had been in earlier. The former throne room of General Sir Max Rashford.

Somewhere in here was the answer.

25

First Vine debated about the lights. The room was dark, the main ceiling lights off and no desk lamp to compensate. Both of the blinds were up. Vine moved over to the windows and, as silently as he could, eased the blinds down. Then he made his way back over to the door and made sure it was shut. He flicked on the main light switch and the room spasmed into reality again.

Vine looked at his watch and fixed on an exit time. Having tripped the sensor, he had three minutes max. By five he needed to be back in the lift again. By six minutes, a full evac, back on Whitehall Court and disappearing fast. That meant priorities. There was no time for the full fingertip search, excavating every corner of this place. He needed to select two or three sites at most, gut them, and then pray that one of them was right.

He glanced across the room now and memorized the space again. He tried the desk first, the most obvious place. Drawers, surface, underneath. Anywhere Rashford could have stashed something like the deodorant bottle in Alexander Ivanov's hotel suite. Rashford had a background in the art of concealment. There would be no clumsy schoolboy sellotape or amateur theatrics. The location would be subtle and invisible to the amateur observer. Vine searched for a minute but came up with nothing.

Two minutes left now. A hundred and twenty seconds, each one vanishing fast.

Vine scanned the room again and decided to try the bookshelf next. It took pride of place next to the seating area, a gesture in itself, piled high with Max Rashford's reading collection. This wasn't the office of some smash-and-grab merchant. The books ranged across different genres: strategy, business, leadership, political memoirs, some hinterland titles on music, sports, even a scattering of novels, given away only by their creaseless spines, unloved compared to the rest.

Vine looked at those more closely and crouched down to catch them on the bottom part of shelving. The titles were all in paperback. Some modern – Mantel, McEwan, Barnes, Smith, Amis – and then a few more literary pieces of non-fiction further along the shelf. Vine counted them along and glanced at his watch: only seconds left until he had to move on to something else. Anything here. He was just about to give up, when something anomalous caught his eye.

Vine took out a handkerchief from his jacket pocket and placed it over his hand. He reached forward and inched the book towards him. The echo from the London Library coming back more strongly to him now. He tilted the spine up until he could see it clearly in the light and read the wording.

Dostoevsky: A Writer in His Time by Joseph Frank.

A biography of Dostoevsky.

Vine could see himself in St James's Square again now, sliding the copy of *Notes from Underground* from the shelf and finding the Special Forces Club ticket inside. He curled the handkerchief further around his hand now and pulled the book all the way out. He looked at the front cover and eased it up, about to flick through the pages.

When, from nowhere, there was a sound. Loud, insistent. An alarm. Not the high fire-alarm wail, but lower and moodier. A blare of sound that seemed to consume the entire building. The walls and floor shook to its rhythms. Vine reacted purely on instinct now. He opened up his rucksack and quickly managed to conceal the book inside, covering it with other papers. He zipped the rucksack shut and hauled it on to his back and was nearly at the door. He was about to reach forward and open it when the door flew open, smashing against the wall, and there was a flurry of activity streaming through the opening. Figures clad in body armour with Glock 17s pointed in his direction and a loud, hoarse voice screaming at him.

'On your knees! Get on your knees. Drop the bag. NOW! *On your knees . . .*'

Vine saw the ring of armed officers surrounding him, most of them prepared to shoot if they had to. He was trapped in the middle of the Chief of the Defence Staff's office on the top floor of the most heavily guarded building in Whitehall.

Don't play the hero. Think your way out. Straight from the Fort playbook.

Always think your way out.

Vine sank to his knees, shrugged off the rucksack and made sure his hands were visible.

The next thing he felt was the cold touch of handcuffs pinching at his skin. He was patted down and hauled up.

Then, unceremoniously, he was marched from the room.

26

As interrogation rooms went, this was one of the more habitable. There was the usual procession of greys, mixed in with other colours, until everything seemed dampened and bedraggled. Grey-green, grey-blue, grey-black. There was a rickety table in the middle and rickety chairs either side. The handcuffs still bit nastily, blood beginning to ooze silently on to his skin. Vine's right thumb was already smudging red.

The armed uniforms had been replaced now by a lone figure in an over-sized jacket. His tie was loosened and the top button visible. A DS, Vine guessed, stuck in the wilderness here, part of a CID outpost stationed at the Ministry of Defence for just this type of occurrence. A legwork copper. A day's worth of stubble bristled under the harsh lights; tobacco-stained fingers itched every few seconds. He was surely dreaming now of bed, home, any-where other than this dank, boxy room.

As the silence lengthened, Vine tried to figure out what the DS would have found so far. The departmental pass, of course. It was taken off him as soon as Vine was appre-hended. The technical wizardry at Hanslope was good, but not superhuman. Still, it provided a barrier of sorts and one Vine could use to his advantage. The cover story would have to be altered and embellished too. The worst scenario would be if they knew about the theft from the Special Forces Club and had been tracking him ever since. These two events umbilically connected, his work in between now null and void.

The man leaned forward in his chair and took out a warrant card from his jacket pocket. He held it up. 'DS Black, MDP. Do you know why you're here?'

Vine decided to play it politely. The Ministry of Defence police – MDP, by their initials – were a specialist police unit that protected MoD sites around the UK. Unlike the Met, they didn't need to engage in handholding or expose themselves to public scrutiny. The MDP dealt with the military exclusively and had acquired similar tics and behavioural patterns. They were brusque and exquisitely sensitive about rank and subservience. Mouthy interviewees were sure to rile them. There was no need to bring up the Special Forces Club incident unless they did. The best option was to sweat it out and pray.

'No,' Vine said, at last. 'I was carrying out an order from General Rashford. I'm not sure why I've been detained.'

DS Black nodded, absorbing the answer. He eased back now and folded his arms. 'Following an order? Is that right? What sort of order would the Chief of the Defence Staff give *you*?'

Vine could hear the instructors at the Fort again. The best lie was always closest to the truth. 'General Rashford rang me tonight. Well, I suppose, technically last night now. He said he needed me to collect something from his office. As per our usual set up, the General had left behind a key in the plant pot in the outer office. Standard protocol in case any one of us at a senior level needed to retrieve something. So, as you discovered, that is what I was doing.'

'Has General Rashford ever asked you to carry out this sort of task before?'

'Occasionally, yes.'

'And if we asked his PA about this, or his military aide, they'd confirm that, would they? About the General's protocol?'

They didn't know about the Special Forces Club, he was more certain of that now. The relief of it coursed through him. Vine let the silence continue, knowing DS Black was watching every flicker on his face. The drab room, the surly manner, the glare of the lighting here – all was designed to unnerve. The fanfare of the arrest and the way the officers had flaunted their weapons should be enough. Any normal mandarin would be singing by now.

'I can't speak for the others,' he said. 'The General always makes the arrangement with me. You know what he's like. If there's a petty health and safety regulation to be broken, the General will break it. Plus, he thinks his assistants work hard enough during the day. Waking them up just to let me into the office would be inconsiderate. The General likes to look after his subordinates.'

The present tense was key. The DS, no doubt, would just have heard that Max Rashford's body had been found at his home in Kensington. What had begun as a simple arrest for breaking and entering could quickly be connected to a far more serious matter. At no point could Vine ever betray knowledge that Max Rashford was anything other than alive and well.

DS Black said: 'When the officers apprehended you, what were you attempting to collect?'

'The General said he'd left behind a briefing paper that he wanted me to look over. It was sensitive. Not something he could ping over via email.'

'It couldn't wait until morning?'

'The General is always indulgent towards junior staff. Not so much to senior staff. Calls you up at all times of the day and night.'

'And what was this special briefing paper about?'

Now Vine waited again – a handful of seconds – and then decided to deploy his riskiest move yet. One that would either save him or backfire in all manner of ways. 'I'm afraid, given the sensitive nature of it, I can't explain much further.'

DS Black stopped, surprised at the answer. He shook his head and folded his arms now, like armour against Vine. 'That's honestly the best you have?'

Vine shrugged his shoulders. 'If I tell you anything more, you really would have reason to arrest me. Describing the document would be violating the terms of the Official Secrets Act.'

'Explain it to me. If this briefing paper was secret, why would the General want you to remove it from the building?'

Vine didn't react. The DS was sharper than he thought. 'There are a variety of classification grades. This particular briefing paper was sensitive. Policy stuff, the sort of paper that causes kittens at Number 10. But it wasn't top secret or classified. Sensitive papers can be taken out of the building. Classified papers can't. Nonetheless, I know what the Official Secrets Act says. And I don't intend to break the letter of it.'

Silence again. The door opened now and a uniform came in. Vine recognized him from the scene in Rashford's office. The uniform had a piece of paper in his hand and he slid it across to the DS, waiting as it was read. The DS glanced at the paper, lips puckering, his face creased with annoyance. Then he handed the piece of paper back. Vine could guess. Confirmation that the technical wizards at Hanslope Park had done their job. The fake ID had a hit on the MoD's internal database. As far as their system was concerned, Will Harding was real enough.

The uniform was about to go, but the DS summoned him back at the last moment with a twitch of his fingers. The DS turned to Vine: 'I take it you won't mind us carrying out another quick search?'

Vine knew he could object. There was no solicitor present. He could kick up a fuss and reach for any amount of mangled legal jargon. But that would only make him look guilty. Instead, Vine nodded calmly. They would have searched his bag by now, of course. They had already searched him earlier. But the intimate pat-down was for their own amusement, one last go.

The DS nodded to the uniform and indicated towards Vine. 'Uncuff him,' he said. 'See what else he's hiding from us.'

Vine waited as the uniform walked over and began undoing the cuffs. He was grateful to have the freedom of movement again, although the blood continued to smear queasily across his skin. Vine got to his feet before the uniform could haul him there, careful to go slowly, no sudden movements that might alarm them.

The uniform approached. 'Both arms out, please, keep them straight.'

Vine did as requested and felt the uniform's hands begin climbing their way up his body. He looked ahead and calculated that he had three seconds, at most, until they found the earbuds and the vaping device. The fake pass had worked, as had the database addition. His visit to Hanslope Park couldn't be the undoing of him now.

Sure enough, Vine felt the hands stop as they encountered the two objects.

'Empty your pockets please, sir.'

Vine reached inside his jacket pockets and took out the vaping device and the earbuds. Everything now depended on whether the uniform and the DS decided to employ full procedure and put the items through the advanced scanners at the front of the building. Or whether Vine had done enough to convince them this was all a misunderstanding.

The seconds ticked by. Vine could see a yawn spreading on the DS's face, clumsily stifled. There was a ring on his finger, a family back home, a spouse who needed him to help with the school run, the chaos of a private life. Vine glanced at the uniform, too, and saw another ring. He placed the two items on the table in front of him and watched as the uniform and DS picked them up and examined them. The earbuds they quickly discarded, nothing to see there. The uniform picked up the vaping device and held it up to the light.

'Quit two years ago,' said Vine, trying to keep the remark as light as possible. 'That thing keeps me going. Don't worry, only when I'm out of the building.' He gave a small smile, nothing too showy. The silence resumed.

The yawn caught up with the DS now. Spreading across his lips and around his nose and eyes, like a sudden rash, distorting all his features. DS Black didn't cover his mouth with his hand, letting the yawn rise and fall.

The uniform placed the vaping device back on the table. DS Black glanced at Vine, indicating for him to take the items again.

'Next time,' said the DS, 'get your bloody papers at a decent hour. No snooping around in high places this early in the morning.'

Vine nodded. He placed the earbuds and the vaping device back in his jacket pockets. 'I'll try and remember that. I think I had a bag?'

The DS nodded to the uniform who left the room momentarily, returning seconds later with the rucksack. Vine glanced at it and saw the odd scuff mark, knowing it had been given the full once-over by the team outside. That confirmed the Dostoevsky book didn't have anything inside it that linked to Rashford. No signature or notes, free of giveaways. Vine put the rucksack back on and was escorted to the door by the uniform. The DS watched him go in surly silence, waiting for the moment he could finally be free of this place.

The uniform accompanied him to the main exit. There was another wordless parting before he stumbled out into the darkness and the bitter cold again, the full impact of everything only hitting him now. Apart from the occasional extramural work for the NSC, it had been three years since his last proper operation. Three years of playing the civilian and denied any real form of fear or danger.

As Vine walked down the steps of the Ministry of Defence and crossed over to Whitehall Court, he realized how much he missed it all. He wondered, for a moment, if he had almost willed them to find him, unconsciously given them a helping hand just for the rush of interrogation, the threat of imprisonment and a reminder he was still alive.

Danger was the drug of any spy. As Vine began to lose himself in the darkness, he savoured the taste of it again. He walked on, waiting for the ghosts to mass around him, those echoes of a world he'd once left behind.

27

Vine headed back to the OCP in Pimlico, the only place secure enough for a full debrief on what had just happened. He made the call to Lockwood following the agreed protocol and then waited for an hour. Finally, Vine heard a knock and opened the door. Emma Lockwood hurried inside, her appearance disguised thanks to an umbrella, hiding the geography of her face. If there were any watchers outside, they would have picked up the mere outline of a figure and certainly nothing they could use to make an identification. After the arrest, neither could be too careful.

It was slightly too late – or too early – for anything other than steaming hot coffee. Vine poured two mugs and then took them up to the top floor. There was something distinctly odd about seeing Lockwood away from the austere formality of the Cabinet Office. Whitehall, the bustle, the obedient aide ushering him through the corridors of power. Here, in this new intimacy, Emma Lockwood appeared younger, for a start. She was dressed casually, the years falling off her. Vine handed over the coffee and then took the seat opposite.

Lockwood smiled and then blew on the drink, steam still circling upwards. 'The dawn protocol,' she said. 'I presume this is connected with the untimely demise of Max Rashford?'

'Is there any confirmation yet of how he died?'

'The Ivanov method,' she said. 'One shot to the head. Right on his temple, mocked up as suicide. Rashford's prints were found all over the gun. Forensics are trying to find any third-party trace at the scene. They're not having much luck so far.' She took another sip of her coffee, then asked: 'So . . . is that why I'm here? Did you find the golden nugget in Rashford's office? Did you figure out where the secret document takes us?'

'Possibly,' said Vine. 'I only managed a few minutes by myself. Then the firing squad entered. I was hauled off to be interrogated by one of the MDP suits. Thankfully the pass worked and the other devices didn't set off any alarm bells. Hanslope still has its uses.'

'You found nothing then?'

'Not quite.' Vine reached for his rucksack and opened it up. He took out the copy of the Dostoevsky biography and handed it over to Lockwood. 'I found this on the bottom of Rashford's bookshelf. None of the other titles made sense. Alexander Ivanov used a Dostoevsky book to hide the clue for the Special Forces Club. I thought there might be a link or some other breadcrumb trail.'

Lockwood had opened the book now and was flicking through the pages. Chasing an inscription, notes, anything hidden in the pages like a bookmark. But coming up empty-handed.

'Tell me I'm missing something,' said Vine.

Lockwood had reached the end of the book. She held it up to see the cover, looking at it from all angles. 'Nothing obvious.'

Vine glanced at the book again. 'The only question is this,' he said. 'How did Rashford hide the treasure?'

Lockwood nodded. 'And how the hell do we find it?'

28

They spent the next thirty minutes going through the book. First they laid the cover out on the table in front of them; then they flicked through each page, both trying to spot any suggestive gap or detail. Finally, they reached the very last page, still having discerned no mark, indent or clue. It was then, however, that Vine remembered an old trick. Those early weeks of training with the Service. A flinty, moustachioed veteran of the Cold War sent to Gosport to instruct each new MI6 recruit in the old-school methods. How to hide behind enemy lines. How to smuggle out messages. Secret ink, one-time pads, the basics of wartime espionage.

Vine picked up the book carefully and then headed back down to the ground floor and the sink in the kitchen. Lockwood followed him sceptically.

'Before you destroy vital evidence,' she said, 'one last plea for sanity. You're sure?'

Vine looked at the tap in front of him. Then back at the book. Recalling again the specific instructions from the Fort, the one instance when he'd performed this trick before. 'Do you have any better suggestions?' he asked.

'No.'

Vine decided the risk was worth it. He began running the hot water tap, waiting until steam began to rise. Then, very gently, he opened the book and eased it in front of the tap, using the water to soak the book for one minute, and counting down the seconds in his head. When he reached sixty, Vine withdrew the book and then placed it on the kitchen table, using his fingers to tease open the endpaper. Gradually, cautiously, exactly as the instructor had taught them all those years ago. Vine felt the endpaper give, courtesy of the warm water, and inside he found the tips of his fingers touching a sheet of cellophane.

Vine could feel the usual sensation. Starting in his back, slowly consuming his entire upper body. He delicately took out the sheet of cellophane as slowly as he could and then laid it on the table beside the book, making sure that nothing was missing or had been lost in transit. When he was sure he had it all, Vine turned to the sheet of cellophane itself. Lockwood joined him now.

She smiled, reluctantly impressed. 'Where did you learn that party trick?'

'Basic training. More years ago than I care to remember. A backup in case any of us were posted to Moscow and had to brush up on our exfil plan.'

'A misspent youth.'

'Not entirely.'

Vine looked closer at the document. This, right in front of him, must be the document that Ivanov had given to Rashford. The document Rashford mentioned just before he died; both deaths linked to it somehow. Once again, Vine was struck by the bizarreness of his own chosen trade. Words, mere words. What secret could be worth a life? And yet so many were.

On closer inspection, Vine saw that the document was a handwritten transcript of a conversation. The conversation appeared to involve two people identified on the transcript simply as P1 and P2. On the surface, the words appeared almost functional, every line scraped clear of any definitive information which could be used against either speaker.

P1: Everything is still in place?
P2: Yes, yes. I can't speak long.
P1: Did the package arrive?
P2: Later than you said. But I picked it up.
P1: You are all set for the big day?
P2: Yes.
P1: The event cannot be repeated. It must go as planned.
P2: I understand.
P1: I'm away next week, hence the urgency in speaking. You'll have to contact the alternative number if you have any difficulties.
P2: I won't need to.
P1: See you on the other side of this.
P2: I hope so.
P1: Goodbye.

Lockwood was also reading, trying to interpret it. 'First impressions?'

Vine continued reading to the end. Then he started again. 'Best guess? I'd say the product from a bugging operation.' Vine looked closer. The transcript appeared to discuss preparations for something; the words 'Operation

EXCALIBUR' had been noted at the side in the same handwriting. Plus, the paper was dated from two months ago. Scribbled at the bottom of the page was another word. Larger, more important, staring out at them both. Another mystery to add to the rest.

'Rosenholz'.

29

Afterwards, they both continued to sit and look at the transcript, hunting for clues. Somehow the information on this page had to relate to the assassinations of Ivanov and Rashford. Vine made them both more drinks and the silence lingered. It was the fate of the spy to spend their life like a linguist, constantly trying to decipher and translate, their trade plied through endless verbal variations. But the journey never stopped. Every time Vine imagined he was nearer the end another find would emerge. Some new secret buried beneath the layers.

'EXCALIBUR,' said Vine. 'We have to assume that's the operation linked to the PHOENIX mole. Logically, that can be the only reason that this would be left behind for us to find.'

'Operation EXCALIBUR has to be Ivanov's assassination then?' said Lockwood.

'Possibly. Excalibur was King Arthur's sword. A weapon that could kill the greatest beasts and demons. The resonance fits.'

The transcript had the studied blandness of the trained spook. The most important secrets couched in everyday banalities. In reality, all those various moving parts had deadly consequences. It was the standard protocol before the start of an operation. One that would see two people end up in body bags.

'And then the final word.' Vine looked again at the strangest one of them all, set apart from the transcript and the other words and lettering. Drawing the eye towards it. 'Rosenholz.'

The silence again. Pure, still, uninterrupted by anything else around them. Vine peered across and saw Lockwood shuffle awkwardly in her seat at the table. The tell on her face. Despite her lofty position in the national security structure, she was still very much the bureaucrat rather than the field-trained spook. Vine let the silence continue and waited for her to speak.

At last, Lockwood put her mug down and sighed. 'That one I do know something about.'

'Rosenholz?'

'Yes,' she said. Another sigh now. 'Unfortunately, as is the way with these things, the secret is not entirely mine to tell.'

'Further clearance.' Yet more acres of knowledge denied to him. 'You're the National Security Adviser,' he said. 'You sit in the building next to Number 10. You have the ear of the Prime Minister and control the entire framework of intelligence in this country. I didn't think there *were* any higher levels of clearance.'

'For everything else, you're correct. But the Rosenholz Files are the one exception. To indoctrinate anyone else into the knowledge about Rosenholz requires an additional layer of authorization. The only layer in the British state that's above my own.'

Vine understood. He was rarely awed by anything. But this was different. He looked back at the piece of paper in front of them again. The scribbles and jottings of a dead man. And felt the full importance and magnitude of this case consume him. The only layer above Lockwood's level was the person who wrote letters to the submarine commanders and gave the final order on using the nuclear codes. The person who called Downing Street home.

'You get authorization,' said Vine. 'I'll finish the rest of the interviews.'

'Four members of the Elders,' said Lockwood, the reality of Rashford's death haunting them both now. 'One suspect down. Three more to go.'

30

Lockwood left the OCP to begin the process of getting authorization on Rosenholz. Vine showered and then crunched through two slices of toast and three large cups of black coffee. He put on his shirt again and stood in the hallway meticulously adjusting his tie. Reviewing the preparation material and everything he'd compiled so far.

His next interview was possibly the most important of all. Dame Olivia Pope was the grandee to beat all grandees. As Cabinet Secretary, she held ultimate responsibility for coordinating the political and intelligence sides of Whitehall. She oversaw the CX reports put into the Prime Minister's red box. She was the person whose fingerprints were on everything. The Kremlin had always dreamed of getting an agent-in-place installed at the top of MI6, a feat almost achieved with Kim Philby. But someone like Olivia Pope made Philby look like a minnow. The Chief of MI6 was an agency head, a departmental manager, a regional governor, overseeing a distant imperial outpost. The Cabinet Secretary ruled Rome.

Vine left the OCP and walked down to Whitehall, giving his name at the gates of Downing Street and waiting while it was found on the list. Then he went through the airport-style security in the hut on the left. He hadn't brought a bag, deliberately, just taking off his jacket. He felt that pinch of nerves again that the earbuds would set something off and watched the police officer's face as they looked at the monitor. The lag of seconds before the cursory nod. Another small victory for the Hanslope team.

Vine dressed again, making sure he looked presentable. Then he continued on the final part of the journey. Looking up at the greyish magnificence of Downing Street and the emptiness of the press area to his left. The Prime Minister was clearly away, preoccupied with a visit or foreign trip. Olivia Pope was the one left holding the reins.

Vine reached the famous front door and saw it ease open before he had the chance to knock. The inside was smaller than he imagined, with the marbled black-and-white floor and the sense of shuffling busyness. The first item requested by the officer at the door was his mobile, safely stowed among the rows of others. He gave his name and waited, marvelling again at the difference of this place, unique from every other Westminster enclave. Nothing here seemed showy or overworked. There were no uniforms or exaggerated grandeur but just the quiet hum of real authority. The wait was followed by the sight of another young aide. Male this time, bright eyed, fumbling Vine's name. The illusion momentarily broken. Dame Olivia had sent for him.

Suspect number three was now ready.

31

There was something about power, Vine thought now, that elevated even the quietest of people. That and the damehood, perhaps, plus the cascade of letters after the name. Olivia Pope was in her mid fifties and there was a bustling quality to her every movement, like an amateur triathlete who never missed a morning run. She had a firm, sharp handshake along with a whispery sort of voice, which seemed to be the latest fashion among the truly powerful. Vine looked at her as a case officer assessing a potential asset. There was something smoothly institutional about her. Yes, if Olivia Pope was the Kremlin's joe, they couldn't have picked much better.

Pope's office was technically based in the Cabinet Office, joined seamlessly with Number 10. But the walk up Downing Street put a flutter into the heart of any visitor. Which, no doubt, was why Pope had told Vine to arrive by that entrance rather than the one further down Whitehall. The entrance and the delay in the foyer were all part of it: the subtle impress of authority.

The office itself was much like its occupant. There was some tasteful art from the government collections on the wall, photos cluttered on the desk of Pope shaking hands with worthies and dignitaries. She wore the same expression in all of them, with the high tilt of the forehead, the clipped and brittle smile, an apparent weariness with show and exhibition, someone who seemingly cultivated back-room power, not front of house, and enjoyed always being the puppetmaster.

The furniture here was grander than the other offices. Newer, plumper, nothing frayed or mothy in sight. They sat and the male aide brought in a tray of coffee and poured them both drinks. Pope held her cup protectively, never taking a sip. As if she'd forgotten how. The cup now merely an ornament, a decorative feature for meetings.

'I'm right in thinking you're *the* Solomon Vine,' said Pope eventually, eyeing the plate of biscuits and then turning away. 'Once our head of counter-espionage.'

Vine wondered whether that was really plucked from memory or whether Pope had quickly had a file sent over and done her homework. Coming to think of it now, someone like Pope always did her background reading. She would keep it in reserve, weaponize it later if necessary, taunting him with those nuggety secrets and facts from his former career. 'Yes,' he said.

'I don't know if I should be deeply worried or simply intrigued.'

Vine smiled. Any flinch now could give everything away. Keep it light. 'If you had enough cause to be worried, I wouldn't have made an appointment. I can tell you that much.'

Pope considered it with the flicker of a smile, as genuine as she ever got. Even that movement was calculated and rehearsed. 'I suppose you're right.'

Vine paused, suitably solemn. 'You've heard about Max Rashford?'

Pope didn't bother to nod, just a dismissive blink of the eyes. 'Of course. Max was growing into his role as CDS. I always thought he had a lot of potential and an interesting future ahead of him. What a waste.'

Spoken as if he was a statistic or some kind of plant which didn't bloom. Vine mentally reviewed the questions he'd prepared. He needed to begin on the front foot, try to unsettle Pope's institutional confidence and not let her hide behind these establishment settings. 'The first question I wanted to ask is simple,' he said. 'The Ivanov operation seems to have been governed by naivety. Why weren't you – the Elders, all four of you – more suspicious of the whole thing?'

Pope was still toying with her cup now, amused by the impudence. 'Because you're not talking to the paper boy, that's why. Between us we had over a hundred years of experience in the security world. We did what professionals in this line of work do. We calculated the risk and made a decision.'

'Was there any attempt to mitigate that risk?'

Pope looked at her watch now. 'Please, I think you'll find that the entire Elders' system *was* one giant mitigation. Think about it. Cutting off the JIC, MI6, Thames House, even Cheltenham. It put us one step ahead at all moments. I don't mean to be rude, but have some manners. This was above your level. The grown ups were in charge and thank God they were.'

Vine didn't react. 'That still doesn't answer my question.

You were recruiting a media mogul with tentacles all over the Kremlin. Why did you ever think you could trust him?'

'Put it this way. Alexander Ivanov knew his history. No Russian ever got as rich as he did and lived to tell the tale. We could offer him a new life and give him the comfortable retirement he needed. He would have been a fool to muck about with an offer like that. And whatever you say about him, Alexander Ivanov had a decent brain between his ears.'

Vine allowed the silence to do the work now. He looked at Pope. He had often wondered with moles whether they acclimatized to it, the risk softening until it was barely there. So used to danger that they hardly noticed it any more.

'A faithful traitor then?'

Pope gave another smile. As neutral as the features themselves, impossible to remember or describe. Spies trained for decades to achieve half as much. 'Aren't we all.'

'How many times did you personally meet with Ivanov?'

'In a job like this you usually rely on other people to do the counting.'

'You can't remember or you don't want to tell me?'

'You were just a head of section at Vauxhall Cross. That *is* right, isn't it? A foot soldier.'

It was said with a mocking humour, somewhere between a joke and an insult. Vine tried not to rise to it, knowing his time would come. 'When you did meet him, how did the protocol work? Are we talking a quick latte at Starbucks or was it the full three courses?'

'Something much subtler, thankfully. Your type of

clumsy tradecraft would be far too obvious. Dead-letter boxes, encrypted mobiles, park benches, signal sites, brush contacts, all that Cold War crap. We kept it simple. Ivanov was a high-profile media mogul. He could plausibly be seen at any major function in London, hobnobbing with diplomats, politicians, sometimes even royalty. It was our open goal.'

'That sounds unusually daring for the British establishment.'

'Like I said, it was. The product was hidden on thumb drives mainly. Ivanov wrote everything down on an air-gapped device and then handed it over. Nothing high tech or overcomplicated. Ten pounds from your nearest branch of W H Smith and you can bring down a government.'

As an old spook, Vine almost smiled at the audacity. Every trained spy was always hunting for the perfect cover, that mix of instinct and tradecraft. He tried to picture Ivanov and Pope together. Both dressed in their finest, champagne in hand. The great and the good of the diplomatic and media circuit all around them. Standing in front of the world and secretly conducting their trades.

Vine saw Pope check her watch again. Restless now, the sign that their meeting was nearly over. Soon the male aide would return, the coffee tray cleared away, the chance gone for good. He was about to speak when Pope got there first.

'Funny. Retired spies usually protect their legacies by staying retired, don't you find?' The mask was back in place now, taut and implacable. As if Vine had broken a last, unspoken code between them. 'The problem comes when they poke their noses into things they don't have the brains or the experience to understand. Like breaking into the office of the Chief of the Defence staff. Or stealing packages from private members' clubs.'

Vine could feel the old rebelliousness surge inside him again and that genetic dislike of any authority figure. She *knew*. It reminded him of school, the beady and all-seeing eye. Perhaps he had been foolish to come here.

Pope looked towards the door, as if Vine was a nuisance, a trespasser. 'Tell Ms Lockwood that your investigation needs to draw to a conclusion. The Elders exist at a higher level than even she is cleared for. I've indulged you this far, but no further. I'm sorry, but game time really is over. For both of you.'

'You're telling us to drop an inquiry put in place by your own National Security Adviser?'

'No,' said Pope. 'I'm *ordering* you to.'

Vine was ready to hear the door open. Whisked outside and never to return again. 'You're not interested in the truth?'

'I know the truth. I'm not interested in a retired spy throwing his weight around. You left the public payroll once in disgrace. It's time to repeat the experience. You were a washout, Vine. A zealot counter-espionage chief who, like all such types, ended up devouring his own.'

'And if I don't drop the inquiry?'

Pope's smile was back now. But dangerous this time, summoning the full power of the office around her. 'Then you will face the ultimate indignity for any spy,' she said. 'You signed the Official Secrets Act. That signature lasts a lifetime. Don't be foolish. This isn't your personal rehabilitation scheme. This is national security. Write up your grubby report on the circumstances, submit it and then rejoin the land of the living.'

'And if I can't do that?'

Pope signalled to the door. 'I wasn't aware of giving you a choice.'

32

As Vine walked the short way from Downing Street to King Charles Street, he felt that sense of shock again. He had expected many things, but being thrown out so cursorily wasn't one of them. He saw the look on Olivia Pope's face and the curl of a smile as she mentioned the MoD break-in and the Special Forces Club. It was rare to provoke someone as senior as Pope into that kind of warning. Usually the cease and desist orders were dished out by subordinates. A quiet word in the ear from a deputy, gently pleading with you to be careful, ushering someone away from danger. How to explain it then? The telltale signs of any agent-in-place who was cornered with no obvious escape route? Or did Pope have the same doubts too? Did she want to find the mole before Vine did, ensure that the decision about what happened next remained in her hands? Either way, she clearly knew far more than she was letting on.

He pushed the memories and questions aside and concentrated, instead, on the here and now. It was time for the fourth and final suspect.

Vine arrived at the Foreign Office and was whisked up to the office and introduced to Sir James Norris. He'd been squeezed into the diary, five minutes tops. No wiggle room. In person Norris could hardly have been more different from Dame Olivia Pope. His title – Permanent Under-Secretary and Head of the Diplomatic Service – sounded similarly pompous, one of the rulers of the mandarin class, part of the network of perm-secs who ran Whitehall. But they came in all forms. Norris had once been an MI6 trainee and was now the most senior diplomat in the British government. The extrovert, the most politically adept, a networker beyond parallel. There was nothing tepid or lukewarm about him. Rather, everything was overcooked and pleasingly exaggerated: the whirl of grey hair, the striped socks, the signet ring. Olivia Pope had the quiet stubbornness of the Number 10 doorkeeper but James Norris was the performer and impossible to hide in a crowd. No wonder he had transferred from the secret world to the open one.

They walked through to Norris's office and Vine took a seat, admiring the surroundings. Still replaying the Pope interview in his head. Wondering whether the flare-up was proof of guilt or innocence.

'So,' said James Norris, plunging straight in. 'I heard about Max. How tragic. How horrific. I adored Max, you see. Not that we didn't have our fights occasionally. The old FCO and MoD rivalry, just par for the course. Too tragic to think about. Emma Lockwood's asked you to tidy things up. Dispatched you from her perch in the Cabinet Office to sort it all out before the press start digging. Very well then. How can I help?'

After his encounter with Pope, Vine wondered how much the Elders communicated with each other. Had Norris been warned what to expect and told to deliver the same warning? Or had Pope been acting alone, trusting that Vine would do his duty and get the message? He went with the second theory for the time being.

This office was more classical than Pope's, the grandeur of the Foreign Office building one of the jewels in Whitehall with its plush reds and lavish paintings. Vine often wondered what decisions would be made in a minimalist equivalent with no grandeur or luxury, the Foreign Office relocated to a business park and all these imperial trappings and illusions stripped away.

'I hear you enjoy ruffling feathers,' Norris continued. 'You had quite a reputation at Vauxhall Cross. May I make a plea for clemency before we begin?'

'You were once in the secret world yourself, I understand?'

'A regrettable dabble, yes. But I soon realized I wasn't cut out for life in the shadows. Open air, daylight, much better for one's health.'

The last sentence was said with an impish smile. The Permanent Under-Secretary oversaw M16, indoctrinated and briefed on almost all the most secret matters in the land. There was virtually nothing that Norris was not allowed to know. 'You can make a plea but it doesn't have to be accepted.'

Norris had that glint of amusement again, a teasing quality. 'The art of diplomacy is letting other people have your way. Full battle stations, then. As you wish.'

Norris took a small bite of a biscuit and then sat back in his chair. Chewing busily through the digestive, wiping away the attendant crumbs. Vine watched him carefully now. It was so easy to underestimate people this high up the chain of command. That was the problem with interviewing them. Pigeonholing each one as some faceless bureaucrat, their secrets and personality long ago forgotten. But no one climbed this far up the pole without being able to play the game.

Vine decided to start with the simplest question. 'Did you like Alexander Ivanov as a person?' he said. 'Was the personal chemistry good or just average?'

'Ha, the gotcha question straight up.' Norris finished crunching on the biscuit, dusting his hands clean of crumbs. The same theatricality to all his movements, as if life was a permanent summit, the act having to be kept up at all times. 'As a diplomat I'll try and be suitably diplomatic and vanilla, shall I? Honestly, Alex was a billionaire and a media mogul. Not to mention being a Russian-trained hood. I am, thankfully, none of the above. So let's just say we weren't downing bottles of vodka together, if that's what you mean. Specifically, I'd heard plenty of rumours from my various diplomatic sources that Ivanov was already on cosy terms with numerous other players in the intelligence game. Not the best start to a beautiful friendship.'

Vine felt that flicker of surprise again. The split second of adrenaline sought out by any long-term case officer, stumbling across a nugget of information that had the potential to reset everything. 'You think Ivanov was two-timing Britain with other countries?'

'Alex was promiscuous, let's put it like that. Though the man had decent, and rather traditional, taste. The Israelis, the Saudis, lots of time spent in the US too, potentially hooked into Langley in one way or another. We could never have absolute confirmation. But, from where I was sitting, I thought it more than likely that Ivanov was already on the books of someone else. Nothing formal. But the usual after-dinner flirtation.'

'Reasonable grounds for a divorce?'

Norris smiled and reached for another biscuit. 'Ours wasn't that sort of relationship. Alex was very Russian, you know, quite a bearish figure. Something of the boxer about him. Sensible people didn't pick a fight. I was one of them. No, we simmered silently.'

Vine absorbed the information and then prepared himself for the next question. He could feel the atmosphere tighten slightly, as if some of the oxygen had been sucked from the room. He went back to the profiles Lockwood had given him at the start of the operation. Each one with their skeletons and secrets.

There was one detail in James Norris's file that had to be raised. He said: 'Why don't you tell me about your time as Ambassador to Moscow?'

33

Norris's body language changed. Not much, he was good, just a slower, more considered rhythm to the breathing. 'I see someone's been searching around my vetting file. That *is* where you're heading, I take it?'

Vine had wondered how he'd respond. Pope had become imperious. Rashford barrack-room matey. Sutherland petulant. Norris, by contrast, seemed almost honest, avoiding elaborate disguise and controlling the confession.

'Your vetting file has an interesting section on one particular episode,' said Vine. 'You were alleged to have had a romantic involvement with a Russian journalist during your time as Ambassador at the Moscow embassy.'

'You're trying to be kind. But you know there was no alleged about it. I did have a relationship with a woman during my posting. That woman was an occasional journalist, among many other things, and a sometime source for the station. I've never sought to deny either of those two things. I still don't.'

'A journalist – Ms Panin – who went missing for six months,' continued Vine, trying to recite the facts as neutrally as possible. 'But who later turned up alive – recanting her former anti-Kremlin rhetoric.'

'Am I missing a hidden question somewhere?'

'Most journalists in Moscow who cause problems for

the Kremlin end up dead. Your lover appears to be the honourable exception.'

'Ah, I see. Did I let my romantic affairs get in the way of my professional duties as Ambassador? That's your worry, is it?'

'You pulled some strings, I imagine. The power of a diplomatic passport and an extensive Rolodex.'

For the first time, Norris's exuberance seemed to desert him. The wattage dimming. 'Rubbish. I'm sorry, but that's total, weapons-grade bollocks. Release suggests she was imprisoned. No one knows that she was. All that's established is that she was there one minute and didn't show up the next. For all I know she could have been with another man. An extended holiday. Our relationship was never strictly exclusive. Any relationship like that rarely is.'

And now, Vine thought, he could see the fault lines. So carefully hidden before, masked by that breezy confidence. But the lies were creeping in. He pressed further: 'Nice try. But this was Moscow in the nineties. It made Gotham look like Disneyland. Everyone had their price. You made a deal. The Kremlin, the FSB, one of Yeltsin's people. Anything else is just wishful thinking. Everyone, of course, would have done the same thing in a similar situation.'

Norris was more serious now. He stared at Vine, an angrier blot of emotion across his face. Old skeletons being resurrected. '*No.* I have never denied being in a relationship with a Russian journalist. But how, or why, she ended up recanting her political views was a mystery to me then, just as it is to me now. I had no part in it.'

'And what if I don't believe you?' said Vine, trying to get more reaction. Provoking Norris. Necessary, if distasteful. 'It has kompromat written all over it.'

Norris didn't get up. Unlike Pope, he resisted the grand assertion of power. Instead, his voice dipped lower, a whisper now and that hint of playful amusement again, as if he found the idea beyond ridiculous. 'Do you have any idea how difficult it is to get this job?' he said.

'My job was to hunt moles, Mr Norris. I'm the one who made it difficult. I have a pretty good idea, yes.'

Norris nodded, intrigued by the rebuttal. 'Then you'll know that what you're insinuating is impossible. Beyond impossible.'

'What exactly *am* I insinuating?'

'That I made some kind of deal with the FSB and agreed to pass on information in exchange for the journalist's release. That I betrayed Ivanov because I feared that the Kremlin would unleash their worst on me if I didn't.'

'Odd things happen in-country,' said Vine. 'We've all been there.'

'In the old days, perhaps, those with chequered pasts could swan into the upper reaches of King Charles Street. But I'm afraid, these days, the lessons have been learned.'

Vine nodded, knowing he'd pushed as far as he could. Still not sure what to make of the concoction he'd been offered: lies, humour, deflection, perhaps some truth stirred in there too. Just like the rest of them. All still running from the sins and ghosts of their pasts. One final question. 'If you didn't, who *do* you think betrayed Alexander Ivanov?' he said. 'Who has blood on their hands?'

James Norris was about to answer when his phone began ringing. The spell broken. He looked towards the phone and his desk and what lay beyond this meeting.

'I'm sorry,' he said. 'That's more your job than mine, don't you think?'

As quickly as it started, the fourth and final interview was over.

34

As Vine left the Foreign Office, he was handed his phone again. He had one new message. It had come through from Lockwood half an hour ago: *Cabinet Office basement. I have something for you. EL.*

This was the way with operations. Spies were like soldiers. So many bare hours of waiting, the tedium of surveillance and planning, before it all happened at once. The events most people experienced in weeks became compressed into hours. Spies looked back on their careers as a series of short moments. Operations were won or lost in a breath.

Vine tried to piece together the chronology of the hours since the phone call came through from the Cabinet Office. That brisk, official summons to the National Security Adviser's office and the news that Alexander Ivanov was dead. It had all become a blur now, each interview and discovery, each hidden part of this case. A tangle of truths and fabulation, impossible to separate one from the other.

He started walking back towards the Cabinet Office. Past Downing Street, up to the civilian entrance on Whitehall. Condemned, in an instant, to become a spectator of Norris and his kind again. The gates and the armed guards like a barrier to all the uninitiated.

Vine saw the suspects in his head now. The four members of the Elders' Committee culled to three: the Chief of MI6, the Cabinet Secretary and the Permanent Under-Secretary at the Foreign Office. Claire Sutherland, Olivia Pope and James Norris. Titled, lauded, three pillars of the Whitehall establishment. The mole to beat all moles. Past, present and future.

Vine reached the entrance to the Cabinet Office and was soon escorted to the basement. Even more secure than Lockwood's usual hideout. A world away too from Pope's office with its quiet authority or Norris's with its flamboyant volume. The basement was the level of the spooks, the technicians and plumbers of the system. It had the same hum of all the buildings Vine had worked in over the years. Vauxhall Cross, the more reclusive parts of embassies, the secure rooms beyond the reach of any technology yet known to mankind. Vine breathed it in again, the sense of something lost. This, yes, was where he belonged.

Emma Lockwood was waiting for him in one of the endless rooms tucked out of sight. All phones deposited in a container outside. A faded sign was plastered to the door with letters and warnings. Vine wondered how redundant the signs were now. Nothing could repair the damage of a high-level double who'd systematically betrayed the country's greatest secrets to an enemy state. All this — the trappings of secrecy — undone by one lone figure at the very heart of things.

Vine walked into the secure room and noticed the small details. The mundane touches that shattered the sacred illusion. The bottles of water. Lockwood's fresh mug of breakfast tea with '007' printed on the side. His own drink was waiting, 'Moneypenny' branded below the handle. A spy's sense of humour. There was no natural light either and the ceiling light was off, just a small lamp in the corner.

'Black coffee. Extra strong. Just as the doctor ordered,' said Lockwood. 'That is your drink of choice?'

Vine appreciated the gesture. 'Ingratiating yourself with an asset,' he said. 'Proper tradecraft. After this, you'd make a good handler. Vauxhall Cross or Thames House could use the help. Is there any reason we're in the dark?'

Lockwood smiled painfully, her left hand massaging the side of her head. 'Sorry.'

'Headache?'

'I wish,' she said. 'Migraines of the worst and most life-destroying kind. They flare up now and then. My curse and flaw, I'm afraid. In my defence, it is my *only* flaw.'

Vine took a sip of the coffee, the strength and heat just right. It burned through his throat and woke him up in the way he needed. That clarity of mind again. 'Anything I can do to help?'

'Solve this case as quickly as humanly possible. And avoid talking loudly or opening the curtains,' said Lockwood. 'How did you get on with Pope and Norris?'

Vine had debated how to frame both conversations on the way down. Olivia Pope and James Norris were used to yielding their power in opposite ways. Mulish perseverance versus unapologetic attack. Both were equally inscrutable. He said: 'Pope was sketchy on details. I tried to get her to go there, but she was almost like a proper hood under interrogation. Kept pushing me away with generalities.'

'Did she seem shocked at the Rashford death?'

'Not as much as I expected. The Chief of the Defence Staff is found dead and it was like another business day. She either doesn't feel much or she was braced for it.'

'You think Pope knew it was coming?'

'If she did, I'd have expected the opposite reaction. The tear ducts to open. Pope to eulogize Rashford, show me how much the loss meant to her. Put on some kind of performance, at least as a deflection. The fact she didn't makes me suspect she was telling the truth.'

'Unless it was a double bluff, of course. Olivia Pope knows how your mind works. How any counter-espionage lifer operates. She outplayed you.'

Vine had considered that too. Logic tangled so completely that it was impossible to ever get it smooth again. It was the problem at the heart of all forms of counter-espionage. Who was playing whom.

'She flared up,' he continued. 'She warned both of us off. Told me to write up my report and then cease and desist with the Ivanov case and the Elders' Committee. It sounded like she thought we might get in her way.'

Lockwood sighed. 'Ignore her.'

'She's the Cabinet Secretary. She's not the sort of person you usually ignore.'

'Pope is an old-school Whitehall hand. She's spent her life on skirmishes, securing territory and then defending it. Now she's at the top, she wants to hoard as much power as possible. She didn't warn you off. She warned *me* off through you.'

'Unless she had a good reason to?' said Vine. 'Dress it

up as a turf war, when really she's hiding something much more important.'

'You think she would be that brazen?'

'All we know is that the PHOENIX mole has managed to operate at the centre of power for thirty years. The mole has climbed right to the very top of the tree without anyone, so far, managing to catch them. That isn't just brazen. That's almost suicidal. A mind that plays games with others as part of daily life. Someone so at home with deception that they can't see the truth any more. If Pope is the PHOENIX mole then, yes, I think it's possible. She could warn me off and take the risk. Dare me to question it.'

'What about James Norris? You brought up the issue in his vetting file?'

Vine nodded. 'He was prepared for it. He's a better actor than Pope.'

'What about Rashford's death?'

'I couldn't get much out of him. He seemed more genuinely upset than Pope, but that's not saying a lot. Norris is a diplomat. He knows how to bury his own emotions and put on a show for the world, convince anyone of positions and policies he doesn't believe in.'

'The perfect mole, in other words,' said Lockwood. She took another sip of her tea and looked deep in thought. Then she turned back to Vine. 'Say you were sitting in Directorate S before it all imploded. Colonel Vine of the KGB. The chance to secure a new asset who you could usher through the ranks until they were planted at the very top. The crowning glory of your service. Which one would you pick? Claire Sutherland, Olivia Pope or James Norris? Who would be your PHOENIX mole?'

Vine thought about Claire Sutherland and her family's financial interests, James Norris and his ambassadorial affair and Olivia Pope's haste to banish him from the office and avoid further questioning. He considered using the politician's response, claiming never to answer hypotheticals. And yet, now, he realized this was far beyond a hypothetical. He saw Ivanov's body in the hotel suite again and the blood staining the carpet. He heard Max Rashford's voice on the phone line. That squawk of terror, breaking through the hard, military exterior. Both doomed by someone they had once trusted.

'It all comes back to context,' said Vine. 'The PHOENIX mole was recruited in the late eighties, the very moment Russian intelligence seemed to have failed. The Soviet dream dismantled, the KGB and its legendary reputation about to be humbled in the most public of ways. Russian intelligence has always been as much an emotional matter as a practical one. They don't want to disrupt the enemy. They want to humiliate them. They have always been willing to spend untold amounts of money in order to achieve that.'

'You still haven't answered my question.'

'In the Cold War, the goal was always to get a mole at the top of MI6. Hence Philby. He very nearly did it, too. The other alternative was to get one of their own into the highest political office. But which is more humiliating for the West? To discover the person in charge of foreign spy ops is working for the other side? Or to find out the person in charge of the entire country is a Russian mole?'

'The latter, clearly. Which means the obvious candidate for the PHOENIX mole is Pope then? Cabinet Secretary beats Chief of MI6 every time. That's where Moscow wanted the mole to end up. Pope has to be PHOENIX.'

'Not quite,' said Vine, finding his way through the sea of information again. All the various strands, all the ways they could connect. 'It means the PHOENIX mole has to be someone who *could* achieve that. Future tense, not present tense.'

'Which rules out Claire Sutherland. No Chief of MI6 will ever take over a secular perm-sec role. Her best hope is to earn some big bucks in the City when she's done. Get as many board seats as she can, the usual portfolio show.'

'Agreed. But the Russians need someone in line to take over the throne. Who better to become the next Cabinet Secretary than the current Permanent Under-Secretary at the Foreign Office?'

'James Norris. At this stage in your investigation, *he's* your prime suspect?' said Lockwood. 'You think Norris is the frontrunner to be the PHOENIX mole? He's the one who gave the whole game away?'

Vine always hated this part. Letting instinct triumph over reason, the worst fear of any counter-espionage type. But that was always the problem with mole hunts. No agent-in-place who had survived for thirty years would be clumsy enough to leave a data trail behind them, a tidy record that could be catalogued and archived. In the end, counter-espionage came down to an unsatisfactory mix of things. Gut, experience, parsing human behaviour.

'At this stage in the investigation,' said Vine, 'James Norris would be my prime suspect. Olivia Pope second. Claire Sutherland third.'

'And this is based on the context?' said Lockwood. 'When the PHOENIX mole was recruited? Not some misguided loyalty to your old service?'

'The context and the facts. Nothing else.'

Lockwood nodded, preparing for something. 'Well, that context might be about to change,' she said. 'I went to the top. I now have permission to indoctrinate you into one of the last great secrets of the Cold War.' She paused, solemn now. 'It's time you finally learned the truth about the Rosenholz Files.'

35

They walked in silence through the rest of the Cabinet Office basement, burrowing down until they reached a level even further below. The first thing Vine noticed was the temperature. A cool breeze gusted through the place, which was like a cross between a freezer and a morgue. Lockwood had a card with her, the magic flick of green followed by the solid click that allowed them through. It felt like an initiation of sorts. It was quiet, too, just the rattle of air and the clunky tap of their steps.

After two more doors, they reached their final destination. Vine read the sign on the outside: 'CO-A (UKEO)'. Cabinet Office Archives, UK Eyes Only. No showing off to foreign visitors. No secret trips by spooks or diplomats on a lunch break. Lockwood presented her card for the last time, then waited for the retinal scan. She stood still before the scanner as it did its work; then they both saw the light blink green again.

Lockwood opened the door and said: 'You've never been to these archives before?'

Vine tried to calculate where they were now geographically. Surely back in those old wartime tunnels underneath Downing Street that were built to withstand Luftwaffe bombs, now converted into archival treasure troves. 'When I became head of counter-espionage, the Chief briefed me on most of our hidden deposit sites,' he said. 'Funnily enough, this wasn't among them.'

'For one good reason. Only the National Security Adviser has access,' she said. 'We employ one archivist with military training who does the basic maintenance. Officially, it still doesn't exist. The one part of Whitehall that managed to escape freedom of information.'

They walked through into the main section of the archive now. This part was how Vine expected it to be. No baubles or finery, just the functional decor and clinical lighting, everything safely stored away in steel cabinets, like an ordinary archive but with the security of a bank vault. The lights were automatic and shimmered on as they walked. There were no signs to direct a visitor, just numbers, only making sense to those already indoctrinated.

'I know why Five and Six need a secret archive,' said Vine, staring round at it all. 'Why do Number 10 and the Cabinet Office?'

Lockwood smiled. 'Because there are things the state wants to keep even from its spooks. Items that would shed light on matters the politicians still want under wraps.' Lockwood clearly had a number memorized, leading Vine down an aisle on their right, faultlessly clean grey cabinets standing at attention either side. 'Welcome to the most closely guarded secrets of the British state.'

'Am I meant to guess?'

'The bulk of the archive is Second World War material yet to be released. Things Number 10 doesn't want aired yet. Or, for that matter, the Palace.'

'On the spy side, I'm guessing the holy trinity are somewhere here too. Blake, Philby and Gordievsky.'

'Guess all you want.'

Lockwood was slowing down now. Vine looked at the number ahead of them and saw they were opposite Vault 701. A pin code was needed to access each cabinet. Lockwood glanced at him and he dutifully turned away, giving her privacy. She typed in a six-digit code and then waited for the final click. She opened the safe and gently eased out several bundles of paper that were well thumbed and weather beaten, as if they'd travelled a great distance. There was a reading table nearby and Lockwood carefully placed the bundles down on top.

'The Rosenholz Files,' she said.

Vine had tried to dredge every memory he could. The Fort, meetings with the Chief, the counter-espionage briefings with his team, every type of historical curiosity and rumour evaluated and reviewed. No one had ever mentioned the Rosenholz Files. 'You'll have to enlighten me.'

'These documents,' she said, 'are the only surviving Western copy of the most important files of the Cold War. The Rosenholz Files were discovered during the fall of East Germany and the dismantling of the Stasi. A list of all assets that the Stasi – and, by default, Moscow Centre – had running in the West. Never released or made public in any way and kept hidden by Britain for all these years. Basically, it's an autopsy of East German intelligence and the Russian machinery of spying. Most of them exist in CD-ROM format. The real diamonds, however, were paper only. The secrets of the Main Directorate of Reconnaissance.'

The Stasi's overseas wing, responsible for all foreign operations. Under the command of the notorious Markus Wolf. 'The HVA,' said Vine.

'Indeed.'

Vine looked down at the bundle of documents again and finally understood. Rosenholz, no. That name was never used outside officialdom. But all spooks had heard of documents like these. They were the Holy Grail, the cross of Christ and Camelot in one neat package. Documents ransacked in the dying days of the Cold War. An almost mythic prize revealing the secrets of the KGB and their outriders in the GDR.

'I was always part of the school of thought that gave the Stasi more credit.'

'You assumed these papers were burned?'

'It's what they did at the Lubyanka. I thought they would have done the same in Germany. It's poor tradecraft to leave every operational detail hidden in one place. And the East Germans and the Russians were always zealots for clean operational work.'

'Zealots ignore reality,' said Lockwood. 'When the crowds turn and the dream's over, there's no time to burn all the documents. Bad news for them, good news for us.'

Vine approached the reading table now and reached down to touch the various bundles. This was always his favourite part. So much of the secret world was conducted in the abstract. Mining the thoughts of another person's head. Here, finally, was something tactile. Vine ran his hand over the surface and tried to imagine the things these bundles of paper had seen.

Lockwood joined him now, both staring at the treasure for a moment. Then she said: 'What if we've been looking at this the wrong way round?'

'How do you mean?'

'What if it all comes down to perspective? We know the Russians' asset is codenamed PHOENIX. We know they were recruited just before the end of the Cold War. We know, or can suspect, that the mission objective was to install this asset at the very highest levels of the British state. And, crucially, we also know that this mole has managed to exist undetected for three decades. Even Philby never managed that long without questions being raised.'

'Why do I sense an objection coming?'

'We have the breadcrumbs from the documents Alexander Ivanov left behind. But we also have basic reason. How likely is it that one agent-in-place could exist for that long undetected? Alone, without support. Since the Cambridge Five, Vauxhall Cross and Thames House have been paranoid about history repeating itself. So has everyone else. JIC, Number 10, the works.'

As she laid it out like that, Vine could feel his own doubts resurface too. The fuzziness around it all, as if something was still missing. 'You don't think one person alone could do it?'

'Do you?'

'Theoretically, it's feasible. If the handler–asset protocol was tight enough, if the agent-in-place was patient, then possibly.'

'What if possibly isn't good enough?'

Vine glanced across at her. 'You think the PHOENIX mole isn't just a single person?' he said.

'What if the PHOENIX asset is far greater than we've been imagining? Directorate S never did things by halves. Why would they recruit one person when they could recruit a ring? You said it yourself. Everything goes back to context. The PHOENIX op was a humiliation exercise.'

'And a spy ring is louder than a lone asset.'

'You can't deny the logic.'

'No,' said Vine, knowing he couldn't. He imagined himself sitting in Yasenevo, months before the great experiment crumbled. The ideological certainty that it would one day be resurrected, old enemies humiliated. A phoenix set in motion to rise again. What could be more potent than another version of the Cambridge Five?

'What if the Centre has been running a spy ring since the end of the Cold War?' said Lockwood. 'A ring designed to reach the very top of the British establishment over the last thirty years? Some active, some sleepers, all of them fully in the service of the Centre and waiting for the right moment to strike? The moment when a new Cold War would rise from the ashes of the old.'

They both stood in silence for a moment. Like a minute of mourning and respect, the weight of the theory making the rest of life redundant. Vine tried to comprehend it. He saw the faces of the Elders again: Olivia Pope, James

Norris, Claire Sutherland. One of them betraying their country was seismic enough. More than one? Penetrating the diplomatic network, embassies, the nuclear codes, the entire machinery of British intelligence.

'If you're right,' said Vine, 'then it means one thing.'

Lockwood nodded. 'Yes.'

'Ivanov had suspicions and so they silenced him. Rashford was next and he suffered the same fate. Anyone who suspects the truth gets taken out.'

'Two down, two to go,' said Lockwood. And then she said it, the hidden truth in both of their minds. 'What if we're the next names on that list?'

36

Protocol dictated that the Rosenholz Files were never to be taken out of the Cabinet Office archives, forcing Vine to work inside the temperature-controlled room. He had a sneaking love for this side of the job. Perhaps it was the closet academic in him. The quietness of the archives, the sense of tranquillity. There were just the bundles of documents and no other sight or sound. The only way to protect themselves now was hard-copy proof. Without that, all they had was theory.

Lockwood was soon called away by other matters. In her absence, Vine pulled up a chair and began systematically laying out each bundle and sorting them into some kind of system. From a first glance, it was clear that no one had tried to sieve the information recently. It was still jumbled from whoever had been in here last. Vine wondered when that was. Twenty years ago, thirty perhaps. These bundles rushed out of the GDR and then dumped here. The tragedy of every generation was forgetting those who went before, a relentless cycle of historical amnesia.

The main thing to notice was the sheer scale of the documents. There were hundreds of pieces of paper with that peculiar, old typewriter font and copious squiggles and additions, crossings out and underlinings, the mix of machine-perfect and amateurishly handwritten. Vine had

German and Russian in his gift, but it had been years since he properly used either. He started reading and it was like revisiting a childhood haunt, familiar and different, full of clumsy beginnings and nursery steps.

He spent the first hour methodically trying to impose some order on the collection. He could see most documents would be of no immediate use. Details of detainees, subjects who'd been interviewed, floorplans and operational details from missions long since burned. He began ruthlessly pushing aside anything not related to agents-in-place, clearing the first four bundles. The next two – five and six – were haphazardly put together. Vine could decode the origin story again, papers jammed into folders, the painstaking filing process discarded in the sweaty rush to get these papers out. Order and logic be damned.

The work was slow and laborious. But time seemed to evaporate even so, hours vanishing instead of minutes. Vine checked his watch and felt his stomach rumble, realizing he hadn't eaten again. Food was always the first thing he forgot when the familiar obsession took hold. The way in which investigating – the thorny details of all counter-espionage hunts – began to consume you.

He was on to bundle seven now. The two preceding bundles carefully ordered in neat alphabetical order, but neither provided what he was looking for. The codenames reached J, and the quest went on to find the first P. Most of the names and the corresponding operational activity referred to sub-agents. Those in-between figures, neither civilian nor spook. The stringers, informants and village gossips who casually betrayed their neighbours. He wondered how many were still alive now. They would have reinvented themselves when the wall came down, of course, this part of their lives quietly forgotten. These paper records were a final indictment for their crimes.

He continued working through the rest now. Alphabetizing and scanning along each codename and date, trying to decipher the scrawls of handwriting in scratchy ink added in the margins, bumping against the limits of his German. Slowly teasing out odd phrases. The familiar mental cramp. Other professions had their visible ends. Counter-espionage was like an endless philological quest, rooting through words and jottings, digging for meaningless notations, knowing the journey would never be over. He was searching for that rare light, the glimmer that illuminated all the rest.

And then, like that, it was there. No trumpets or fanfare. Instead, the summit was inherently normal, just another mark on another page. Vine looked at what was in front of him again. The rumpled texture of the paper and the faded type, the thumbprints still visible around the top. Two thirds down, stowed there like any other entry, was the magic word.

'PHOENIX'.

Across from that, under the subsection reserved for handler codenames, was another two-syllable word: 'ARTHUR'.

The first new piece of data to add to the rest. Vine flicked back through the other pages to double-check. But he was sure. From the position on the document, ARTHUR had to be the senior handler for the PHOENIX asset, the intelligence officer monitoring PHOENIX's progress from HQ. Handler, mastermind and mentor. Alive or dead, this codename was the only trace. Next to ARTHUR was '(DRES)'. The HQ for this operation was Dresden and not, as might have been expected, East Berlin.

Vine checked the entry once, then again. He flicked further on to see if there was any other material linked to the PHOENIX entry, but the 'P' section ran out. He turned back to the entry and kept studying it, trying to divine any more clues, waiting for the patterns and implications to properly form.

But the first order of business seemed already clear. PHOENIX was the codename for the asset or, possibly, the spy ring. ARTHUR was the name of their handler. It would be run through the Stasi to give distance, but the Centre always exerted full control over an op of this magnitude. What was EXCALIBUR then? The codename written on Ivanov's transcript of the bugged call. Where and how did that fit into the picture?

The initial link was obvious, no doubt. EXCALIBUR was King Arthur's greatest weapon. Operation EXCALIBUR had to be linked to the KGB handler ARTHUR. Some kind of inside joke. Vine turned back to the older bundles now, thumbing hurriedly until he reached the 'E' section, scanning down to see if EXCALIBUR made any appearance. But there was nothing. He spent the next hour looking through the rest of the papers – those categorized and those still formlessly uncategorized – but there was no mention of EXCALIBUR in either. Why would Ivanov include it, and yet it was omitted here?

Vine could feel the pieces turning, slowly slotting into formation. Perhaps it post-dated this? The EXCALIBUR operation was – no, *is* – the handler ARTHUR's final flourish. Yes, something only hazily envisaged at the time the Rosenholz Files were compiled. Ivanov had given the piece of paper to Rashford for safekeeping. Rationally, P1 and P2 from the transcript, then, had to be involved in EXCALIBUR too. But as what exactly? Asset and handler? PHOENIX and ARTHUR? Or, perhaps, two of the PHOENIX moles conversing together. In station parlance, PHOENIX 1 and PHOENIX 2.

Vine sat back and closed his eyes and let the various options play out. The mathematical probabilities. There were so many ways in which history could have formulated itself. His eyes were still closed when he heard footsteps behind him. A light shimmered on further back. He had only just turned and opened his eyes again when he saw Emma Lockwood standing behind him.

She looked drained, as if she'd just thrown up, shock hollowing her out. It was like a nightmare recurring. The queasy reality of the enemy and their invisible might. 'What's happened?' he said.

Except, on some level, he thought he already knew.

PART THREE

37

By the time they arrived at the crime scene, the place was already crawling with lights and uniforms. A portion of the South Bank had been cordoned off at either end. Members of the PaDP team had been drafted in to temporarily patrol the scene. The body had already been retrieved from the Thames and was now being examined by forensics.

DCI Kate Calman was ahead of them now, marshalling her team of plainclothes and uniforms, glancing warily at the two intruders. Vine heard the snippets of radio chatter and talk all around him. But there was only one thought pounding through his head, like an alarm blaring at his temple.

The third victim. The most senior member of the Elders' Committee.

The person he had interviewed only hours before.

Olivia Pope was dead.

Eventually, Calman bowed to the inevitable and came over to brief them. 'We got the call-out half an hour ago,' she said, brusque and unflappable. 'A tourist saw the body floating down the river. The Marine Policing Unit were called in to retrieve the body and that's when we had the first hint of an ID. Given the sensitivity, it had to go straight to the top. The Commissioner made the decision to bring in the SFOs and cordon the whole thing off.'

'Any idea yet how it happened?' said Lockwood.

'From the distance travelled, and calculated against the current, we think she jumped from the South Bank.' Calman stopped before the barriers, the Thames churning ahead of them. 'Around about here, I'd say, where the barriers are low.'

It was pitch black now. Vine looked out at the greyness of the water, interrupted only by the sprinkle of lights from Portcullis House on the other side of the river. The middle of Westminster Bridge was on their left, a remnant of tourists still clustering round. Vine tried to imagine Olivia Pope standing here, looking down at the limitless expanse of water, knowing she had only seconds left. The balletic fall and then the hellish coldness of the river.

'Why jumped?' said Vine, turning towards Calman.

Calman looked at him with the same accusatory stare from the Savoy Hotel. 'What do you mean?'

'It's still too early for the tox to come back. Why do you say jumped?'

'I see,' said Calman. 'As a spook, you have an in-depth knowledge of forensics, do you? You think she stumbled into the river?'

'Were there any signs of struggle on the body? What about any indication she might have been pushed?'

'Do you know how difficult it would be for an assailant?' said Calman. 'Picking an open location and a high-profile target. Opposite Parliament and New Scotland Yard, in direct view of hundreds of police officers.'

'Unless the assailant needed the target to be silenced quickly.'

Calman shook her head. 'The woman jumped. Forensics will back me up. That's the only way this could have happened. Trust me.'

Vine was about to respond when he saw Lockwood warn him off. There was little point getting into a needless spat with Scotland Yard now. 'Thank you,' he said.

Calman nodded. 'Is there anything else you lot need? Or can I get back to my proper job?'

'That's all we need,' said Lockwood. She took out a card and handed it to Calman. 'My direct number. Anything else happens – statements, fast-track forensics – call me.'

Calman took the card and then hurried away back to her team, shouting out orders to the CSIs and the huddle of uniforms trying to keep warm. Lockwood buttoned up her coat and they began walking back in the direction of Westminster Bridge.

'I know what happens when a monarch dies,' said Vine. 'And I've heard rumours about when a Prime Minister passes away in office. What's the protocol when the Cabinet Secretary goes?'

'Welcome to my world,' said Lockwood. 'The Cabinet Secretary makes and enforces the protocol. Normally we'd ask them.'

They'd reached the start of Westminster Bridge now. Vine looked to his left and saw a few lights still aglow on the House of Commons Terrace, the building casting an awesome shadow over the river, dominating the skyline. He could see Calman's point, although he disagreed with it. To strike at Pope here – directly opposite Parliament, Portcullis House, New Scotland Yard and the Ministry of

Defence – was bold. For ordinary mortals? Impossible. But this was a flash job, hurriedly adapting to circumstances, another statement by the Centre. No, they weren't – and never had been – dealing with ordinary mortals here.

Alexander Ivanov, Max Rashford, Olivia Pope.

Vine wondered again at the scale of it. The SVR had endless freelancers on their books. Wet workers of the highest calibre who could vanish instantly. But they were summoned only for missions of overwhelming importance to the Russian state. This latest move confirmed that protecting the PHOENIX secret counted as such. No one – no matter their position, wealth or status – was beyond Yasenevo's reach.

'What will you do now?' said Vine.

'Liaise with the Prime Minister for starters,' said Lockwood. 'The death of the Chief of the Defence Staff was bad enough. The death of a serving Cabinet Secretary now makes this a category one matter of national security. We'll have to go into full damage limitation mode. A DSMA Notice to the press to stop this getting into tomorrow's papers. And an urgent call up for the three agency heads. The PM will want to chair a COBRA meeting before we plan our response.'

They were almost at the end of Westminster Bridge. A selection of cabs swished by, the odd pedestrian making their way home, a smattering of medical staff heading over to St Thomas' Hospital near the crime scene. Lockwood's phone was pinging constantly. They stopped just before crossing over to Bridge Street.

Lockwood turned to him, tiredness and stress playing

around her eyes. 'I need you to do something else for me,' she said. 'Even though you've already done so much.'

'Of course,' said Vine. 'Anything.'

'I want you to continue with your clear-up operation. Ivanov and Rashford left material behind just before they died. If our suspicions are correct, there's every chance Pope wanted to alert us to something too. See what you can find out.'

'Anything in particular you want me to search for?'

'You said Pope sounded like someone who was conducting her own investigation. She warned us off because she didn't want anyone getting in the way. If that's correct, then tonight must have happened because she was getting too close.'

Vine considered the request. After so long, he could feel the pinch of fear. An old acquaintance he'd hoped to never meet again. The sort that rose behind the throat and paralysed everything. He looked back at the crime scene, seeing Calman and her troops still busy down below. And he thought of his bed and all that had happened since answering the call. Wishing, once again, that he could wind back time. Undo what had already been done. 'And what happens if we get even closer?' he said, looking out at the river and its black-blue embrace. Remembering the warning from before. 'What happens then?'

'Then,' said Lockwood, a similar note of fear entering her voice, 'we pray.'

38

The first angle to try was the cameras. Vine was almost sure that any assailant trained by the Centre would have memorized CCTV positions and expertly ducked them all. But it didn't hurt to rule out the possibility of a mistake. Each murder was a more daring play, yes, but also a more reckless one. The Centre was improvising now, desperately trying to protect their asset, hoping some other crisis or event would turn the state's attention away from the PHOENIX case. And improvisation always led to errors.

Back inside the OCP in Pimlico, Vine brewed himself another mug of strong black filter coffee and then returned to the top floor. This was another aspect of the job so many hated. The new recruits, especially. All enticed into the secret world with the lure of covert action, the lingering comparison with the CIA's Special Activities Division, a paramilitary fable of the spy's life. Instead, they ended up immersed in the painstaking grind of real investigation. Document review, conversation transcripts, hunting through hours of CCTV footage to spot the one pearl of information that could be a genuine lead. After twenty years, Vine was convinced intelligence officers came in two breeds: performers and analysts. Despite his fieldwork, he had always been an analyst at heart.

He loaded up the raw CCTV footage and took another sip of coffee. He pressed play and then sat forward in the chair and began watching. The footage contained everything from the main CCTV cameras around Downing Street, allowing the viewer to piece together the exact chronology. All the way from Olivia Pope leaving Number 10 through the main gate right up until her body was found floating in the Thames.

The first hour was the real legwork, scrolling through CCTV footage from the Number 10 cameras themselves. The Cabinet Office, the Foreign Office, Richmond House, the obscure Parliament Street entrance to Portcullis House. Each camera to be watched separately, like a film editor splicing the best shots together, building a scene with forensic slowness. Another cup of coffee followed. Now Vine had the best angle for every step. Pope swaddled up in her formal coat, that brisk sense of establishment smartness. The first curiosity, of course, was Pope walking at all. The Cabinet Secretary and the National Security Adviser both had permanent access to the government carpool. A way to avoid a rucksack being snaffled on the Tube and state secrets revealed. Why breach protocol and head out on foot?

The second curiosity followed soon after. Vine rewound the footage now and made sure there were no visual tricks being played. Then he fast forwarded, looking at all the various angles at the start of Westminster Bridge. The route Pope must have taken to reach the point on the South Bank where the police believed the incident happened. He checked once, then again. But it was unmistakeable. Pope exited Number 10 on foot and then – quite clearly – went dark before getting to Westminster Bridge.

Vine rewound the footage. And spotted the exact moment it happened. Dame Olivia Pope, Cabinet Secretary, joining the migration towards the entrance to Westminster Tube station. Vine fast forwarded again, did his usual trick with the various camera angles, and saw Pope proceeding towards the start of Westminster Bridge from Bridge Street.

For the next half hour, Vine rewound and fast forwarded, playing every possible variation. Every spook knew the unreliability of camera footage. The Centre enjoyed nothing more than manipulating visual imagery into Hollywood CGI, the improbable turned into mundane reality. And yet he was sure the footage he was seeing was real. The details correct. Small recurrences that were tiny, almost unnoticeable. Vine slowed down the milliseconds of footage and zoomed in as far as he could. Then he slowed the footage even further until he was watching it frame by frame.

Pope about to enter Westminster Tube station. Surrounded by a cluster of others escaping the office at such a late hour. Pope glancing up, breaking the fourth wall. Looking for a split second – nothing more – directly down the lens of the camera placed above. As if she knew what might be about to happen, the chance of someone reviewing this footage later. The simplest and most elemental tradecraft in the book. Old school in every way.

Vine loaded up a map on the monitor and double checked his hunch. Any pedestrian wanting to get to

Westminster Bridge from Number 10 would simply cross at the lights and make their way up Bridge Street on foot. Elbowing through the crowds in Westminster Tube station was a timewaster, an illogical diversion. Unless the logic was for something else. The secret rationale of a person who knew her life might be in danger. Who had no easy recourse to a dead-letter box. Someone forced to use what she had in the moment.

Olivia Pope had left him a signal.

39

When he had memorized the footage, Vine left the OCP in Pimlico and began the short walk back to Westminster. He replayed the CCTV footage in his mind, convinced that Olivia Pope's look-to-camera had been an indication. Pope entering Westminster station from the Parliament Street entrance could only have been for tradecraft purposes. Servicing a makeshift DLB, perhaps, or a brush contact. Pope had never been trained as a hood, but she had been in contact with them throughout her entire Whitehall career. She knew enough for when the moment came.

There were still a few late-night drinkers and stragglers milling around. Otherwise, the streets had a churchy quiet to them. Vine carried out his precautions, taking a variety of decoy routes. Almost fearing the absence of a tail more than the presence of one. A watcher echoing his movements meant routine surveillance, the sort Vine had become used to throughout his career. The absence of a tail meant something far more worrying. The snatch job. A van skidding to a halt in an empty street. Or now – and worse – the more brutal option. A kitchen knife in and up, butchering through the stomach. Bleeding out on the pavement. Another stabbing quietly erased from the record the next day. Solomon Vine would be as anonymous in death as in life.

He arrived in Westminster now and headed down Whitehall to recreate Pope's movements exactly. He reached the entrance to Westminster station and noticed the small camera eye just where Pope had looked. Hidden away to avoid attention. The glance had to be deliberate. Pope knew where the cameras were. The decoy stop in Westminster station was not accidental. Something was in there which could shed light on all the rest.

Vine headed down the steps into the station now. Struck, again, at the decrepitude of it all. The dirty floors and the lights with their hospital brightness, colourless and unnatural. The only relief were the posters, adding some vibrancy. A busker sat in his usual position tunelessly serenading the last few travellers with snatches of old Beatles songs. Vine walked on towards the main concourse and the ticket barriers. The exit to Bridge Street was on his right and a trickle of people were still heading up. Vine stood for a moment and looked around.

The newsagent's. The coffee place. Then the barriers and the platforms and the odd tubular architecture of the lower levels, commuters welcomed into a space-age dystopia. Picking a dead-letter box, or DLB, was always an impossible task. DLBs were designed to help both parties share and exchange items while avoiding surveillance. The greatest drop was an illusion. It was invisible but also easy to access, allowing the second party to service the drop without drawing attention.

That made any of the shops difficult. It would be nightmarish to service without being caught by the shop assistants. Vine discounted the shops, looking instead for other alternatives. Locations that were a permanent fixture but weren't often used. He saw a pile of free newspapers waiting to be thrown out for the day. He wondered if Pope could have hidden something in the bottom there, trusting that the last copy wouldn't be taken. But, again, the risk factor outweighed the opportunity.

Vine walked back and decided to try the time-honoured alternative. The bathrooms were located in the long passageway that joined the two Parliament Street entrances to the main concourse. He checked it was empty and then walked into the women's bathroom. The cisterns were the usual places to hide something, but that involved preparation. Pope didn't seem like someone who had that kind of time. This drop was instinctive. A desperate last attempt to leave a trail for someone else to follow before the worst happened. Placing something in a cistern or taping it underneath the sinks was too onerous. Too public. Vine checked for anything obvious, but his doubts were confirmed. No, there was nothing here.

It was just as he was walking back up towards the main concourse that he realized his mistake. What if Pope had decided on something more interesting than an ordinary dead-letter box? A piece of tradecraft that would have pleased even the best minds in Vauxhall Cross and Thames House.

Vine could hear the instructors at the Fort again. The easy lessons over, turning now to the proper intricacies of the trade. The tricks passed down from generation to generation of spooks. Only one thing trumped a dead-letter box. That was the live letterbox. The living and breathing equivalent. Not just hiding in plain sight, but existing right in front of you.

Vine walked back from the bathroom area and looked at the busker again. The music was so familiar it barely counted as background. As baked into this place as the dust on the floor and the cracks in the ceiling. The busker always seemed to be of indeterminate age, hovering anywhere between late twenties to early forties, the contours of the face disguised by the tangle of beard, curling up until it merged with the sideburns and overwhelmed any distinct features. He had a battered old guitar and was strumming the chords for 'All You Need Is Love'. The guitar case in front of him contained a scattering of loose change.

Vine watched from a distance for a moment and then decided to trust his gut. He headed back up to the main concourse and straight to the cashpoint, tapping in his PIN and withdrawing two hundred pounds. He was the last devotee of cash, trusting its wonderful physicality. The one thing that couldn't be traced.

He returned to the tunnel now. The rest of the place was empty, not even the tap-tap of imminent souls about to pass by. Vine felt unusually nervous. He had strategies to pitch to most types: the banking classes, the politicos, the fellow spooks. But he'd never approached a busker before on operational duties. Knowing how many ways this could go wrong.

And so he made the offering first. Bending down and showily placing the hundred pounds into the guitar case. Hoping that would buy him an audience. The busker looked at the notes and kept lazily strumming, the tune filtering out until it was just a hazy progression of chords. But quieter now, giving room for Vine to make his case. Addressing judge and jury.

'I think you know a friend of mine,' said Vine. 'Five-six, mid fifties, brown knee-length coat with a fur trimming on the collar. She was here earlier this evening?'

The busker didn't indicate anything as he listened to the description. He kept strumming, then glanced again at the guitar case. Nothing direct, just a flick towards the hundred pounds as he turned his head away. Vine acknowledged the gesture, opening his wallet again and taking out the next portion of the money. The same routine repeated. He bent down and, with some fanfare, respectfully placed the next hundred pounds in a different part of the case.

'I think my friend left something for me,' continued Vine. 'Something which she asked you to pass on if I came looking.'

The second financial contribution seemed to have satisfied the busker. He glanced again at the case and then ceased strumming. He looked up at Vine. When he spoke, his voice was hoarse, rasping out each syllable. 'Password.'

Vine moved closer to hear properly. Crouching now, too. 'I'm sorry?'

'Password.'

Of course. Basic operational security. No one could service the live letterbox unless they also furnished a password. A simple, if surprisingly effective, way of avoiding an SVR hood from the Russian embassy or a NOC making the same journey.

Vine stood up again now, relieving the pressure in his legs. It had to be assumed that the events of the last few days were linked. Ivanov, Rashford, Pope. Each victim leaving behind a trail to be continued. The three of them aware of what went before. All of them knew their lives could be in danger thanks to the activities of the PHOENIX mole. The answer, surely, was buried somewhere in those facts.

Vine went back over everything. Searching for a common thread he could cling on to. Ivanov's body in the hotel suite. The note guiding him to the London Library. The book by Dostoevsky. Rashford's office and the bookshelf. The biography of Dostoevsky and the transcript carefully hidden inside the endpaper. Now, at last, Vine looked around and saw the third and most obvious clue. The location of the live letterbox. There was no way to be sure, but it was the best guess he had.

The book in the London Library.

Westminster station.

One last password. One last hoop to jump through.

'Underground,' he said.

There was silence. Vine wondered if Pope had attached further conditions. Was it one guess at the password or more? Or could this really be it? The last truth of Dame Olivia Pope trapped for all eternity. Vine could hear another sound break the silence now. Hard leather soles tapping down the concrete stairs to their right. Another commuter, or worse, about to round the corner and observe them both.

And then the busker reacted. He reached behind and

pulled out a single manila file with one official stamp on the front. Vine took the file and read the wording.

'CSEY'.

Cabinet Secretary Eyes Only.

The top level of classification, far above the strap grades. Strictly speaking, a file like this was never allowed to leave government premises. Pope had broken the law even by bringing it here. By implication, Vine was about to repeat the same sin.

For a second, he debated what to do next. He was working under the authority of the National Security Adviser. He was retired and yet – now – semi-official. As a former head of counter-espionage, he knew there was only one proper option. He should hand this file in. That was the only way the system worked. His training demanded it. And yet – and *yet* – the system was compromised, infected from the inside. Vine checked behind him one final time and quickly stashed the manila file in his bag.

The other commuter was nearly at the bottom of the stairs now. Vine nodded to the busker and then turned swiftly away.

40

The sensible thing was to go back to the OCP in Pimlico. But Vine let his instinct override operational security. Yes, it was possible that Wellington Square had been under some kind of surveillance from the start. But the OCP was still state-run. Seeing the manila file with the CSEY stamp on it brought an even greater reality to things. Olivia Pope – the Cabinet Secretary, the person in charge of it all – hadn't trusted her own structures. She'd broken the law she was tasked with enforcing and betrayed her own code. Vine didn't want the stale, official comforts of the OCP. Now, more than ever, he wanted a taste of home.

The route back to Wellington Square was suitably convoluted. Vine changed cabs three times, making some of the journey on foot to confuse any watchers. Anything to avoid another repeat of the Special Forces Club or MoD experience. Forced into losing his anonymity and cover. As the last cab pulled up outside his front door, Vine was confident he'd dry-cleaned himself. Wellington Square was still empty at this hour, the banking classes soon to rise, creeping out for their early dawn vigils.

Vine took a shower and ate for the first time in forever. The food allowing his brain to function properly. When he was fortified, he picked up his bag and headed towards the library, his favourite place in the house. It had been his sanctuary ever since buying the place. This was where he made his bets on the market, filling up hours, sometimes days. The library was the place to take the ultimate decisions in a case. Now would be no different.

He opened up the bag and slowly removed the manila file. It was something that wouldn't have looked out of place during Vine's early years with the endless documents that swilled around Century House and Vauxhall Cross, the legacy of a vanishing world now returned. Paper couldn't be hacked. Paper didn't leave a digital trace. It could be burned, completely eliminated from the face of the earth, locked and secure. Paper was the spy's ultimate weapon.

Vine opened the file Pope had left behind and carefully began flicking through each page, photographing each one with the vaping device from Hanslope so he had a record for later. From the dates on the opening pages, the file appeared to have been compiled over the last few months. It contained numerous highly classified documents relating to the service of British diplomats and civil servants in the late eighties and early nineties. Lists of names, embassy postings, personnel evaluations, photos, training records. Pope was conducting her own off-the-books investigation into a possible mole. Hunting through the archives to try and join the dots. When Vine finished photographing the pages, he reached for his mobile and dialled the only number stored inside, cancelling the call after the third ring. The pre-agreed signal.

Half an hour later, the doorbell rang. Vine placed the file down and went over to the window. He saw a car heading back out on to the King's Road. A cab rather than anything official. Sensibly, she was taking even more precautions this time.

He glanced around the rest of the square, then headed down to the door. He opened it and Emma Lockwood walked in silently, neither speaking until they reached the library. Her hair was already dewy from a smattering of rain.

'The signal,' she said. 'That means you have something?'

Vine walked over to the drinks tray and found two clean tumblers, pouring a finger of Scotch into each. 'Yes,' he said, handing the first tumbler over. 'More than something.'

41

They sat in two armchairs opposite each other, the manila file on a coffee table between them. Vine tried to remember the last time he'd had someone over to the house like this. But he couldn't. Wellington Square was his private place, a fortress protecting him from the outside world. Even in the early days, a visitor felt like an invasion, sullying what had just been his.

Yet, now, he felt the opposite. It was always the way with operations. The intensity was like a political campaign, throwing disparate people together at such close quarters. The usual fumbling and awkwardness cast aside. Two people forced into a relationship by circumstance, marooned in the middle of something they still didn't fully understand. Wellington Square was almost an embassy now, the one piece of ground where they were nominally safe. Everything beyond seemed thorny and hostile.

Emma Lockwood took a sip of Scotch, her face still damp from the rain. 'Pope did leave something behind then?' she said.

Vine put his tumbler down. 'Yes,' he said. 'A file. I accessed it through a live letterbox at Westminster station.'

'Impressive tradecraft for a civil servant.'

'She obviously absorbed more than we thought.'

Lockwood nodded. 'Either she had something to hide,

or she hated the idea of a third party trampling over the evidence.'

Vine opened the file and picked up the first page, handing it across to Lockwood.

She put down her drink now and glanced at the title on the first page. 'Ivanov?' she said. 'Pope *was* directly investigating the Elders' operation?'

Vine had other parts of the file out now, handing them over in turn, the words almost falling out of him in a heady rush. 'As you can see, the centrepiece of Pope's file is an intelligence report written in her own hand.'

'Centrepiece?'

'It claims to be an interview with a senior Russian defector in Britain, one of the many former KGB hands being housed and protected by the government. According to the file, this senior defector recently summoned Pope for a meeting in the Cotswolds and told her that he had information concerning a long-term agent-in-place. Someone at the top of the Whitehall hierarchy who was reporting back to Moscow Centre.'

Lockwood looked at the second piece of paper. Trying to decipher Pope's spidery scrawl. 'Did this senior defector name a price?'

'The defector was Russian. Naturally, he always had a price. Again, according to the file, the said defector claimed he would trade this information in exchange for greater protection from the Security Service and Scotland Yard. Plainclothes at the end of the road, that sort of thing. The defector appeared worried that the GRU would come for him next.'

Lockwood continued reading, trying to get a sense of it. 'And Pope agreed to the demand?'

'It appears so. According to her own report of the case, at least.'

Lockwood put the piece of paper down. Reaching forward for more papers now, thumbing through them. Concern etched across her face. 'Do we know if this defector's product was chicken feed or the real thing?'

'According to Pope's report,' said Vine, 'it was pure gold. This Russian defector – never named in Pope's report for basic op-sec, it seems – was exfiltrated from the Soviet Union just before the end of the Cold War. But the defector tells Pope a story from a visit he made to the KGB station in Dresden. He claims that Moscow Centre succeeded in recruiting a double right at the heart of the British establishment before the wall came down.'

'PHOENIX.'

'Yes. The defector also goes on to provide numerous other personal details. First, he claims the asset known as PHOENIX was recruited as a student in the late eighties. Second, that the asset was a brilliant linguist. And, third, that the asset was educated in Cambridge as a scholar.'

'That was the place of recruitment?'

'The defector claims the PHOENIX mole was recruited in Cambridge, not abroad, and has worked within the government for their entire career.'

Lockwood stopped reading again. She looked across at Vine. 'So this defector claimed the PHOENIX mole was a single asset? Not a network?'

Vine nodded. 'One individual mole. Someone now at the very top of the tree.'

'Which explains why Pope resented us being involved. We were looking at the Elders in the round.'

'Olivia Pope was ahead of us. According to the file itself, she'd already narrowed it down to two possible candidates.' Vine reached for another part of the file, handing the next cache of papers over. 'I've read through it all. The second part of Pope's file concerns the history, vetting and career activities of two of her fellow members of the Elders' Committee.'

'Claire Sutherland and James Norris.'

'Yes. The Chief of MI6 and the Permanent Under-Secretary at the Foreign Office.'

'Profile-wise?'

'Both fit almost all of the criteria. Both Sutherland and Norris studied at Cambridge University in the 1980s. Both are fluent in multiple languages. Both have worked for the Crown for their entire working lives.'

'What about the other details?'

'Some aren't exact. But, for me, that makes the defector's account even more plausible. He was giving this information to Pope almost three decades after his defection. Realistically, we'd expect some slippage.'

'Too perfect and it becomes suspicious.'

'Rehearsed, exactly, learned rather than heard. Neither Sutherland or Norris ever technically had scholarships to Cambridge, but that's a minor mistake. Either an error from the defector's original source in Dresden or a detail lost in the mists of thirty years.' Vine picked up the very final piece of paper from the file and handed it to Lockwood.

She looked down at it. Two photos – one of Claire Sutherland, the other of James Norris – with a word written in Pope's unmistakeable handwriting at the bottom: 'PHOENIX?'

Lockwood lingered on it; then she glanced back up at Vine. She held the papers in her lap, reaching over for the tumbler and draining the rest of it. 'I think it's finally time, don't you?'

'Yes,' said Vine, knowing she was right. 'I think we need some reinforcements.'

42

The backup couldn't be official. Or have any links with Vauxhall Cross. Those were the first two basic rules. Between them, Claire Sutherland and James Norris controlled the entire diplomatic and intelligence machinery. They oversaw embassies, consulates and stations all over the globe, the distribution of CX reports to Number 10 and the face of Britain to the world. No, backup couldn't come with a sanctioned intelligence past. It would have to be a contact from the old days, then. Vine had one name in mind.

The first task was to arrange a meeting. Lockwood soon left Wellington Square to head back to Whitehall. Vine, meanwhile, showered and skipped breakfast, his mind too full of what needed to be done to eat properly. He drank another round of black filter coffee instead and then rooted through his drawers to find what he needed. One last memento from his time at the Fort all those years ago. A single piece of bright yellow chalk. A vital tool now.

The next part of the protocol was the most exposed. Vine left the house and headed down the King's Road, checking his tail every minute or so. He entered Sloane Square Tube station and pretended to buy a paper ticket from the self-service machine, checking if anyone had followed him in. When he was sure they hadn't, Vine left the Tube station and walked the few yards towards the Royal Court Theatre. He paused nearby for a moment, stooping down as if picking up some litter from the ground. He took out the yellow chalk from his coat pocket and left a small X mark on the wall. Obvious enough to be visible, but not distracting enough to be washed off within the next few hours. He checked the mark and, once satisfied, took another decoy route back up to Wellington Square. The mark had now been left at their usual signal site. The first part of the plan was laid.

The rest of the rules were similarly specific. The second stage would wait until the afternoon. Vine occupied the time by going through Pope's file again, committing every word to memory. He fidgeted restlessly and paced the floor of the library and prayed that the signal site was still monitored. Hoping the plan would work.

That afternoon, Vine dry-cleaned himself on a route back towards Westminster, stopping before he reached Whitehall this time. He bought a copy of the *Economist* in cash and inserted the necessary information half-way through. Then he headed up the stairs towards the entrance for the National Gallery, walking up to the top floor at three thirty exactly. The second part of the set up was always more finicky than the first. His job was to wait in the middle of the top floor. He took a seat on one of the benches and patiently bided his time. The other person was meant to find him. A simple brush contact. Straight out of the Fort's textbook.

Eventually, Vine saw a woman sit down beside him.

Late fifties, bunched grey hair and an anonymous jacket. She was cradling a copy of the *New Statesman*, as instructed. No words were ever exchanged. The woman put down the copy of the *New Statesman* and Vine did likewise with his copy of the *Economist*. The woman waited for several minutes until she rose from the bench again, this time absent-mindedly taking the copy of the *Economist* with her. Vine had checked the rest of the room religiously for any potential troublemakers, the civilian classes who interrupted ops through no fault of their own. But no one looked as if they were going to take the seat immediately. So Vine waited another minute before rising himself, the old spook in him a stickler for the finer points of trade-craft, properly inhabiting the role.

When the wait was over, Vine scooped up the copy of the *New Statesman* and walked away casually, the most natural thing in the world. The information slipped into his copy of the *Economist* had two lines on it. The first line gave the time for the meet. The second the location. The brush contact had done its job. Everything was now set for the third stage of the plan.

Vine returned to Wellington Square to endure the next period of waiting, feeling like an actor condemned to their trailer. The hours seemed to drag and he went back over Pope's file once more, scouring it for any details he might still have missed. Then, after an eternity, the moment was upon him. He left Wellington Square and took a variety of cabs – interchanged and with intersecting routes – before arriving at the Coleridge Hotel in St James's at seven thirty exactly. In addition to the embassy hoods, others could still be looking for him after the Special Forces Club exit. Those with more muscle than morals. Able to make anything – and anyone – disappear without a second thought.

Numerous rooms had been booked out across different hotels with free cancellation policies in London. The real meet was occurring here in Room 34. Meets like this required putting an asset at their ease. Vine had planned ahead and began arranging the preferred delicacies. One bottle of vodka. A selection of cigars, some eye-wateringly expensive chocolates, and more alcohol of all varieties and flavours, in case this meet carried on far into the night. The same ritual as always. The chores of the seasoned agent-runner.

At eight exactly, there was the knock on the door. Two knocks, then a gap, then a further three knocks. Vine waited, and heard a further two knocks timed precisely ninety seconds after the last. Their own code for each other. Vine opened the door and saw Andrei standing in his usual state of merry dishevelment.

'Thomas!' said Andrei. 'My old friend.'

That's how he was always known. Neither of them ever did surnames. Everything was strictly on a first-name basis. Vine was 'Thomas', a British embassy hand with an abundance of connections in the secret world and helpful access with the Cousins. Andrei was a former KGB analyst, currently a freelance fixer in demand across the globe, operating in the gleefully misunderstood world of 'security consultancy'. His primary base was now London. He never advertised and had no public presence. His client list insisted upon it.

Andrei gazed round the hotel room and alighted on the vodka. 'The emergency protocol,' he said. 'The last time you triggered that must have been a decade ago. It's that serious?'

Vine closed the door and nodded. 'I'm afraid it is.'

43

They sat opposite each other like leaders at a summit, the grandness of the hotel room and the space around them gaping emptily. It seemed big enough for a function or a ball. Vine had already performed the basic checks. The light fittings, the en-suite bathroom, disconnecting the phone lines. There could be no third-party listeners to what he was about to say. Andrei busied himself with the vodka and the cigars, alternating chaotically between each.

'I take it this sudden meet is about Comrade Ivanov then,' said Andrei, eyeing up one of the cigars. 'The news is all around town.'

News travelled, no matter the precautions. Andrei would know about Rashford and Pope too. Chapter and verse. Vine sketched in some background on the case, nonetheless, but Andrei was too skilled in the ways of the world to give much of a reaction. He always had two modes: the neutral professorial look, the analyst in him busily crunching through new data and trying to find the most logical pattern; and then the broker he'd become, the showman who entertained clients, the man of hollow legs, the hugger and brawler and fighter.

Andrei remained silent for a while. He was finished with the vodka now. Instead, he was dipping his hand indulgently into the chocolate box, holding each chocolate up to the light like the finest ornament. 'So the rumours on our side are true,' he said. 'The British government does indeed have a copy of the Rosenholz Files?'

Vine knew there was no point lying. In such a wilderness of mirrors, Andrei and his type valued only the truth. A mark of brotherhood. 'Yes.'

'And you're sure that this PHOENIX asset is singular, yes? That it's not a spy ring of some kind. Fellow travellers, sympathetic souls who couldn't forget the cause? The sort of sub-agents still littered all over Europe. Annoying, but harmless. Agents of influence, as we once called them.'

Vine nodded. 'We considered the possibility of a ring. But Pope's report contradicts that theory. The information she received from the Russian defector clearly stated that the PHOENIX asset was one person.'

'That was all?'

'No. The defector also claimed that the PHOENIX asset was fluent in multiple languages and studied at Cambridge University in the 1980s.'

'Do you have any suspects?'

It was important to tease Andrei with glimpses of information. Enough to tempt him to speak, but no more. 'We have two.'

'Don't be coy. This is me you are speaking to.'

Now Vine was clearer, tougher. 'I asked you here for the meet because you know the Centre and you know the shadow world,' he said. 'PHOENIX isn't just garden-variety. The Centre doesn't run someone this high up for office gossip and dinner party chatter. What's the product for this op? What is PHOENIX's mission brief? Why is the Centre going to such lengths to protect them rather than pulling them out now and giving them a full pension and medals in Moscow?'

Andrei decided to eat the chocolate, the theatre of chewing a neat way to buy time. Getting a definite answer from a former spook was like trying to bottle air. They wriggled and writhed, obfuscated and downright lied. When the chocolate had all gone down, Andrei said: 'There is always gossip, you know that, Thomas. Put three former spies together and there are moles in every garden.'

No, he couldn't be allowed to duck out of an answer. Not now. Vine went again. 'But this time particularly,' he said. 'The Centre taking out two high-ranking members of the British establishment. Wet work on Ivanov himself. Why are they showboating, Andrei? Why are they throwing all caution to the wind? What's the endgame for them here?'

Andrei had a look on his face that Vine had seen before. For Andrei, secrecy was fun. It was to be toyed with, enjoyed, rolled around like a fine wine. He said: 'You ask too much, Thomas. All a person hears are rumours. All a simple member of the rank and file like me can tell you is that it's something big. Something major. The crown jewels themselves.'

'Rumours are a first step. Tell me the rumours.'

'It was Western naivety that allowed it, Thomas, you have to understand that. You and the other Whitehall liberals were fools. And the Centre knew it. Public weakness leads to private strength. The moment when the world is discounting you is always the perfect moment to strike. As the Cold War was ending, that is what the Centre did.'

'What could the Centre want then that it still wants now?'

'They knew the fight wasn't over. And, unlike your tribe, they took the long-term view. The Centre didn't evaluate operational performance in months or years. They saw it in decades. They plant a seed in the late eighties. By now it has grown into something. The Centre knows that tactics change but the world remains fundamentally the same.'

'The meets were conducted through the embassy then?' said Vine. 'The Centre would send a handler to run the PHOENIX asset through the usual channels? That's how the product was handed over?'

'That would be too easy. No, for an operation this big, the handler would have been an illegal. Someone with no ties at all to the Russian embassy or Moscow itself. A cut-out of some kind. They call them Special Reserve Officers. They hail from Department 1 in Directorate S. The fabled Special Reserve Unit.'

'The same SRO continuously for all this time?'

'That would be risky. Plus, the PHOENIX asset was working their way through the ranks. No, Thomas, listen to me. The Centre was prepared to bide its time. They could receive nothing for two years, possibly three. But happy in the knowledge that the asset was in place and ready to be reactivated when the Kremlin needed something.'

Vine paused, ordering his thoughts. 'What were they after, Andrei? Was the product economic, diplomatic, security-related or military even?'

Andrei smiled now. 'You're not seeing the full picture.'

It was always the ultimate analyst retort. If something didn't make sense, the fault wasn't with the world but with you. 'Help me see it,' said Vine. 'What am I missing?'

'A double who's been hiding in plain sight for thirty years,' said Andrei. 'We're talking once in a generation brilliance. Someone beyond Philby or Blake. Someone beyond Judas. This is a traitor at the very height of their powers. If they stumble, they die. So they learn never to stumble. Tell me. Are there any other codenames or pieces of data that can't yet be explained? Is there any part of the picture which you haven't found an answer for yet? An outlier? A deviation in the pattern?'

Another analyst question. Vine nodded. 'Yes,' he said. 'Just one. A meeting transcript was left behind by Alexander Ivanov, passed to me through General Rashford. It mentions an operation called EXCALIBUR.'

Andrei seemed intrigued. 'That was all? Ivanov just left the word behind? Excalibur, nothing else? No context?'

'No, just the word.'

'Then the word should be your guide. The Centre taunts you like that. Think about it, Thomas. Moscow has openly poisoned two traitors on UK soil. They have been behind the killings of many more, struck down on your own streets. What could be a final humiliation? Both public and secret at the same time. Something big enough to show the world? Real shock and awe?'

Vine had run through every possible target in his mind. He saw the faces of the two remaining suspects: James

Norris and Claire Sutherland. The Foreign Office and MI6. More than that?

At last, he said: 'Some form of attack.' He was desperate now for a nod, a clue, the merest hint of something. 'Taking out the bedrock of the special relationship, the UK and US intelligence-sharing partnership. A joint attack on both nations. That's the only thing that could be bigger. You're telling me *that's* what EXCALIBUR is?'

Andrei was smiling again. He rose from his chair now, scooping up the rest of the chocolates and unceremoniously tucking them into the baggy outside pocket of his jacket. Loot for the journey home.

'I told you the prize was big,' he said. 'Something worth waiting thirty years for. The UK and US helped destroy the Soviet system three decades ago. They have been waiting all that time to return the favour. Watch your back, Thomas. Tell your friends to do the same.'

44

Andrei left the hotel room and Vine made sure to clean up afterwards, ensuring there was no trace of them left behind. By nine fifteen, Vine had made his way towards Horseferry Road for his second assignment of the evening. The lights in Westminster mortuary were still on and Emma Lockwood was waiting outside, changed out of work clothes into mufti. Neither of them wanted to draw attention.

'How did it go?' she said as they began walking in step with each other. 'Did your secret source have anything to help us?'

Vine had been mulling on the Andrei meeting as he walked over. He had the same regrets of any interrogation, always wondering if he could have got more. 'Rumours in the shadow world suggest the Centre is going big,' he said. 'A full-scale attack against the UK and US high command. Something to make Litvinenko and the Salisbury poisonings look like child's play.'

Lockwood nodded sombrely, digesting the news. 'So ... you ready for this?'

Vine had only ever been inside a mortuary on two previous occasions. He always brandished a fake ID and muttered something vague about being attached to the Home Office. Now, though, Lockwood's status did all the work for them. One call to the loftier ranks of the Met and both were granted a private meeting with the forensic pathologist and sight of Pope's body with no police interruption or interdepartmental warfare.

Despite Vine's preparation, he found the smell was something else entirely. Clinical with an aftertaste of chlorine. The place seemed without colour, merely a procession of watery blues and insipid greens. The floors were hard and easily cleaned. The whole place was raw, all sharp elbows and edges. It reminded Vine of the tunnel area in the Tube station. The same pitiless light. But, this time, there was no hurried passing through.

The pathologist was a rake-like woman in her fifties. She had a matronly voice that could be heard two corridors down, and a ruthless busyness, blind to the dead person before her and upbraiding her assistants over tiny points of etiquette. Her various tools were laid out like cutlery near a plate.

Lockwood and Vine stood either side of the metal table, slowly adjusting to the sight of Pope. Once again, Vine was glad he chose Vauxhall Cross rather than Scotland Yard. There were few post-mortems in the spy world. People vanished, quietly sent into the great beyond. No one had to dig through their flesh afterwards.

The pathologist flicked a harried glance at them both, much like DCI Calman, and said: 'She drowned, in case you were wondering.'

'We weren't,' said Lockwood, matching the pathologist's tone. 'You said you had something else to tell us?'

'Yes. It looks like she was drugged as well. Nasty

business, fatally slowing down her reaction once inside the water.'

'Do you know what type of drug was used?' said Vine.

The pathologist directed another glower at him. Once again, he wondered if his presence triggered some kind of allergic reaction in law enforcement. The pathologist said: 'Not one I've come across much before, to be honest. In the trade it's known as SP-117.'

Vine nodded. 'Sodium thiopental.'

A fleeting look of respect that was gone as soon as it arrived. 'Yes. SP-117 is sodium thiopental mixed with barbiturate-anaesthetic. It's psychotropic. Completely tasteless and practically invisible.'

'One of the favourites of the KGB.'

'If you say so. For the man or woman on the street, it's more commonly known as a form of truth serum. Works like a charm, every time. Or so I've heard.'

'So whoever killed Pope got her to cough what she knew before killing her,' said Lockwood. 'Extract a full confession.'

'It's certainly one possibility. There are also bruising marks on her shoulders, indicating that she was pushed into the river.'

Vine saw the queasy implications and the horrible possibility of Olivia Pope spilling out all her secrets before dying, including their identities and mission. He feared the next logical step. 'That means she could have given away everything. The whole damn lot. She might have compromised the mission and everything she knew?'

'Yes, I suppose she might.'

'Is there anything we should be aware of from Pope's medical history?'

The pathologist shook her head. 'I had a quick glance through. Her notes show some battles with depression in her younger days. But I don't think that's what did for her.'

'There's no chance this was self-inflicted?' said Lockwood. A note in her voice, almost like hope. Anything other than the messy reality.

The pathologist stared at them both. 'No,' she said, her look softening, becoming even slightly apologetic. 'Sorry. But I'm afraid there's no chance of that at all.'

45

It was getting colder outside. Lockwood and Vine bought some takeaway coffees and then continued walking. Operationally, the open air was always the safest place for a debrief. The strategic use of their coffee cups – held up directly in front of the mouth when not drinking – allowed both to talk without the fear that someone could be lipreading too. The darkness did the rest of the work for them.

'I've had a read through the initial scene notes from the police team,' said Lockwood. 'So far, they've found no trace evidence left behind by the killer. The SP-117 is the only hint of foul play. The killer knew how to avoid the cameras near the South Bank and Westminster Bridge. Just like the Savoy and Rashford's house.'

Vine expected nothing less. 'Wet workers on the books of Moscow Centre have been trained for decades,' he said. 'They're expensive because they're the best. Chasing after them is hopeless. The exfil's probably already happened. Some private flight out of London City, halfway across to safety by now.'

'Unless they're waiting to kill again.'

'What about the Whitehall front?'

'The usual. Since Pope was found, Vauxhall Cross is demanding full control of the investigation.'

'Giving Claire Sutherland a bird's eye view over everything.'

'It gets better. Technically, the role of Cabinet Secretary has to be filled, at least on a temporary basis. The best-qualified candidate usually slots in until the full interview process is completed. In this case, that candidate is James Norris.'

Vine almost smiled at the symmetry of it. 'The new acting Cabinet Secretary.'

'The very one.'

Vine processed the thought. 'I'm not sure which is neater. If Sutherland's the mole, she can clean up all the mistakes and deflect blame. If Norris is the guilty party, he has the entire machinery of government at his disposal. Odds equally weighed. Both have clear motive.'

'In either scenario,' said Lockwood, 'Moscow Centre now has its ultimate wish. The PHOENIX asset firmly at the levers of power. Sutherland manages to move up from MI6 and get closer to the centre of things. Or Norris makes the acting Cabinet Secretary role permanent. The PHOENIX operation is nearly complete.'

'Not to mention that any concrete proof disappears too.'

'It looks like either Norris or Sutherland were bugging Rashford's phone and listening in to all his calls. When they saw that Rashford was calling you, they had someone on standby.'

Vine nodded and took another sip of coffee. 'And Pope?'

'Either they were bugging her office, or, more likely, Pope got careless and told Rashford that she was working on something. Rashford liked a few drinks. A bottle or two down, he mentioned it to either Norris or Sutherland.'

'The ring theory again.'

'Yes. Despite what the Rosenholz Files say, I still think we have to seriously consider that Sutherland or Norris aren't working alone. The PHOENIX operation is bigger than just one person. It would certainly explain how they've managed to survive all this time. I also did some more digging into Norris's and Sutherland's movements on the night of Ivanov's murder. It took a while, but I finally got their schedules.'

Vine was taken back to the start of the case. 'Ivanov's right-hand man, Sebastian Quinn, said he thought Ivanov had opened the door to someone he knew.'

'Precisely. Sutherland, it turns out, was stuck in an emergency Five Eyes meeting which went on into the small hours. James Norris, however, is unaccounted for. Not at the office, not at his home. Staff say they were trying to get an urgent message to him but he wasn't answering his phone either.'

'Norris does the intro and then Moscow Centre's finest does the rest.'

'Most likely. If we're going to have a chance to convict, we have to gather something that sticks. Theory won't be enough for the CPS to authorize charges, no matter how watertight.'

Vine looked at Lockwood. She seemed in pain again, trying not to clutch her temples. As though pins were pressed against her eyes.

'Migraine?' he said.

'My genius with disguise is clearly better than I thought,' she said.

'How bad?'

'DEFCON 3. Bad but not quite nuclear.'

'I'm sorry.' Vine was about to ditch the takeaway coffee and begin the dry-clean back to Wellington Square. 'This job always gets you in the head eventually. We've all been there.'

'Really?'

'Too many bodies, too many assets who never came back. You don't survive that unscathed. None of us do.'

Lockwood nodded and said: 'In terms of reinforcements, how would you feel about running this past another contact?'

Vine was intrigued. 'Higher than the source today?'

'Yes. I was thinking about putting this by Alexander Cecil. He's the only person alive who knew both Norris and Sutherland back in the day. He might be able to give us something.'

Vine considered for a moment. 'Conditions?'

'Your own cash. A different passport. Nothing official that links back to the Cabinet Office or the National Security Council. The whole thing would have to be completely deniable.'

Vine looked up and saw the night draw further in around them. Wondering how many eyes were on them now. 'If I do this, you have to rest up. You can't function in that sort of pain. Time is a healer, or so I'm told.'

'I'm the National Security Adviser, Vine,' said Lockwood, managing a rickety sort of smile, the pain still clearly throbbing in her head. 'How much time do you think I have?'

46

There was one last task Vine needed to complete before he headed off to his next destination. He left Lockwood and headed down to Pall Mall. He entered clubland and glanced up at the gold statue atop the grand entrance to the Athenaeum Club. He signed in at the front desk and then picked up a newspaper from the rack and took a seat near the entrance.

Pattern of life analysis was more often used to find terrorists. But one detail had emerged from his searches through James Norris's background. Once a week, without fail, he dined at the Athenaeum, a few minutes from King Charles Street. The same corner table, the same meal. Getting an invite was a seal of approval and a chance to sample Norris's gossipy style, catnip for journalists on the hunt for spicy briefings about all manner of ministerial failures. Vine wasn't waiting for an invite.

Instead, he sat for nearly an hour on the ground floor until he saw Norris grandly making his way down the long club staircase, the glare of the loud tie and pocket square jutting out of the front pocket. Vine was up, carefully folding the newspaper, and waiting as Norris was helped into his coat by one of the staff. He approached, waiting for Norris to see him. Vine watched the flash of surprise being replaced by a knowing calmness.

The head of the Foreign Office alive to anything, alert and ready.

'You do realize stalking's a crime,' said Norris. He looked different now, the easy confidence gone and a watchful desperation creeping in. Haunted by the fate of the others. 'Max Rashford and Olivia Pope, two of my closest colleagues, have both been murdered. I'm not exactly in a trusting mood for strangers.'

'I need some more answers.'

'Let me guess,' said Norris, 'you have more theories. I'm Putin's man in London. I helped mislead the world on WMD. No, wait, I was always the third man. Kim Philby was just pretending.'

It was a peculiarly English affliction, thought Vine, the idea that attempted humour was a way out of even the most lethal scenarios. 'Can we talk somewhere more private?'

Norris sighed. 'If you promise to leave me alone after that.'

'That depends if I believe you.'

'Strangely enough, your beliefs are of very little interest to me.'

They found another, more secluded room within the club walls and shut the door. The lack of official protection was always one of the oddities of being a civil servant. The Foreign Secretary and other Cabinet grandees had police protection and drivers; they were hidden within tight cocoons of safety, on a level with the secrets they held. The Permanent Secretaries, bar the Cabinet Secretary, had to make do with pool cars or shoe leather. They knew so much, the state's most important secrets stored inside their heads, and yet they were left exposed and isolated. Anonymous figures patrolling the streets of London. The perfect type of asset.

'I wanted to ask about your time at Cambridge,' said Vine.

The question seemed to rock Norris. 'Did I have an affair with anyone famous? No. Did I star in the Footlights and dream of a thwarted career onstage, giving me a pathological need to steal the limelight by betraying my country? No. Did I decide while studying Russian during the eighties that Gorbachev was better than Reagan and that the USSR was the land of the free? All together on the count of three . . .'

Vine nodded, resigned. He had been overly blunt before, getting in the face of all the suspects. He decided to try the more personal route now and see if he could coax something out. 'Recruitment is like a form of seduction.'

'I see. Now it's confession time.'

'I can remember every detail of my recruitment to the secret world. I thought I was going for a job at the Treasury. I had no idea I was about to be taken into a career in intelligence.'

Norris was more literal now. Melancholy, almost, as if remembering shards of his own past. 'Trinity, yes? We always used to like picking people there. Not the Hoorays or the sporty types. The hidden ones, overlooked in the college, but desperate to prove themselves.'

'I was brought up in care,' said Vine. 'The Service got its hooks into me. I walked straight in and never looked back.'

'This was post 9/11?'

'No. It was just before. I signed up in the old world and got my posting in the new. I always think that must have been what the Cold War was like. One day we were fighting the Russians and the next we were friends again. Like the war, even. Moscow has been our ally and our enemy so often it's easy to confuse the two. You must have been aware of recruitment during your time there?'

Norris stared at Vine. 'Of course I was. I was studying Russian at Cambridge, for goodness' sake. I'd clawed my way up there from a school no one had ever heard of. I was the first person in my family ever to go to university. I knew about Philby and Burgess and the Cambridge Spies. Perhaps I even thought about emulating them at some stage. I was a student in the eighties. All of us were young and stupid and headstrong.'

Vine waited. Norris seemed even more vulnerable now, stripped of the armour of his office. He was just another human being. Vine was fishing for anything. The merest hint of regret, the personal aside.

Anything.

'I know what you want,' said Norris. 'In my experience, there are two types of traitors. The ideologues and the rebels.' Norris reached out with his left hand and cast it across the grand room. 'I wanted this, you see. The halls, the beauty, the power. I wasn't contemptuous of this country. I loved it, too much perhaps. The others seemed born to rule. I wasn't. It took me so long to get here. Honestly, I never had enough time to think about betraying it.'

Vine watched Norris carefully, unable to decide whether

he was in the presence of a traitor or a master performer. Someone so versed in diplomatic ways that any real motive was impossible to fathom.

'Does that answer your question?'

'Almost.'

'And I mean it,' said Norris. 'If I see you hanging around this club again, I'll know who to call.'

47

After the detour, Vine headed back to Wellington Square, teasing over the contradictions. He packed lightly before unlocking his safe and reaching inside. He took out the new passport mocked up at Hanslope Park and checked the security system for the house was set.

The first part of the journey was the simplest. The flight across the Channel from London City to Rennes passed without incident, the fake passport working as seamlessly as intended. Vine hired a rental car at the airport and travelled the seventy miles to Vannes. He used the two earbuds from Hanslope and listened to all the interviews again, checking his memory against the cold reality of the recordings. Hunting for any nuance or detail he'd missed.

The initial part of the journey was easy. The next part, however, was considerably trickier. He searched for two hours before he found the house he was looking for, a neat little three-storey place. It looked suitably clandestine, the eye passing straight over it for the smarter houses either side. There was no grandeur or pomposity, the surroundings nondescript too. Some former Chiefs of MI6 liked to live it up in retirement. Cameos on the conference circuit and pricey speeches to bankers and rooms of corporate suits. Others traded on their secret reputations and became advisers to equally shadowy consultancy firms, doyens of the prawn cocktail circuit and brokers for hire.

Vine parked the rental car and looked out at the house in front of him. Even now, despite all that had passed, the idea of this meeting still caused a schoolboy dread. Vine knocked on the door and almost prayed that the house would be empty. But there was the sound of a wheelchair being rolled. A mumbled curse. Finally, the door opened and an elderly man looked up at Vine. The leonine crest of hair and the same judgemental stare as ever, as if Vine had committed sins he wasn't yet aware of.

There were many titles to describe Alexander Cecil. Former Chief of the Secret Intelligence Service. Former Master of Trinity College, Cambridge. And once upon a time raised to the peerage and installed as Lord Cecil of Burford. The man who had stood atop British intelligence, commanding his fiefdom with a ruthless authority, now condemned to his continental exile.

The house was pleasant but decidedly modest. Looking round, Vine realized the money must have gone too, lost in a misbegotten business scheme or other. Cecil had always cultivated his social standing, a regular with the Prime Minister at Chequers, checking in on the Foreign Secretary at Chevening, first-name terms with the inhabitants of the grander establishments – Blenheim, Chatsworth, Althorp. The exile had followed disgrace, with an official government report delivering a damning verdict over Cecil's handling of a covert US–UK drone programme during his time as Chief. The sinecure at Trinity had ended; the raft of board appointments dried up. Cecil was sent abroad to nurture his cabbage patch and ruminate on his crimes.

There was no maid or help today, just Cecil in his wheelchair, and the place looked in need of a good dusting. There was a scattering of books and newspapers on the central coffee table and a large TV dominated the rest of the main sitting room. Vine remembered his previous meetings with Cecil. They all seemed to occur in grand offices and luxurious hideaways. But all of that was now part of a former world, an Eden before the Fall. Even Cecil's presence seemed to have changed. The man himself had always been physically imposing, large and inescapable. From the start, his nickname within MI6 was the Fat Controller. Now the weight was gone and his skin seemed to sag on the frame. Age had crept up until it almost obscured the handsomeness, his face decorated with lines and sags, like a rock exposed to weather.

Vine poured them both a drink and took the armchair opposite Cecil. That was the thing with their peculiar trade. Other Whitehall lifers could move on. For spies it was always more personal. The lingering paranoia, the faces of the people you shadowed, the weight of secrets kept. Retired spooks didn't fill their diaries with cruises and liberation, but too much booze and leathery old regrets. The past was always in danger of becoming present. Vine wondered again if coming here had been a mistake after all.

Cecil took a sip of his drink and said: 'Can I call this an official visit or an unofficial one?'

'Very much the latter,' said Vine. 'This is strictly off the books. If anyone asks, I'm afraid it never happened.'

Cecil nodded. 'I take it you didn't come all the way for a social call then?'

Vine had debated how much he could tell Cecil. Lockwood had given her tacit blessing but had never officially approved sharing operational information with someone no longer cleared. Even someone who had once held the rank of Chief. In his past life, Alexander Cecil was renowned for being too political for MI6. The schemer and consummate Whitehall player. Vine looked at him now and wondered how much the old man still enjoyed his politicking and his games.

'I wanted to get your advice on something,' said Vine. He looked around the room again, checking the ceiling corners.

Cecil watched him look. 'Don't worry,' he said. 'I know someone good, former DGSE, who lends me a hand. We ensure the place is spotless. You can speak freely here.'

Vine recounted the details of the case – the call, Ivanov, the trail and the deaths that had followed – and Cecil didn't respond immediately. He glanced around the room as if it could give him inspiration.

Then, at last, he turned back to Vine and said: 'Based on what you've just told me, you seem to have it all covered. Why this bit of extra-curricular activity? Why find an old spook in retirement and pick his brains? Why *me*?'

Every pitch had to be designed around the source. Vine moved into case officer mode now. Cecil had an ego that needed to be massaged. Only then would he talk.

'Because you have a unique vantage point,' said Vine.

'No one else knows as much about the history of the Service in the late eighties and early nineties. The files won't tell us and the official record is useless. The only way we can solve this case and discover which of the two remaining suspects is the PHOENIX mole is by knowing what really went on in those days. You, it turns out, are the only person who can tell us.'

There was a long silence. The faint grumble of a car rolling by outside. Cecil drained the last of his drink, and then a smile emerged: smooth, arrogant, the old piratic hint to it; every conversation a power play which had to be fought and won. For the first time, Vine saw the man of old struggling through.

'Consider my ego thoroughly stroked,' said Cecil. 'Now . . . where would you like to begin?'

48

The question was rhetorical. Cecil settled back in his wheelchair and took a deep breath. He cleared his throat and said: 'The first thing you have to understand about both Claire Sutherland and James Norris is that they're schooled in our trade. This was the period when the Service still did things properly. The Fort was staffed by people who'd actually seen thirty years of combat behind enemy lines. The best of Sovbloc, the masters of Russia House. They'd done their time under diplomatic cover or as NOCs in all corners of Mother Russia and lived to tell the tale. There was nothing about tradecraft the instructors didn't know or understand.'

'You met both Sutherland and Norris early on?'

Cecil nodded. 'The Service was looking to diversify. Five had already scored some political points by embracing the equalities agenda and loved nothing more than painting us as dinosaurs. A Service stuffed with the product of Eton and Harrow, a gravy train that ran all the way through Christ Church and ended finally in my office. The intake needed a greater balance, all backgrounds and creeds. Sutherland and Norris were the top two trainees in their intake. I interviewed them both personally. Ask anyone at that time, and I'm sure they would tell you that Sutherland and Norris were part of Cecil's brigade. The new band of modernizers.'

'And the vetting on both Sutherland and Norris found nothing?'

'Not a whisper. Both of them were fluent in multiple languages. Both were flying high at Cambridge. Both from middle-income backgrounds. They were the epitome of what the Service needed to become. Their records were clean. Their academic merit impeccable. Even then I predicted that one of them would eventually take my place. And so it proved.'

'You're telling me that no doubts emerged at all?' said Vine. 'No questions that needed answering, either during initial training or afterwards?'

'There were some odds and ends, of course, as for everyone. But nothing untoward, no. It was clear after a few years that Claire Sutherland would continue as the career hood. She never sought glory, happy to work away in the shadows and let others take the credit. James Norris was always the other way inclined. He began to find the anonymity of the secret world constraining. After a few years, he decided to take the secular route and move over to the Foreign Office. I tried to make him stay, but even I could see it was the right decision. Thankfully, history tells the same story. Staying at MI6 would have been an eternal frustration for him. At the Foreign Office, he was able to gossip and network to his heart's content. The fact he has risen to the top job at King Charles Street rather proves the point.'

Vine could feel his early optimism fading. He was like a reporter looking for scandal, anything to back up his suspicions. He tried one final time. 'What about as they both moved up the ladder?' he said. 'To reach the top, they must have encountered enemies. Surely there was some pushback at the speed of their ascent?'

'Ah, typical Vine,' said Cecil. 'You want to know if my enemies inside the Service thought two members of Cecil's brigade were getting promoted ahead of them? Who stabbed whom in the back? Hunting for some Shakespearean drama at court.'

'I'd make do with grubby office politics if that's on offer.'

Cecil sighed. 'The secret world works on patronage, as you well know. It's secret. There is always a limit to accountability. The success or failure of operations can't be assessed by an independent panel with outside experts. It has to be judged by someone inside the organization. In this case, *me*. Claire Sutherland was always the least controversial one. I had no doubts about appointing her to be Sovbloc Controller at Vauxhall Cross. She was seen as my successor and a leading member of my faction. Some of the old guard made complaints, but nothing of substance. Sutherland had a razor-sharp operational head and she produced results. Some of the more overtly ambitious were off running the Afghan and Iraq sagas, angling for promotion by chasing the counter-terror brief. Sutherland played the more intelligent game. She nurtured Sovbloc and won out in the end.'

'What about James Norris?'

Cecil shifted in his wheelchair again. The smile resurfaced. Cecil was teasing, Vine knew, drip-feeding information and making him beg for more. 'James Norris, admittedly, was always more problematic. He was more political. In my own image, I suppose. He liked to curry favour with the ministers. And he was good at it too.'

'That can't have been the only reason he left the Service though? No one crosses to the other side for that reason alone. What was in Norris's vetting back then? What was the skeleton?'

Cecil remained silent, debating with himself. Reluctant, then exhausted. As if he had a last secret left. Something to be unburdened. Then he said: 'You really want to know why James Norris gave up the priesthood?'

'Yes.'

'If you must, then. His personality was one reason. Whatever else you might find out, let's be clear on that. To be strictly accurate, however, there was also another reason why he went down the secular route, later quietly removed from his file. A previous scandal which, I assure you, in my view is quite unrelated to what came later. I presume you're already familiar with the saga involving a certain Russian journalist when he was Ambassador to Moscow in the nineties?'

Vine nodded. 'I asked him about it when I interviewed him.'

'Of course you did. And, magician that he is, I'm sure he thoroughly outfoxed you then as well. No, this scandal was earlier in his career. I was keen to promote some of the new intake. I approved the posting of James Norris under diplomatic cover to our embassy in Berlin as a Second Secretary. It was a medium-level post in terms of danger. But the politics could be messy. Technically, spying on a European ally was considered bad manners and it was imperative that Norris knew how to play the game. He was performing excellently. A convincing diplomat even though, at that time, he was still a spy. Then I received an urgent call from my head of Berlin station and, well, all hell appeared to have broken loose.'

The theatrical pause again. Vine obliged. 'What type of hell?'

'It seems James Norris – our erstwhile Second Secretary – was being investigated within the embassy for receiving hush money from a former Stasi informant. Allegedly, the money was being deposited in a numbered Swiss bank account. Norris, of course, claimed it was all nothing. Just a portion of old family money, a secretive Swiss account passed on from his late father. The supposed Stasi informant was now a reputable merchant banker and was simply doing the paperwork. But, all the same, it caused quite a stink internally at the time. I gave him the benefit of the doubt and stood by him. But I was facing a rebellion from within the ranks. Eventually, I was forced to recall Norris. He was then rather brutally cashiered by his section chief. The evidence was evenly balanced on both sides and I felt mildly guilty for what happened. So I set about finding him some gainful employment across the river and rustled up contacts at the FCO.'

Vine felt energized again now, slowly piercing through Cecil's egotistical shell. Payments, a Stasi link. *Finally.* 'Do you still buy Norris's story? Do you think he really was innocent?'

'My view then is the same as my view now. The whole thing was an office spat. To make sure we were leaving no stone unturned, Norris underwent a full investigation at the time in case he really did have outside sympathies. But nothing was found. Officially, it was deemed a mistake rather than something nefarious. That was why the transfer to the FCO was ultimately approved. That's why the blemish was quietly excised from his file.'

Vine debated what to say next, deciding eventually to put aside his usual caution and see if he could get a rise from Cecil. 'To some people that might sound like a classic Whitehall cover-up,' he said. 'The Chief of MI6 stepping in to help one of his own.'

'Conspiracies round every corner, yes. Like Philby or Blunt all over again. No, now I think it would actually be seen the other way. An innocent man from a humble background framed by a bunch of jealous aristo managers and turfed out through no fault of his own. Making sure he had a berth at the FCO wasn't a cover-up; it was the decent thing to do. Spies don't have employment tribunals. He had no realistic means of complaint.'

Now to deploy the secret weapon. Vine kept his eyes firmly on Cecil, watching every flicker. 'One of the main pieces of evidence in this case are the so-called Rosenholz Files. Stasi records smuggled out of the GDR giving a full list of Stasi and – by default – Soviet assets at the end of the Cold War. Given that context, James Norris's link with a former Stasi informant could be crucial. We also know that Norris went AWOL on the night of Ivanov's murder. He wouldn't be stupid enough to pull the trigger personally. But his face might have been needed to get the Centre's man through the door.'

Cecil smiled now. The familiar mocking look building on his face. 'Come on, Vine. Your powers are wilting with age. You know as well as I do that most of East Germany was a Stasi informant. I could give you thousands of perfectly reputable bankers who had some misbegotten link with the Stasi back in the day.'

'What better way for the PHOENIX mole to be paid than the transfer of assets to a Swiss bank account by a former Stasi informant? Norris played you then and he's playing us now.'

Cecil was serious again. 'Back then, we put our best people on it. People just as good as you. I did my homework and I reached my conclusion.'

'The PHOENIX mole is the Centre's prize asset. Better than good. They could fool you. Fool any of us.'

Cecil was more restless in his wheelchair now, momentarily forgetting the constraints on him, the old baritone in full force. 'Even if James Norris *is* your mole, an old bank account and a brief link with a Stasi informant isn't proof. Nor are sketchy hypotheses about his movements on the night Mr Ivanov was taken out. At least not the sort of proof you need.'

'Let me guess. You're worried your reputation will fall further? Lord Cecil, the former intelligence baron, failed to spot the greatest Soviet double nestling in his ranks? It would be your last humiliation.'

Cecil seemed to retreat slightly now. Age catching up with him until the momentary burst of energy dissipated.

The wrinkled, papery skin looking even more distressed in the fading light of the room, haunted by memories. 'Trust me, Vine, I have nothing more to lose. My job has gone. My college has gone. My reputation and board appointments and money along with it. This isn't ego. This is fact. The truth is useless unless you can *prove* it. And, at the moment, it doesn't seem you can.'

The mind games. Of course. No trip to see Cecil would be complete without them. 'We know an asset codenamed PHOENIX was funnelled through the books of the Stasi,' said Vine. 'We know this asset is fluent in multiple languages and studied and was recruited in Cambridge. Only two people fit that profile. Both of them were members of the Elders' Committee, tasked with recruiting and handling the Ivanov operation. One of them has a link to the Stasi in their past. The other has a financier spouse with fingers in every Russian pie imaginable. Both have motive. Both had ample means and opportunity.'

Cecil stared at Vine. The old arrogance gone now. 'Then you've forgotten the one lesson we taught you,' he said. 'The golden rule of all analysts. Say James Norris or Claire Sutherland are your mole. They've survived for thirty years. Do you really think you can rattle them without proof? That you can interrogate them like some Thames House newbie and get a confession? Norris and Sutherland would rather die than confess. You have nothing.'

Vine could hear those words beat at him again. EXCALIBUR and ARTHUR. Operation and handler. The looming threat and menace of both. 'Unless that's exactly what the asset's counting on,' he said. 'We wait for all the evidence and thus we wait forever. James Norris is on the verge of assuming complete and total control of the Whitehall machine. He's eliminated anyone who can stand in his way. Unlike you, we don't have time to sit back, drink Scotch and debate first principles.'

'Wrong,' said Cecil. 'Forget first principles, and Norris or Sutherland get away. No case, no charge, nothing.'

Silence again. This small, boxy old house seemed even stiller than before. There was just the creak of it and the absence of any human warmth. This was the final resting place for spies, Vine realized now. Haunted by eternal solitude.

Cecil's voice was parched and cracklier. The conversation exhausting him. 'You're an analyst, Vine,' he said. These last words quieter, almost gentle. Cecil reaching out to the nearest human connection. 'Build your case or watch the suspects walk. It's entirely up to you.'

49

The words stung. It was stupid, and Vine knew it, but nevertheless a cloud seemed to follow him away from Cecil's house and into the rental car. He found his way out of the village and drove back towards the airport, the rest of the world almost ceasing to exist. It felt like the old days again. Vine gaining an audience with the Chief, being shown his manifold mistakes and then left with his wounds afterwards, trying to figure out how to heal each one. Time broke apart now, memories colliding with present-day reality until it was impossible to tell them apart.

And now a newer feeling too. The threat of despair. One side of his brain was seeking an answer: no puzzle or pattern was too hard to crack; the mysteries of the case should fall away like scales from the eyes, leaving truth in all its glory standing before him. Except not this time. Age and rustiness were blunting the edges. His student days and arriving at the Fort and those initial chaotic operations, the very tempo of those years, were gone now. Never to be felt again.

Vine realized he was driving too fast, checking his tail and then reducing his speed. Perhaps Cecil was right. Even now, despite everything, it was necessary to return to first principles. Lay each piece of the investigation out and fit it all together again. First, and most urgently, that one word: 'EXCALIBUR'. The word Alexander Ivanov had left behind and entrusted to the care of Max Rashford, written on the transcript of the bugged call between the mole and their handler. P1 and P2. Everything now, surely, depended on what EXCALIBUR was. If Andrei was right, it could be an attack that would reshape everything. A statement. Plunging the world into a new type of chaos.

Vine drove on and reached the airport and remained there for a while longer, not yet ready to move. This is what happened to spies past their prime. Each thread of connection slowed by moral doubt and indecision. Reason and logic crushed by the weight of past mistakes.

Vine sat in the car and looked out at the bustle of other flyers and closed his eyes, willing the pieces to somehow become whole.

50

The flight to London City was full of business types and wealthier tourists. Vine sat near the back and put his headphones on. He loaded up some Handel, one of his favourites since university days, and then sank back against the headrest. He looked out of the window and saw the sky seemingly motionless around them. The feathery trace of clouds, like a carpet suspended in the air.

Vine loaded the photos he'd taken of Pope's file with the vaping device. He lingered on the words in each photo now. Making sure he understood every shade of meaning Olivia Pope might have been trying to convey. Resurrecting all those old tricks analysts used when consuming raw intelligence and longing for the days when he was young enough to dissect it in his sleep.

Cecil again. The booming laugh and vestigial double-chinned smugness. Vine could see himself almost twenty years ago, walking those familiar halls to his desk. Giddy with the secret world. The history, the aura, the mystique. The mathematician in him hungry for more numbers to crunch. Scouting for the anomaly. Spying out the error.

What was it here? Pope recorded in her file how she met the Russian defector. One of the many former assets that Britain gave safe harbour to in the nineties. The defector was never given a name in the file, or even a codename.

Pope's trust in him supposed to be an unquestioned guarantee of the man's testimony. What flaw, though, was there in the defector's testimony? What error? What entry point that unlocked the rest?

None, though, except the scholarship. Surely. Vine paused on that one detail again, the insignificant morsel in Pope's file that hadn't made sense before. The file was clear. The Russian defector said the mole codenamed PHOENIX had been a scholar during their time at Cambridge. The exact word was even repeated two more times in the testimony. Used by the defector in that unabashed, very un-English way. Being a scholar was an endorsement, even a badge of pride. A scholarship verified the competence and desirability of the asset. A key factor in Moscow Centre's recruitment.

And yet Vine had double-checked through Claire Sutherland's and James Norris's background files. There was no doubt at all. Neither Sutherland or Norris had ever received a scholarship to Cambridge. They had no exhibition or any kind of commendation. They were ordinary undergraduates. Why would the defector repeat the mistake? Once, yes. The defector heard the detail from his contact within the KGB. The gossip of the chosen ones in the First Chief Directorate. But twice? No, that was different. A distinctive feature of the asset in question. A concrete part of the profile.

Had the PHOENIX mole lied to their handler? Pretended to be of scholarship standard to impress their recruiter, hoping for elevated status or, more probably, extra pocket money? Possibly. Yet even that didn't hold for long. The KGB might have been on the verge of disintegrating, but they never ignored the basics. London station could tap up any of the Bollinger Bolsheviks at King's and get them to check the Cambridge University records. Ensure the asset wasn't lying to them from the start. One exaggeration like that from the PHOENIX mole and the recruitment would have been over before it even began.

Spot the flaw. See the mistake. Vine looked back at the photos from the vaping device again. No, the lie theory didn't hold. It failed the most basic test of reason and plausibility. The defector Olivia Pope interviewed was certain the PHOENIX asset had, first, studied in Cambridge and, second, been there on a scholarship. Cambridge, logic, Wittgenstein and Russell. Now – for a split second as the plane continued around him – Vine was pitched back to his own first taste of Cambridge. The court, the smell, the scale of it. The tests they set before the interview. Deductive reasoning at its purest.

Premise one: the PHOENIX mole attended Cambridge with a scholarship. Premise two: Claire Sutherland and James Norris did attend Cambridge but not with a scholarship. Conclusion: therefore, Sutherland and Norris cannot be the PHOENIX mole.

Two premises with the wrong answer. Cecil's words again.

You're an analyst, Vine. Build your case or watch the suspects walk. It's entirely up to you.

The old man was right. And, like clouds dispersing to a faultless blue sky, the answer was suddenly in front of him.

51

It all came down to the preposition. That small, often-ignored grammatical function. Passing like traffic before the eye. The blur between the verbs and the nouns, the brain immediately discounting the rest.

The answer went back to the exact wording in Pope's file. It was contained here thanks to the wonder weapons supplied by Hanslope Park. Vine looked at the photo again. Those carefully transcribed words from the defector.

'The PHOENIX mole studied in Cambridge.'

Not studied *at*. Studied *in*.

The preposition.

And now, like a fever dream, Vine wondered if he'd committed the cardinal error. Reading the data through his own experience, the one blind spot of every analyst. How many times had he talked himself of studying *in* Cambridge? 'In' and 'at' sounded so interchangeable, and yet not for an outsider. Not for a Russian defector carefully selecting the right word in a foreign tongue, someone repeating exactly what he'd been told three decades earlier. It was there in the operational sense too. The Centre was allergic to anything overly direct. Spies talked of general geographic areas, never specific institutions. There was comfort in the abstract.

Not *at*. But *in*. The PHOENIX asset had studied *in*

Cambridge. They had received a scholarship. And now Vine saw the full extent of his myopia. The failures of logic and reason. Cambridge, England, in the 1980s wasn't a land of scholarships. There were no fees. Living expenses could be covered by maintenance grants. It was a land of milk and honey when education didn't incur a charge. Cambridge, England, could never – logically, rationally, on any level – have been the answer.

The premises again. That smooth, deductive reasoning.

Premise one: the PHOENIX mole attended Cambridge with a scholarship.

Premise two: Claire Sutherland and James Norris did attend Cambridge but not with a scholarship.

Conclusion: the Cambridge in question is not in England.

The data points could be satisfied no other way. The scholarship detail wasn't a mistake, but the attribution had been misinterpreted on his side. The PHOENIX asset wasn't studying at Cambridge, England, in the 1980s. But another Cambridge. One almost equally famous.

Cambridge, *Massachusetts*.

And now, like the best types of mathematical equations, Vine could see the neat elegance of it all. The PHOENIX mole could still have been recruited while studying. They could still have been of sufficient calibre to interest the highest ranks of Moscow Centre. They could still have ascended through Whitehall on the back of a stellar education. But Cambridge US rather than Cambridge UK meant something different. The PHOENIX mole was a scholar.

Cambridge, Massachusetts.

A Kennedy Scholar.

Harvard University.

Now, like dominoes falling, the rest of it began to move into place. Every jagged edge fitting. Vine looked around the plane and felt a sudden, queasy realization. What if there was another way in which the mole could have known that Rashford had the document from Ivanov? That Pope had indicated she was already on the trail of the mole? A way entirely distinct from either Sutherland or Norris?

Vine spooled back through everything he'd done over the last few days. Going to each crime scene and cleaning up the mess. Finding the trail that all three victims had left behind. The deodorant canister, the London Library, the Special Forces Club, Rashford's office, the document left inside the book, the busker and the live letterbox. Collecting the entire trail that would lead back to the asset. He had handled the most incriminating evidence and eliminated it all.

The plane was about to land. The seatbelt sign came on and the tables were tucked away. Vine looked down and saw London rise up before him. And he saw it now as clearly as anything before.

The different pieces, at last, making sense.

52

There was no one waiting for him at London City airport. Not that he thought there would be. A public spectacle was still too obvious. No, they would bide their time, let him slip back into his normal routine before moving. He was certain of that much.

As he passed through the airport, he took out his secure mobile again. The one constant throughout the entire operation. Vine didn't need another trip to Hanslope Park to know all the ways it could be turned into an active listening device, able to pick up any conversations and record his every move. He didn't switch it on or begin taking the device apart and teasing out the SIM. Too obvious, again, the sort of clumsy tradecraft an amateur stringer would stumble into.

Instead, he began the first part of his plan. He entered the men's toilets at London City and saw a bag resting by one of the sinks, the owner otherwise engaged. Vine pretended to drop his phone, bending down and quietly placing the secure government mobile deep into a side pocket of the bag. With any luck, the commuter wouldn't notice until putting away his things at home. For now, it would buy some time.

Next, Vine bought a cheap burner phone in cash. He waited until he was out in the car park before loading up the browser and typing in the address. He thumbed through to the page he needed, bringing up the profile.

He looked at the page and scanned down the paragraphs of text. The realization beating at him, a constant tattoo in his head. The hazy anxiety of the plane journey now morphing into a horrible, undeniable reality. That logic again. Painfully clear. He saw every event from the beginning, each part of it now imbued with a different meaning. The reason he was called out of retirement and asked to investigate the case. The close calls at the Special Forces Club and Rashford's office. Gathering up the trail left behind, ensuring his fingerprints were smeared all over it. He had done the asset's dirty work. Setting himself up to be arrested for the very crimes he was investigating. He had played right into their hands.

Vine looked down at the webpage on the screen. He read the sentence at the start again, the words that finally confirmed everything. A biographical detail that appeared as innocuous as any other but which unlocked the entire case. The sentence read: 'Following a Kennedy Scholarship at Harvard University, she joined the Civil Service in 1988 . . .'

Vine stared at the official government photo above the biography. The face he had come to know so well over the last few days. The person who had summoned him from Wellington Square and asked him to serve his country. The confidante for all the information he had found.

The only true candidate now for the PHOENIX mole.

Her name and title proclaimed for all the world to see.

'UK National Security Adviser – Emma Lockwood.'

PART FOUR

53

It had been so long since Vine was operational that it took him some time to adjust. A different part of his brain activated again. He was no longer the distant analyst viewing the various pieces, unable to pursue the case through official channels. No, he was in the heat of battle again, long-term strategy replaced by short-term dangers. Denied the comfort of credibility. Few, if any, would now believe him. Vine tried to calculate all the mistakes he had already made. The cameras that might have picked him up. The data points he had already left behind. If he was going to make it through this, he couldn't afford any more careless errors. Everything – *everything* – had to be finely calibrated.

Alongside the adrenaline came that old instinct. The basic rule of survival was to assume that you were always being watched. Placing the secure phone in the bag would help, confusing the SIGINT trail and giving Lockwood contradictory information. Now it was time to play some games with the CCTV. Vine headed for the car park and found a taxi and ran through the instructions with the driver, paying upfront to avoid any complications later.

They began crawling away from London City and heading towards Vine's stated destination. The key with any deception of this kind was convincing a watcher – whether on foot or digital – that everything was normal. As far as Lockwood was concerned, Vine had returned from an off-the-books meeting with Alexander Cecil. It would be perfectly natural to head back in the direction of the OCP in Pimlico to report on the meeting and debrief Lockwood in person. That, Vine assumed, was when Lockwood would move. The location would be private and away from the glare of the world. Yes, it was vital that Lockwood believed the OCP was his intended destination now.

The traffic back to Pimlico was heavy. Vine ran through everything he needed to do from this point onwards. The parts he could plan and the slices of luck any operation like this required. Given the nature of the case, Lockwood would be using a small team, eager to avoid an army of uniforms creating an unnecessary scene. The sort of officers trained in discretion, perhaps culling some of the best from the PaDP contingent near the Cabinet Office and some A4 watchers from Thames House. Armed, highly trained, able to minimize all fuss. Vine would be carted away and smothered with the vaguest subsections of the Official Secrets Act. His case never heard in open court; the sentence never revealed. Merely another piece of nameless collateral damage.

He looked out and saw they were finally approaching Pimlico, the OCP a matter of minutes away. Vine couldn't be sure if a team was already waiting for him. He repeated the instructions to the driver again and then prepared himself. They were near Victoria station now.

Everything as normal. Until, out of nowhere, the cab made a detour and headed down to the covered section of Bridge Place by the station exit. Vine didn't wait for the car to stop, already jumping from the cab as soon as they reached the black spot, all coverage now obliterated in one fell move. The cab kept going, emerging at the other side of Bridge Place, seemingly continuing without incident. Vine managed to land neatly, avoiding an ankle twist and cushioning himself for the fall.

Now for the next part. There were two rough sleepers in the covered section, both curled up in their sleeping bags and wearing military-style coats to retain the vanishing warmth. Vine took out his remaining cash and approached the younger of the two, offering a trade. Three hundred quid for his coat and beanie. To be swapped with Vine's own jacket and jumper. The deal was soon completed and Vine made the exchange, threading his arms into the military coat and adjusting the beanie. Then he emerged from the other side of the covered section, head down, subtly changing his stride pattern and stooping in order to alter his height. Lockwood, and whatever team she had, would be glued to the progress of the cab heading round to the OCP. As per Vine's instructions, the cabbie was to head past the OCP address as if he was going to stop – before, at the last minute, continuing onwards.

He had kept his wallet and quickly disposed of his credit and debit cards now, and the burner. He walked on until he reached Chelsea and found a cab near Sloane Square station, handing over another generous wad of money and specific instructions for his next location. Now for phase two of the plan. Vine changed cabs again halfway through, the journey taking over an hour in total. By the time he arrived at his second destination, Vine was confident he was clean.

The storage facility near Paddington had been rented under a fake name. A safety net in case old operations ever resurfaced. Vine found his storage unit and changed his clothes again, this time altering his appearance even further. He shaved his head and used glasses to play with the aspect of his face. Every part of his dress sense was changed in the same calculating way. The shirt exchanged for a t-shirt, brogues for trainers, tailored jacket giving way to looser sportswear, the beanie now replaced by a baseball cap. He looked like a tourist – a visiting American or Canadian – as far away from the all-English spy as possible.

Vine turned his attention to the other details. There was two grand in cash stored in a variety of gym bags, carefully added to every month to avoid suspicion. He had access to a crypto account too and had long since memorized his personal access codes. Vine collected as much of the cash as he could as well as three new burner phones. He put a further change of clothes and some other toiletries into a rucksack and then left the storage facility, careful to avoid any cameras. His mind already turning to the third part and what lay beyond this.

It was getting gloomier now, night beginning to set. Vine continued on foot, the walkabout specifically designed to lure out any watchers. But there was still nothing.

The initial two phases of the survival operation had been completed. The decoy with the cab and the change of clothes had worked as intended. But he needed to keep outpacing Lockwood and buy enough time to put in place the final stage of his plan.

The clothes from the storage facility were designed to be durable for a night in the open air. With the burners turned off and his face obscured for cameras, food was now the only thing he longed for. As he went on walking, Vine saw a crumpled newspaper left behind at a bus stop and quietly snatched it for himself. He found an empty corner nearby and looked again at the front page. There was a photo of Olivia Pope and another of the crime-scene tape on the South Bank by Westminster Bridge. And then the headline beneath, screaming out at him. The harsh, accusatory glare of it:

WANTED: EX-SPY ON RUN FOR CABINET SECRETARY MURDER

Vine read the story in full, following it through to page four where his old MI6 photo was now recycled. At the end of the article was a quote from Emma Lockwood. Vine read it once, then again, memorizing every word:

> We have found very concerning evidence suggesting that Mr Vine could have been paid by pro-Russia groups to work on their behalf. We know he is highly trained and therefore warn the public not to approach him and to call the police if they believe they have seen this man.

There were footsteps coming his way. Vine ducked further into the alleyway and saw a group of drunken locals passing by. He could trace out the grim logic in full now. His entire career exposed and revealed, every controversy and incident painstakingly revisited. Framing others was the time-honoured tactic of any agent-in-place. The double's only excuse and strategy. He didn't have days, then. A mere handful of hours at most.

He composed himself and tried to focus on that word again. The last remaining data point that had yet to be explained by the rest. The meaning still coiled and hidden. Not past, but prologue. As Vine moved on, the single word wouldn't leave him.

EXCALIBUR.

The worst still yet to come.

54

Everything now depended on using the one advantage he had. Lockwood wasn't trained. Yes, she knew her stuff. Tunnelling her way up through the civil service fast-stream, proving her smarts at the Home Office and then the leap from the secular route through stints at GCHQ, before eventually landing back as the National Security Adviser. But that was management. Budgets and updates and interminable meetings. Lockwood had never been at the Fort. She'd never served under diplomatic cover. She didn't have the battlefield experience of those who had sweated out their twenties on the frontline of the war on terror.

Training gave you the basics. The shortcuts. The hacks. It taught you, for instance, that professional counter-surveillance always played with basic human logic. Lockwood would have discovered Vine's trick by now, the cab from the airport failing to stop outside the OCP. She would have found the slip occurred at Bridge Place. Her team would be backtracking through the CCTV footage, but the trail was ice-cold. Lockwood would rationally assume that he was out of London, smuggling his way into the countryside, judging how to make the final break and skip across the Channel again to a borderless European mainland.

Amateurs did the expected. Hoods did the opposite. And so Vine made his way back from Paddington to Victoria and headed towards the railway arches. Finding sanctuary among the misfits and the overlooked. No one bothered to search here. Vine found a spot and then took out one of the fresh burner phones from the storage facility. The next decision pressing on him, defining everything from here on in.

Vine loaded up the browser on the fresh burner and began searching. He wanted any publicly available information concerning the movements of the top Cabinet Ministers, the Great Offices of State: Prime Minister, Chancellor, Home Secretary, Foreign Secretary. Speeches to be given, summits being hosted, announcements pre-briefed to the media. Any likely contender for the EXCALIBUR attack.

He searched and logged the information. Then, once he had it, Vine used the photos from the vaping device again. The transcript that Ivanov had left behind and the conversation between P1 and P2.

P1: You are all set for the big day?
P2: Yes.
P1: The event cannot be repeated. It must go as planned.
P2: I understand.

P2 – person two, as he now knew – was Emma Lockwood. Person one, surely, was Lockwood's handler on the Russian side. Or perhaps one of her many handlers. The transcript was a bug of Lockwood, as National Security

Adviser, talking with her handler. The fact that Ivanov had written EXCALIBUR on the transcript implied Lockwood and her handler were discussing operational matters. The handler had clearly delivered something which would help EXCALIBUR come to fruition.

There was the sound of an ambulance flashing by. A police car threaded past too, heading in the opposite direction. The net closing in now. Vine knew time was draining away. He closed his eyes and settled on his plan again, trying to summon any final alternatives. But, no, there was only one option left. This had to be it.

Vine got up and started walking, still looking through the profiles on the browser of the two people he was investigating until only a few hours ago: Dame Claire Sutherland and Sir James Norris. One now leading the Pope investigation, the other in post as acting Cabinet Secretary.

The only two people with the power to help. Those with enough might in Whitehall to counter Lockwood and her reach within the security establishment.

Sutherland or Norris. Vine glanced at the two profiles and thought back to the two interviews. Rolling through everything he knew about either of them.

One, or both, could be his saviour or his destroyer tonight.

And this next move might well be his last.

55

The evening was closing in by the time Vine reached his destination. The house was near to Wellington Square. An imposing five-storey affair on Smith Street, the millionaires' or billionaires' row, the sort of places only inhabited half the year. This one was more noticeable for another factor too. Outside stood a uniformed and heavily armed Pa DP officer, a similar sight to that found outside the doors of Cabinet Ministers and the senior members of the Windsor family. He was armed with the typical accessories: Glock 17, a Heckler & Koch G36C, ballistic body armour, a taser and, for good measure, an airwave radio.

Vine waited at the end of Smith Street for half an hour, watching the traffic and footfall, getting the rhythm of the street. Eventually, forty minutes into his vigil, he got his break. A courier bike pulled up outside a door on the right. Vine watched as the delivery driver checked the address and then began unloading his cargo, removing three pizza boxes and heading up the flight of stairs towards the front door.

The window of opportunity was tight. The delivery driver was wearing a thick helmet which he didn't take off, obscuring the view and any clear sense of peripheral vision. Vine walked past and saw a spare Deliveroo bag stored inside the trunk. He checked to his right to see the driver still waiting. Then, seamlessly, he bent down to tie his shoelace in front of the bike and rose again, walking away quickly. When he was sure he was out of sight, Vine relaxed his left hand and looked down at the spare Deliveroo bag. Empty for now. Vine removed some items from his rucksack and placed them inside before zipping it up again, the bulk masquerading as food.

He made sure his baseball cap was low, the peak masking his brow and eyes, as he approached the correct house. He took out some earbuds from his jacket pocket and slotted them in, clicking on a Spotify shuffle and forcing the volume up. He could see the protection officer becoming aware of him now. Vine copied the approach of the delivery driver he'd seen, checking his mobile as if the order details were on the screen, then stopping as he saw the protection officer. Earbuds in, music blasting away, the cap and poor light a worthy disguise.

The protection officer glanced at the Deliveroo bag. He was weary, Vine saw, probably towards the end of his shift. Young, too, which always helped. Bored of the street corner with no threat or excitement. Vine played it politely and waited for permission to go up to the main door. The protection officer sighed tiredly and then nodded him through.

Now for the obstacles. Vine paused the music from his phone and took out the earbuds. He rang the doorbell and waited, rehearsing each move. Too deliberate and he'd have no chance. Too slow and the moment would be gone. The difference between professional tradecraft and amateur bungling was always in the exact nuance. The actorly craft again, so easily fumbled.

There was the sound of footsteps inside and then the door eased open. It was one of the daughters. Eleven or twelve, old enough to know what a takeaway was but young enough never to have paid for one. Vine didn't give her time to react, carelessly dropping the bag inside the door as he attempted to open it. He got a step over the doorway and the daughter instinctively backed away and let him through.

Vine was inside the hallway now. The door easing shut by itself.

'Mum!'

He waited, knowing this would be the moment that determined everything. The next ten seconds primed to go one of two ways. The daughter was about to shout again when her mother emerged from the sitting room, fixing an earring, dressed as if about to go out for the night.

'I don't think we ordered any—'

Vine felt instinct take over again. He removed his baseball cap. The speech carefully prepared. Every word weighed and debated during the vigil earlier.

'Wait—'

'Alert the protection officer standing outside,' he said, 'and I'll release notes from Dame Olivia Pope accusing you of being a Russian agent-in-place. I'm not armed and I have no backup. I'm innocent of all the charges made against me. All I need is five minutes to explain how.'

The daughter glanced confusedly between the stranger and her mother.

Claire Sutherland, however, kept her eyes firmly on Vine.

The house was more modern than Vine had imagined. The artwork in the living room was jagged and bold, the book selection decorative rather than educational. There was no TV but a selection of tablets and headphones in varying sizes scattered among cushions.

The memories of their earlier interview were gone now. The persuasive brilliance of a handler controlling an asset gave way to something new: cold, wary, more like a prison officer surveying an inmate. Claire Sutherland didn't sit; she perched instead on the armrest of one of the sofas, still fiddling with her earring. Letting Vine stand and make his pitch. Outside, obscured by the thin curtain, Vine could almost feel the presence of the protection officer. He wondered again if this whole endeavour was simply a ruse to get him to stay in one place. Trapping him here. Nowhere else to run. Her chameleon brilliance again, playing the interested party until more support arrived.

Sutherland looked at her watch. 'You have four minutes and thirty seconds before I call the guard outside,' she said. 'I'd start talking.'

And so he began. Like the initial speech, the rest of his pitch had been honed during the evening, whittling away the incidentals until he was left with the bare essentials. He laid it out chronologically. The summons from

Lockwood, the documents Ivanov left behind, Rashford's call and the interview with Pope and the material he'd picked up in the wake of both. He told her about the Cambridge confusion and the profile given by the defector in Pope's notes. Then, with the background shaded in, he mentioned EXCALIBUR. The subject of the phone call between Lockwood and her handler and the last remaining piece of the puzzle.

Sutherland didn't say anything at first. She remained emotionless, with a hard and almost glacial scepticism. She finished adjusting her earring and looked at the floor in contemplation. Then, at last, she said: 'Last time you were accusing me of having helped kill Ivanov. Now you're telling me that Emma Lockwood's the agent-in-place and you're merely the decoy?'

'Yes.'

'Why on earth should I believe you? Why, in fact, should I trust anything you've just told me?'

'I went hard in my interview because that's what we do,' said Vine. 'That's how we're trained. You know my record at the Service. You know how closely I was vetted and the operations I conducted. You know my training and the section I led. And you should trust a fellow officer. That's why.'

'Surely that could all have been in the aid of cover,' said Sutherland. 'Unmasking moles, building your legend. What if the Centre authorized those discoveries?'

She was asking questions, which surely meant she believed the story. Or so Vine told himself. The real doubters didn't get this far. She would have ended the conversation and alerted the protection officer, or never have allowed him to make the case to begin with. He had spent his adult life conducting assessments of agents and sub-agents, spotting the subtle tells of others. He had to trust his gut now.

But time was still draining away and Vine decided to go further. 'I've analysed all the movements of key government figures over the next few days,' he said. 'Even the next few weeks. I can't see any obvious target that the Centre could be aiming at, but I need your help to identify what EXCALIBUR is and what Lockwood could be planning.'

'How can you even be sure that EXCALIBUR is a physical operation?' said Sutherland. 'It could be referring to anything.'

'Why else did Ivanov leave that transcript so specifically? Lockwood was confirming something. Everything tells me that EXCALIBUR is the final masterstroke. Something that will make the last ten years of Russian aggression on UK soil merely a warm up.'

'And ARTHUR is the handler name from the Rosenholz Files?'

'Yes.'

'Then I ask again. How can you be so sure EXCALIBUR is urgent? Facts, this time, not speculation.'

'It's the only way anything that's happened so far makes sense,' said Vine. 'Taking out Ivanov, the Chief of the Defence Staff and the Cabinet Secretary. The Centre doesn't announce itself like that unless it's preparing for something that's worth it. Ivanov was still in an evidence-gathering phase. The fact he had to be taken out now – the fact the Centre had to silence anyone who might get in the way – confirms that much. Trust me, this is happening *now*.'

Sutherland paused again, collecting her thoughts. There was the sound of a motorbike rattling outside on the street. The pause seemed to extend for a fatally long time. Then, eventually, Sutherland looked up at Vine and said: 'I may have one idea.'

Relief, now. Purer than anything Vine had felt before.

'Emma Lockwood has been organizing a secret summit to discuss the ongoing Western military and intelligence partnership,' continued Sutherland. 'So secret, in fact, that MI6 and even the Cabinet Office have been largely shut out of proceedings, much to our collective annoyance. The whole summit has been entirely controlled by the National Security Adviser's office and run by Lockwood herself.'

'But the summit's official? It has the Prime Minister's blessing?'

'That depends on your interpretation of the word official. Lockwood's been playing a skilful Whitehall game. Technically, she has the blessing of senior ministers. In reality, the summit is being conducted strictly off the books for fear – rightly or wrongly – of any diplomatic leakage.'

'Who's attending?'

'Like most things to do with the summit, the final details about attendees have been kept under wraps by Lockwood herself. But the rumoured names are the

Foreign Secretary, the Defence Secretary and the US National Security Adviser.'

Vine let that new information sink in. The foundation of the special relationship, the key players in the Western intelligence alliance. The ideal target. He tried to run through all possible options. 'Just the four of them?' he said. 'Lockwood and those three?'

'As far as I've been able to gather.'

'You said it was off the books?'

'Masterminded by Lockwood herself. Supposedly for their own protection.'

Vine started pacing now, the detail of the room becoming a blurry mix of colours. EXCALIBUR. He had always known that it would come down to the meaning of that one word. But something this audacious, this bare-knuckled. No, he'd hoped for something other than that.

'If Lockwood organized the meeting,' he said, teasing the logic through, 'then she arranged the security details. As National Security Adviser, she knows every gap in the armour. If the Russians wanted to cause chaos and derail the West's attempt to unite against them, what better place to do it? The Kremlin eliminating anyone in their way.'

Sutherland's phlegmatic calm was receding now. The facts had an inexorable symmetry to them. 'A direct attack would effectively be a declaration of hostilities,' she said. 'An overt challenge to the West.'

Vine looked at Sutherland. 'I need your decision now,' he said. 'If you're with me, we still have a chance. If you're not, then I need to find someone else.'

Sutherland looked caught, still processing it all. 'Except you may not have as much time as you think.'

That deep hit of unease again. Gripping his insides. 'Why?'

'The US side touched down this morning. They're meeting for a working dinner tonight and then leave tomorrow. In-country for twenty-four hours only.'

Vine stood in the room and calmed his breathing rate. The key was to stay focused. 'Do you know specific timings?'

'Only what I've heard. The working dinner is due to start in an hour.'

'Location?'

'There I really can't help you. Lockwood's paranoia over security knew no bounds. Only principals and their CPOs were briefed on the final location. It's why she got the nod for off the grid. Deliberately sealed from the usual government channels. The whole thing's impenetrable.'

'The US agreed?'

'They practically insisted on it.' Sutherland paused, searching for the clearest solution. 'There's a chance I can pull some strings at Vauxhall Cross.'

Vine had already considered it. 'No, Lockwood will have anticipated that,' he said. 'It will burn up time we don't have.'

'You have some other idea?'

Vine felt the pieces in his brain stop now. One idea emerging from the fuzz. 'We need to use your phone.'

57

Sutherland's home office upstairs boasted a PC with enhanced security features and a secure phone installed for emergencies. Given the existing search for him, Vine knew he was condemned to work behind the scenes rather than out in the open. Technically he was still a wanted man. But decamping here was the best option for now.

He sat and watched as Sutherland rang James Norris as acting Cabinet Secretary, the only person with the authority within government to do what they needed. He was only half aware of the bizarreness of their surroundings with the cramped, low-ceilinged home office and the selection of family photos and mementoes decorating the shelves. Sutherland used Norris's personal mobile number and repeated the agreed lines: the Prime Minister needed to be evacuated from London as a precaution and taken to Chequers; the other most senior Cabinet Ministers likewise deposited somewhere outside the capital. And then, as anticipated, the bureaucratic fight began. Norris was unable to confirm immediately, the usual boilerplate about consulting others. It was a partial victory – if one at all – but warnings had been duly given. Their duty done.

Next, Sutherland instructed the analyst team at the Joint Terrorism Analysis Centre to find a source at the Government Car Service. Despite the shadowy nature of the summit, logic dictated that a fleet of cars must have been requisitioned for the high-profile guests, whisked from their flights to the summit location. Vine might not have details of the location, but the GPS locators did. It was their one last, vanishing hope.

They waited another ten minutes until the secure phone rang again. James Norris for a second time. Now he was the bearer of worse news. Sutherland listened respectfully and put the phone down before, finally, turning to Vine. 'Norris has refused to authorize the Cabinet evacuation.'

'On what grounds?'

'Lack of evidence. Red tape. The need for Whitehall to form a sub-committee before it ties its bloody shoelaces.'

Vine saw something else in Sutherland's expression. An old dread resurfacing. 'What else?'

'I'm afraid you were spotted en route,' she said. 'A police team are heading this way and will arrive in the next few minutes.'

It was the lifecycle of any operation. A rollercoaster lurch from possible success to certain tragedy within the space of seconds. 'Lockwood wins then,' said Vine. 'EXCALI-BUR goes ahead. The Kremlin upends everything.'

Sutherland looked round the room, trying to decide. Then turned her eyes back on to Vine. The final judgement for any spook.

'Only if I give you up,' she said.

58

Outside there was just the distant glitter of police vehicles and the melodic chime of sirens. Sutherland increased her speed, turning the corner before the cavalcade descended. The Mini Clubman pitched forward, tarmac skidding noisily beneath them.

Vine lay on the passenger seats, his body stretched the full length until the soles of his shoes were brushing the opposite passenger door. Sutherland was in the front, keeping watch through the wing mirrors. As the speed increased, Vine knew he needed his mental powers to work properly now. For so long – ever since retirement – his brain had existed in a half-life. The early fire diminished. He looked up at the car roof and heard the background wail of the sirens and forced his mind to concentrate, analyse the problem in its purest form.

Think.

EXCALIBUR.

A location.

What could he deduce so far? To allow the EXCALIBUR operation to take place, Lockwood had been forced to choose a unique meeting spot. A venue approved by the highest echelons of the US security establishment. It couldn't be for public consumption, which ruled out a government building. Anything in Whitehall, meanwhile, would draw protestors and the paparazzi. Even the more fugitive corners – the Foreign Secretary's official residence in Carlton Gardens, say – were vulnerable. The summit was not on the official calendar and not for the eyes of the press. Logically, Whitehall was strictly out of bounds.

Where then? For starters, somewhere used to high-profile guests. And, importantly, where guests of this calibre – a US National Security Adviser, the Foreign and Defence Secretaries – could blend in. That had to be enough data to work with. Vine let those various premises linger in his mind before he settled on a result. Only one type of location fitted, surely. The sort of heritage luxury that London still excelled in. Parading its stars. A fixture of guidebooks. The lure of the promised land.

A hotel. Yes, a five-star hotel.

They turned another corner, now far enough away from danger. Vine sat up and moved forward in his seat. Claire Sutherland saw him, craning her head back to listen.

'You have something?'

'Tell me. The Foreign Secretary is one of five Cabinet Ministers, including the Prime Minister, who have round-the-clock protection details, right?' said Vine. 'CPOs by their side at all times.'

'What of it?'

'If we're right, then Emma Lockwood circumvented security protocol by keeping the summit off the books and not official business.'

'So?'

'But, no matter how hard she tried, Lockwood wouldn't have been able to get round the Royal and Specialist

Protection detail assigned – day or night – to protect the Foreign Secretary. They get full coverage, just like the PM.'

'RaSP protocol is the preserve of the Met Commissioner and Home Secretary. That procedure can't be altered without the approval of both, yes. As NSA, Lockwood would have no say in it.'

'Logically, then, that's the only chink in Lockwood's armour,' said Vine. 'We have to get the RaSP officers on the FCO detail to give away their location.'

'How?'

'Contact the lead officer over secure channels. Say the Chief of MI6 needs urgent sign-off for a wiretap operation that concerns the safety and security of the Foreign Secretary's family.'

Sutherland saw it now. 'Manipulate the SIGINT protocol.'

'The Foreign Secretary has to personally approve all new wiretaps. You tell the officer that a secure courier will send round documentation. All the detail has to do is provide a location.'

Sutherland looked torn. 'They'll try and delay until morning.'

'Not if you personally make the call. A direct order from the Chief.'

'You realize issuing false information over secure channels could land me in jail.'

'Possibly.'

'But you think I should do it anyway.'

'Being the Chief of MI6 who launched a new war with Russia won't be much fun either,' he said. 'Consider this your chance to rewrite history. Before that history happens.'

Sutherland glanced at Vine and then began slowing. 'On one condition.'

'What?'

'It's your turn to drive.'

Vine took the wheel and Sutherland made the call, her voice never displaying a moment of doubt. She issued the disinformation and was asked to repeat it. The rest of the world seemed to pause as they drove on, waiting in readiness. The uniforms would already be at Smith Street now, Vine knew, searching a house with a husband and children. But no Chief and no prisoner either.

The silence seemed to extend forever when, out of the nothingness, a codename came back. Sutherland ended the call and turned to him. The quiet still lingering.

'CAESAR 4,' she said, at last. 'The summit is being held at the Ritz Hotel.'

The first order of business was, in effect, the simplest. Piccadilly was thronged by the time they approached the Ritz and the famous front steps. The opulence of it all made the reality seem impossible. The secret world intruding upon a fantasy one. Danger was an alien concept amid the chauffeurs and the limos, the flash of cameras, the sparkle of jewels and the playfulness of it all. Here the rest of the world appeared to be forgotten.

Sutherland went through the entrance into the hotel first and Vine followed. He held back once inside and watched as Sutherland approached the reception desk and found the hotel manager. As she followed the plan, Vine moved towards the doors leading through to the piano, afternoon tea, the bar and, beyond that, the dining room. And saw it destroyed, for a moment, the permanence turned to ashes.

EXCALIBUR. Any moment now.

He looked back and watched Sutherland and the hotel manager locked in conversation. Her script was clear and rehearsed, acted out in the car. She gave her credentials – Ministry of Defence rather than MI6, naturally, a card proving the matter – and said she had an urgent message for the RaSP team assigned to protect the Foreign Secretary. Nothing more, nothing less. There was a backup number to confirm should the hotel manager wish.

The hotel manager took the card and called the number and waited as he confirmed her identity. The number led back to a forger team in Vauxhall Cross who manned the phone line in shifts, a backstop for agent-runners and so-called diplomats the world over. Sutherland's cover was verified in every detail. Then, finally, the hotel manager put the phone down and led Sutherland back across the reception floor, the two of them soon disappearing from sight.

Vine continued looking towards the crowds of visitors. Their flutes of champagne, the piano playing mellifluously in the background. The scene so at odds with why he was here, the mucky plumbing of his world. Everything seemed to be calm and glittering. For a solitary moment, Vine wished he could step through the looking glass and join them all. He was sick of this life, tired of secrets, willing it all otherwise. To be a civilian. To be normal. To be other than himself. Free from the burden and the knowledge.

Then, with an appropriate delay, his burner phone pinged.

The first message.

The messages came in quick succession after that, Sutherland texting Vine's burner with the directions and enabling him to follow. Vine had studied a map of the hotel on the way over. He knew they were heading in the direction of the William Kent house located next to the Ritz. It was home to some of the most renowned rooms and deeply private, hidden away from the other guests. The perfect location for a secretive political summit, dodging the glare of press attention.

The next part was logistically complicated but necessary. Vine held off getting too close to Sutherland and the hotel manager. He waited, instead, for Sutherland to perform the final part of her act. A security detail was standing outside the entrance to the house, a collection of RaSP officers and equivalent CPOs from the US side, and Sutherland switched into distraction mode, engaging the senior member of the RaSP team in conversation, both quickly embroiled in confused discussions about messages and letters to sign and instructions needing to be urgently verified.

Which left the back route open. Just as Vine intended and as the plan dictated. The various members of the security detail clustered round now, trying to sort through the confusion. Vine followed the path from the map, a snaking trail that led through the William Kent garden and round to the door of the house itself. Darkness was his ally now. There was no glare, no lights or alarms. Even so, one mistake would announce him. One tiny, sly, human error would unleash their wrath.

He reached the side door and waited. There was still the distant sound of the security teams arguing and Sutherland using the privilege of her position to give as good as she got. The house had no immediate view inside, either, the curtains drawn at each window. Vine took a breath, knowing every part of his analysis had to be correct. One wrong deduction, a flaw of reasoning, and this was it. Custody for him, exile for Sutherland. Both eternally condemned.

As expected, the door to the William Kent house was locked. But the security team outside meant everything was still manual, trusting humans not electronics, impervious to hackers. Vine bent down and used a piece of wire he had extracted from the boot of the car and, thirty seconds later, managed to jimmy it open. The Fort again, like muscle memory, and those tricks of a misspent youth.

According to the map, with every detail safely memorized, the Wimborne Room was before him now. The final door. Open, this time. The cymbal sound of voices inside and Lockwood, the Foreign Secretary, the Defence Secretary and the US National Security Adviser. The summit.

EXCALIBUR.

The end.

60

The first thing Vine noticed as he walked in was how unsurprised Emma Lockwood seemed. He had always mistaken her general demeanour for calmness. But now he realized it was something else entirely – her face existing in a neutral gear, above the petty emotions of others. She was seated at the head of the table, a rucksack next to the table leg beside her. The three others were positioned at different points either side of the table. All looked up now as Vine entered. The Foreign Secretary with her unbreakable calm; the Defence Secretary muscled and combative; the US National Security Adviser the most perplexed, glancing towards the others for a signal how to react.

'Vine,' said Lockwood, absorbing his presence with barely a blink. 'I hate to break the news, but you're not on the invite list.'

The rucksack.

He knew he had only seconds now. He stared at the rucksack more closely. It was the more formal kind, newly bought. Anonymous, but noticeable.

'I'm sorry,' said Lockwood, looking towards her guests. 'Excuse me while I deal with this.'

And yet still he was distracted by Lockwood. He knew the variety of reactions from those he'd apprehended over the years, each one noted and recalled during those wakeful hours when sins rose up and became real again. There was no time to produce the documentary evidence proving treachery. That Lockwood was the mole known by the codename PHOENIX. That she was using this summit as part of a final operation – EXCALIBUR – to launch an attack and propel the West on a path of inescapable conflict with the Russian Federation.

And still the rucksack.

Lockwood was speaking into her phone now. 'Zero Eight, we have an intruder. Yes, this is Red One. Repeat: this is Red One.'

Disbelief, confusion. The seconds draining fast. Other doubles, Vine knew, kicked and screamed. They invoked curses and spells on their accusers. They played the innocence card and tried to laugh off such baseless accusations. Doubles strained every boundary to save themselves. But not her. Not now. She was calm, controlled, normal.

She never took her eyes off Vine, either. He felt her gaze stick to him, knowing the mark would prove indelible. He was drawn in by it, almost captivated, before his senses prevailed and he discarded all thoughts of anything else but the rucksack still in the middle of them all.

The rucksack.

EXCALIBUR.

The rucksack.

Soon this place would be too filled and too packed. Busy with bodies and activity, so many voices crossing each other until nothing could ever be clear again. The cacophony of sound, each tending to their own duties.

Vine rushed forward and did the only thing he could

do. He picked up the rucksack and felt the weight of it. Debating whether to run out until he was in the open air and nearly to safety. Take full control until bomb disposal was called; knowing, or at least hoping, that the last vestiges of his life as a wanted man were now surely over and never to return.

'There's a bomb in this room,' he said, scanning the faces of the four of them. 'You need to evacuate now. This is not a drill. *Move.*'

'Ignore him,' said Lockwood.

Vine looked at the others. Already seeing the lack of fright on their faces. There was bemusement, instead.

The stocky one now, soldierly almost: 'You were in the paper. The *manhunt.*'

And then Vine looked down inside the rucksack. He tried all the compartments, all the pockets, desperate to disprove the evidence in front of him. But there was only a file inside. He took out the file and looked through the pages and saw the handwritten scrawl. Then he looked up at Lockwood, still standing resolutely at the head of the table. He saw the puzzled look of innocence and the sense of shock around them.

There was more noise to her left. 'In here,' she said.

And Vine had only seconds to turn around, seeing the uniformed RaSP officers entering, justice about to be completed. Claire Sutherland, at last, entered the room too. She looked at him first, then turned her eyes on Lockwood. Believing one, distrusting the other.

Vine put the rucksack down and tried to see where the error had crept in. He looked at the people seated around the table – the Foreign Secretary, the Defence Secretary, the US National Security Adviser – and worked through every chain of logic that had brought him to this point.

Something was wrong. Something was very, very wrong.

Vine was about to turn to Lockwood, the pieces still colliding in his head, when he felt a force in his back pushing him to the floor now. The carpet was against his mouth. One of the RaSP officers held him down at the front while another applied the flexicuffs. Everyone in this room was security trained. The first rule was never to try and take out the hostile yourself. Apart from Lockwood, they were all still seated.

'I didn't kill Rashford or Pope,' he said. 'I've been framed.'

'A wonderful story, Vine,' said Lockwood. 'You always were quite the fantasist.'

Sutherland was standing in the doorway, the room turning to her.

'She can vouch for me,' said Vine. 'Wait, she can . . .'

Then he saw it. Sutherland glanced at Lockwood, then back at Vine. Surrounded by the great and the good here. The flicker of belief was waning now, scepticism taking hold again, that moment of indecision and raw, political survival. Finally, Sutherland said: 'Take him.'

As Vine was hauled up, he saw the Defence Secretary reach forward and reclaim his rucksack. Carefully slotting the file back inside. It wasn't a bomb. It wasn't even Lockwood's possession. It was nothing.

Nothing.

The two RaSP officers turned to face Lockwood. For

the first time, Vine caught the millisecond glint of triumph, carefully hidden behind the neutral veneer. 'Move him into the security room,' she said. 'I want two on the door. I'll finish up here and deal with him later.'

Vine looked at her for one last time. Still unable to see his error. Then, like rubbish being removed, he was led away.

61

The security room was based at the back of the William Kent house. It was decked up in makeshift fashion with everything needed for such a confidential summit, including a bank of CCTV cameras and radio links to each of the various protection details. Given this was on UK soil, the RaSP detail was the lead force, in charge of coordinating the security arrangements during the visit of the US National Security Adviser. They were plugged into JTAC and marshalling the combined wisdom of Five, Six and Cheltenham.

Vine was placed in a chair behind a table in the middle of the room. Proper cuffs were applied this time, chaining him there. Cuffs also went on his legs to avoid any theatrics or escape attempts. And now he began to realize his mistake. The fear that had lingered at the back of his mind as the routine had been cycled through at Claire Sutherland's house. Had Claire Sutherland played him? Had she calculated that Vine might overpower a single RaSP officer outside her door and played along to bring him here? Or was it only when the rucksack proved empty that her courage deserted her, going along with Lockwood's order to arrest him, a cowardly dash for safety? Either way, Sutherland had vaulted to the top of Vauxhall Cross by being the expert politician, the chameleon incarnate. She would wash her hands of him now, claim a victory in leading him here to be captured. The Chief proving her field smarts once and for all. She was a survivor. Damn the evidence and the theories.

There was sound outside, and footsteps. One of the RaSP officers opened the door and Emma Lockwood and Claire Sutherland both made their entrance. Behind them, Vine could see handpicked waiters arriving at the William Kent house laden with silver trays. The summit guests could be left to talk among themselves. A tale of two worlds: he sat here shackled; out there, dinner was about to be served.

The door closed again. Lockwood walked over to the bank of CCTV monitors and carefully ensured that the camera link and audio for this room were turned off. Then she took a seat on the opposite side of the table with Sutherland. The two senior members of British intelligence. Two people who could ensure that Vine spent the rest of his life behind bars. Two people who *would* ensure that, if only to protect themselves.

Vine looked at Sutherland, trying to read her. Spot any tells. Still figuring out exactly where he had lost her.

'I hope you've had your fun,' said Emma Lockwood, a note of regret in her voice. 'It may well be the last you have for quite some time.'

He was in legal limbo. That much Vine knew for sure. They had detained him but not officially arrested him. He hadn't been taken down to a police station and he hadn't been given the option of a lawyer. Lockwood had brought Sutherland along to make one thing abundantly clear.

There was no way out of this. No legal chicanery and no fancy footwork. The entire might of the British establishment was ranged against him. For the next few hours, he was in no man's land. Not a citizen with rights and demands, but a disgraced spook, a shadow hunter whose nine lives had finally run out. This was a show of force. A reality check.

'It's clear you need some kind of help,' continued Lockwood. 'To be honest, I should never have brought you back. You went through a lot in your career. More than most people could ever handle. I'm not sure what you hoped to find in that rucksack. But it looked like PTSD symptoms to me. Bombs round every corner. Danger with every house alarm. What was it you called it? Too many bodies, too many assets who never came back. You said yourself that no one survives those traumas unscathed. You're not in a good place, Vine. Medically or otherwise.'

It wasn't the card Vine had expected Lockwood to play. This was for Sutherland's benefit, he was sure. Lockwood's diagnosis sounded reasonable and moderate. The inevitable endpoint for a spy who had seen too much, known too much. He would be carted from here to a secret psychiatric hospital before being deemed fit to stand trial. The rucksack had been too obvious, of course it had. What then?

'There's nothing wrong with my mental state,' said Vine. 'My thinking is as clear as ever.'

That mournful look from Lockwood again. As if this was all regrettable, sad, another consequence of war. 'You inserted yourself into the investigation precisely to clean up your own evidence trail,' she said. 'You were the best counter-espionage mind we ever had. Who better to sell their soul to the Russians and ensure they never got caught? You knew all our tricks. Hell, you even wrote the manual.'

Vine watched Sutherland again now, and tried to figure out what he'd missed. 'I didn't kill Alexander Ivanov,' he said. 'I wasn't behind the murders of Max Rashford or Olivia Pope.'

Lockwood looked weary, checking her watch. One hand clutching the top of her forehead again, the migraine clearly back. Eating away at her eyes. A building, excruciating pain. She battled through, determined not to be put off her stride. 'You wanted revenge on the Service that had cast you into the wilderness. Someone offered you that opportunity and you took it. It was masterful, Vine. But it's over. The sooner you accept that the better.'

Now, at last, it was time for Claire Sutherland to speak. Vine held her gaze. He still couldn't be sure whether she had played him all along or had once believed him. But he hoped it was the latter. Somehow he had to persuade her again.

She said: 'No one wants to see this country embarrassed, Solomon. Enough scandal has already been caused. We've spoken to the Attorney General and the Director of Public Prosecutions. If you agree to confess to everything you've done, Her Majesty's Government is prepared to offer a reduced custodial sentence. The offer is one time only and will never be publicly acknowledged by the Crown Prosecution Service or by HMG. If you refuse, of course, you're on your own. The rest of your life inside.'

So this was it, Vine knew. This was the end. If he confessed to crimes he hadn't committed, he might taste open air again. If he did not, the rest of his days would be spent pacing a cell floor. Solitary, no visitors. An inhuman existence.

'Take the deal,' said Sutherland. 'Use your head and take the deal.'

There was a moment of silence. Terrifying and absolute.

Before, finally, Vine understood the whole damn thing.

62

He didn't say anything at first. Vine went through the logic of it in his head, checking and rechecking, until he was sure he had it. The answer was always in the incidentals, the half-glimpsed detail. He conjured up the scrawl of handwriting in the file he had taken from the rucksack. Memory obscured by the tension of those precious seconds. Then he looked up, staring towards Emma Lockwood this time. Keeping his voice calm, his expression focused. Everything he had always prided himself on: analytical, reasoned, interested only in the truth. Proofs for the ultimate equation.

'It was the wrong type of bomb,' Vine said. The simplicity of it striking him afresh. The answer settling in his head, cursing himself for missing it. He had been right and wrong at the same time. So close and yet so far.

Lockwood glanced at Sutherland, feigning confusion now. The hand at her forehead, blinking her way through. 'Vine,' she said. 'Please tell me you understand what we've just said. This deal is a lifeline. If you refuse it now, it will never be offered again. We are giving you the chance for a reduced sentence if you confess to your involvement with the Russians. You are already a wanted man. *Tell* me this is getting through.'

Vine couldn't resist a small smile now. All the

complications that reason could throw up and yet the ultimate answer was so unavoidably obvious. 'I wasn't wrong about the bomb,' he said. 'My only mistake was what type of bomb it was.'

Sutherland was silent again now. Lockwood's migraine had to be worsening: more glances at her watch, more fidgeting. The pain was drilling away at her head. The stress overwhelming.

'You're not making any sense, Vine,' she said. 'There *is* no bomb. There never was. The bomb and the attack are the illness talking. This summit is one of the most secure places on earth. We have teams of RaSP officers protecting this place to the nth degree. I need to know that you understand the offer we are giving you. I *need* to know you're following this.'

Vine turned his attention to Sutherland once more. Ignoring Lockwood. Trying to verbalize everything he had already deduced. 'It all goes back to the fundamentals of the case,' he said. 'We know Moscow has gone all out on this. Wet work on a media mogul, the Chief of Defence and the Cabinet Secretary. Why? What could the PHOENIX mole know that was so important? What is the *one* thing that still makes the United Kingdom a major intelligence and military power?'

'Was that rhetorical or were you expecting an answer?' said Lockwood, getting up from her seat now, pacing the floor, the migraine taking hold. 'The time for theory is over, Vine. You can't talk your way out of this. *Accept* the deal in front of you.'

'There is only one reason why an island of sixty-seven

million people is still on the UN Security Council,' he said. 'Why we can still hold our own against countries with billions of people. The final legacy of the Second World War that has ensured another century of relevance.' Vine held Sutherland's gaze with his own. 'I was right about the bomb. It's just a *different* kind of bomb.'

Finally, Sutherland spoke again. Quiet, as if processing the information herself. 'Nuclear.'

'The Russians have infiltrated our financial system. They've infiltrated the political system. With the Cambridge Spies, they nearly brought down our intelligence system. But none of that was ever the ultimate goal. The crown jewels. The one secret they would do anything to find. What would happen if the Kremlin infiltrated our *nuclear* system?'

Lockwood, still pacing, turned to Sutherland. 'He's toying with you,' she said. 'Don't indulge him.' She looked at Vine. 'The offer will expire in the next twenty minutes. Take it up or rot in a cell. Flip a coin for all I care.'

Lockwood was already walking towards the door, in obvious difficulty. The migraine splitting through her. Vine watched Sutherland, trying to assess her every movement, knowing that the next second could determine it all. The same moment he'd experienced in the field a hundred times. The handler pitching an asset. Triumph on one side, despair on the other. Life and death hanging in the balance.

'Wait,' said Sutherland, still seated.

She was listening. In that moment, Vine could feel the same buried elation as he had before. The pitch landing, the asset about to step over the line, the seduction and persuasion becoming real. There was a window now.

He made his move. He took out the earbuds from his pocket, hidden neatly enough that the RaSP officers hadn't found them. Vine set them on the table and then pressed the button on the side to play, the correct moment already found. Listening to the words from Sutherland's interview at the very start. Watching as she heard them too.

Moscow already seemed to have its claws in every area of British life. Few areas – only the blockbuster secrets – were still ours.

'You made the point in our first interview,' said Vine. 'But neither of us understood its true significance. P1 and P2 in the transcript Ivanov left behind were Lockwood and her handler preparing for this exact moment. That's what they meant by the big day. That's why the event couldn't be repeated and had to go as planned. Even one of my Russian contacts talked about shock and awe. I thought he was talking about a physical bomb. But they don't have the power to shock any more. He was talking about something much worse. Ivanov found out Moscow had someone inside the operation and he was being betrayed. Rashford had his suspicions too. But it was Pope who went the furthest. She almost solved the whole thing. She didn't reveal her hand to anyone in case they proved to be the insider.'

Sutherland was still listening. 'That's why they all had to be taken out.'

'Yes. The government is replacing the UK's fleet of nuclear weapons, a once in a generation move from the Vanguard class to the Dreadnought class,' he said. 'The designated official in charge of that operation is the National Security Adviser, coordinating intelligence and military wings for the first time. Given the state of our finances, we now rely on the US side to help keep the new nuclear fleet operational. *That* is what this summit is for. *That* is why the Kremlin had to let it go ahead. Tonight is the moment that the US side signs off on the details of the deal. It gives the UK National Security Adviser full power and knowledge over our nuclear secrets for the next fifty years. That's why it was off the books. *Tonight* is the most hallowed prize. They get control over the block-buster secret to end them all.'

Sutherland almost mouthed the word, still not wanting it to be true. 'EXCALIBUR.'

'That is what the entire thirty-year mission has been,' he said. 'EXCALIBUR is the magic weapon that protects the kingdom from all foes. *This* is what it's all been for.'

Vine could feel the impact of the words ricochet around the room. Until he looked at Lockwood, still by the door, and saw her eyes close. Blinded by pain, the stress devouring her. The migraine overwhelming everything else now. In the end so very human.

And, quite suddenly, it happened. Claire Sutherland rose from her seat and Vine felt the suspicion lift from him just as Lockwood pitched forward. Vomiting violently all over the floor. Again and again, racking her body, breaking it. A sickly tidal wave pouring out of her. Forcing her to her knees. Helpless, isolated, desperate.

The pain screaming in her head.

63

Things moved quickly after that. The sickness continued, Lockwood's body heaving until there was nothing left but air. Now occupying the netherworld, a liminal space. The migraine gripping until she was almost paralysed and totally immobile. The summit was hastily disbanded and the guests told to return to their rooms, the Foreign Secretary whisked away by his protection detail and back to the safer enclave of his official residence in Carlton Gardens. Sutherland began taking control now, ensuring that the news wasn't relayed to the Met through the RaSP officers, instead preferring to keep the distribution list as tight as possible. Vine called an ambulance from his personal mobile, the safest way to ensure word didn't get out.

Sutherland made sure Lockwood was being tended to by guards before taking Vine to one side. She said: 'I need you to ride in the ambulance and get a debrief at the hospital bed. I can't give you reinforcements in case of a leak. I need to take it directly to the PM and get authorization from Number 10. This is beyond top secret, Vine. Beyond strap four. Are we clear?'

Vine nodded. 'You realize what we may have just avoided,' he said.

Sutherland looked shell-shocked, unable to comprehend

it all yet. 'There'll be time for celebration. For now, don't let her out of your sight.'

'Of course.'

The ambulance arrived ten minutes after Vine's call and the scene began to fully disperse. Vine watched the paramedics load Lockwood into the ambulance and then forced his way into the back to ride along with them to the hospital. Sutherland stayed behind and continued master-minding operations. As the ambulance began pulling away, Vine looked back at the odd sight of the William Kent house, knowing what had just taken place inside. The silent terror of what could have been.

As the sirens started and the ambulance began slicing through the busy traffic, Vine glanced at Lockwood laid out on the medical bed. Thirty years of hiding in plain sight. One mission, clear and almost impossible. Storing away a secret so vast it could render the defence of an entire state useless. Did that explain the featureless expression and look of serene, almost preternatural calm earlier? Did Emma Lockwood know that the prize would elude her just seconds before she was due to claim it? The scale of the task, the sheer ambition of it, too audacious – too unlikely – in the end. Hubris always punished by the gods.

As the ambulance jerked through the gaps in the traffic, Vine knew various essentials had to be preserved nonethe-less. The last, instinctive ethic of the secret world. It was vital that the paramedics had no idea who their cargo was, nor those at the hospital. The press couldn't be allowed to get wind of what had happened. Sutherland was paranoid over further leaks and rightly so. If this was made public,

Britain's reputation would never recover. Everything, including the seat on the UN Security Council, would be called into question. A mole at this level with their fingerprints on the nuclear codes? There could be no return from that.

Vine turned back to the scene ahead and watched uselessly as the paramedics continued to help Lockwood. The initial steps hadn't worked and now they embarked on another remedy. A needle filled with fluid. They injected Lockwood's right arm solemnly and the plunger was slowly pushed down. Both of the paramedics stood back, eyes unblinking. Like pilgrims before a shrine.

But nothing. Lockwood lay as still as she had been throughout, her body locked. The violence of the attack pushing her beyond her limits. And now Vine felt the shock begin to wear off and something else take its place. He could still feel the weight of the RaSP officers pinning him against the floor, the physicality of what had happened to him only minutes earlier.

Yes, disaster had been avoided. But still they had failed. Her secrets – three decades' worth of them – would disappear with her if she failed to recover properly now. He had been within touching distance of knowledge few spies would ever encounter. The facts beat at him, loud and agonizing, once again.

Emma Lockwood was still paralysed.

That is, until she wasn't.

64

Afterwards, Vine would only remember the events as a blur. The ambulance veered off from the main road, heading away from the hospital. Second, there was activity inside the ambulance itself. The two paramedics hovered busily over the stretcher as Lockwood's body began to stir. A twitch, at first, before it became a spasm. The head jolting backwards and then, from nothing, some movement appearing around the eyes.

The ambulance began speeding up now. The driver accelerating until they were shooting down the side road even faster than before. The sirens still wailing. Vine was about to shout out, to tell them that the driver was heading in the wrong direction, when there was motion on the stretcher again. Colour returning to Lockwood's cheeks. The sound of her breathing. The monitors showing her pulse climbing steadily and the paralysis breaking.

The ambulance veered sharply right, then left. And Vine looked back at the two paramedics, both still fully concentrating on Lockwood, verifying the injection was working. Lockwood's eyes were flickering open now, her hands beginning to move normally. One of the paramedics checked the rest of her face and muscle responses.

The ambulance turned for a final time. The speed picking up again. And Vine did the calculations in his head and understood the route entirely, calculating exactly how much time he had left. The full, horrifying truth – the secret – burning into him now. Sense, at last, prevailing.

He saw it all for the first time. Every detail, every accent had been copied to the highest level of perfection. The paramedic uniforms, the equipment, the way the vehicle was dressed. A piece of stagecraft so immaculate it was invisible to the human eye.

Not salvation, but a living nightmare.

And the very final pieces of it all fell into place. The last remaining data points cohering.

The world was roaring past them now. Tyres squealing on the road. The distant sound and sight of cars and lights. And the rattle as the two paramedics, the two operatives, began unstrapping Emma Lockwood from the stretcher, helping her sit up. Vine knew the door was still locked shut. That everything – the call on his own mobile, keeping the distribution list tight – had been planned to the very smallest detail. His reactions profiled and taken apart. Reason trapped and manipulated. Logic used against him.

One terrifying truth. One inescapable secret.

This wasn't an ambulance at all.

65

He saw Emma Lockwood sit up fully now. Finally, the mask slipping. Her cover wilfully broken.

'Why?' he said. It was all he could say. Nothing else seemed to matter. 'Why?'

'I'm an instrument for my side,' she said, her voice still croaky. 'You're an instrument for yours. The difference between us is just a matter of perspective.'

'No . . . *no*.' Vine kept looking at Lockwood, this new creature inhabiting the features of someone he had once known. This stranger in front of him. He waited – five, four, three – knowing it was down to her to give the final nod. The thumbs up or thumbs down. The ultimate power of life and death.

They were continuing down a side street now. Soon the vehicle would stop and the next phase of the operation would begin. And then he saw it, the flinch, Lockwood nodding to the two men. The attack order. An emperor approving an execution.

'*Go.*'

Vine tried to comprehend what was coming at him, although the profile was as clear as anything. The two men were both special forces trained, of course, veterans of the Thirteenth Department. The Directorate for Special Tasks.

People who had performed this routine many times before. Yasenevo and Moscow Centre's finest.

The people who'd taken out Ivanov, Rashford, Pope. He was just one more victim to add to the roll call of killings. This last piece of theatre, the very final flourish.

The ambulance was slowing now, allowing the two assailants more control. Vine tried to make an initial move, but the first assailant launched at him, using the thick and heavy press of both hands to attempt to subdue Vine. The first assailant was the muscle man, trained to overpower. The second – thinner, a long-distance physique – was the genuine medical practitioner, the person holding the syringe and calculating the exact dose required. Nothing was left to chance. Everything was forensically prepared.

Once the needle hit, Vine knew, it would all be over. The first assailant was pressing harder now, trying to stop Vine kicking and flailing. And Vine could hear the self-defence instructor at the Fort again. Coordination. Use every limb in sync with the other, until the assailant feels attacked from all directions, losing any sense of orientation. Vine was pounding with both fists, using his right knee to smash into the assailant's chest, his left foot to cut upwards into the assailant's back, aiming for the middle of the spine.

The first assailant was unable to stop Vine's wriggling, uncatchable rhythm. The man arced back on top of him and landed the first serious punch, the fist slamming down into Vine's face until it seemed to crack his nose. He barely had enough time to duck away from the second, feeling the fist collide with his jawbone, the sound of another break. Blood, now, smeared and dribbling around his face, his eyes the only thing intact.

It was time. Darkness overtaking him. The other assailant still waiting for the moment to plunge the syringe into his neck. Any second now, though, as Vine saw the first assailant work up towards the next punch. The brutal, final, bloodied effort.

The backup. Yes, any second now.

Vine turned to check it was still in place, just as he had been taught. That brief hiatus at the very start, way back at the house, when he had hauled himself up into the ambulance. Using the memory of basic training again. A lifetime in counter-espionage and the paranoid misery of the field.

The backup. He always had a backup.

An escape route, an emergency number to call, a fake passport primed and ready. There was nothing as elaborate now. Merely a simple stone placed into the jamb of the ambulance door when he had entered and closed it behind him. A small pebble that stopped the ambulance door from locking completely. It was one of the oldest tricks in the book, improvising with anything to hand, a form of divine insurance.

The first assailant was about to strike again. The second assailant had moved round now, ready to jab the syringe through the skin. Vine saw the first assailant poised to pummel his face, when he summoned every last piece of energy he had and kicked at the ambulance doors with both legs. Battering them harder than anything in his life, feeling the bone in both legs crunch at the impact.

The sound was changing too now. The riot of the outside world feeding in through the ambulance. The right-hand door flying open, the stone theory working. Vine kept his foot in place to stop the door shutting again and used the millisecond of distraction. The move had created enough space to prepare fully for what came next. The first assailant smashed down into his face again; Vine avoided the worst of the blow by rolling sideways. And, before the second assailant struck, a gap in time emerged to make his last move.

Vine rolled his body until it built a momentum of its own. He felt the sheer drop of the open air, the speed at which the ambulance was catapulting forward. The movement was unstoppable now, despite the attempt of the first assailant to hold his legs. Vine was clawing free – every last bloodied piece of flesh – as he felt the roadway burn horribly beneath his body, skinning him alive as the speed of his exit met the hardness of the tarmac. Until, right there, the pain was almost deafening.

The ambulance was still speeding off ahead. Unable to stop. And the world was becoming lighter now. The next stage would be seamless and planned to the final degree. The exfil was almost complete. The last part of the operation to spirit the PHOENIX mole to safety nearly done.

The road was empty and Vine lay there for a second. He felt only the hot, acidic pain over his body and the agony on his skin.

He lay there and wondered if he was still alive.

And, for a moment, if he still wanted to be.

66

It was all too late by the time reinforcements arrived, the operation vanishing before them. The police cars and blacked-out vehicles covered the street, but there was no trace. The whole thing spotless, rehearsed to the second. Vine gave full descriptions of the two people he had seen: the operatives play-acting as paramedics. He walked through the statement with a detective inspector, and then repeated it for various officers from Thames House. All the while, he looked up at the stars speckled above him and saw the world stare back accusingly.

The initial part of the process was soon over. The 'package' referred to in the P1 and P2 transcript had clearly been an enhanced version of the 'sick pill', a medical device to induce sudden and authentic illness, distributed to all sleepers and illegals hidden behind enemy lines. The imaginary migraine episodes, then, were legend-building at its best. Vine watched as uniformed police and plainclothes spooks trawled the scene to see if they could recover anything more. A forensic team patiently excavating each step. An MI5 officer reported that CCTV had tracked the ambulance to the Russian embassy at Kensington Palace Gardens and, from there, to a private diplomatic flight out of the country. Lockwood and her accomplices were already untouchable. Far, far beyond reach.

Vine sat there now looking at the street and cursed them all. He cursed Lockwood herself for the betrayal. He cursed the people around him. And, above all else, he cursed himself. It had been that moment of empathy, the twinge of the human spirit, that had given Lockwood her opportunity. His logic and order and patterns predicted and manipulated.

The proper medics arrived soon after and Vine received some rudimentary medical attention for his injuries. His body was still raw with pain. The breeze beat at his face and he had to tear himself away from the sight ahead and the memories crowding in, all of them useless now.

She was gone.

67

Afterwards, he was driven back to Vauxhall Cross where he recovered and nursed his injuries. He lay awake all night, unable to settle. He woke early and emerged again as dawn broke and saw another car was waiting for him. Official this time, a Jaguar XJ from the government car-pool. Vine was ushered into the back seat and then driven in silence to Whitehall.

As the morning sparked into life, they drove into Number 10 by the private entrance with just the briefest glimpse of the Treasury and the start of St James's Park. Once inside, Vine was escorted to a secure room in the depths of the Cabinet Office, another journey underground. The greetings this time were muted, but respectful. Claire Sutherland nodded and shook hands. James Norris muttered something about an eventful night. Coffees were poured for all three of them. Then, at last, they got down to business.

'Firstly, I want to thank you for the work you've done,' said Norris. He sounded different now, the extravagance dimmed slightly. The new Cabinet Secretary – confirmed via press release that morning – was presenting an official face to the world. 'We should have listened to you, Vine. Both of us. If we had, perhaps last night's events might never have occurred. You were the one who uncovered the PHOENIX mole. You spurred the Russians into action. They knew our weaknesses and they used them. We were blind, not you.'

Vine was surprised at their generosity. He could still feel the weight of it all, as if his very essence had been split. But they were wrong, naturally. 'Thank you,' he said.

It was Claire Sutherland's turn now. All distant charm, as if her moment of indecision at the house never happened, unable to ever apologize. She spoke in her recruiter voice, leaning forward and looking at him directly, like a handler sweet-talking a new asset. 'We asked you back here to consider a proposal,' she said. 'We know the Centre fears you. That much is clear from the events of the last few hours. And we, above all, want to use that fear. Show that our side won't back down. After much discussion, I – *we* – want you back at the Service full time.'

Vine let the news land. He was still angry at Sutherland for doubting him. Now, though, he wondered if this was an even worse punishment. A return from exile. 'In what capacity?' he said.

'Your old job. The job you should never have left. We need a head of counter-espionage at Vauxhall Cross who strikes terror into the hearts of agents-in-place wherever they may be. You're the best mole-hunter we have and the threats are growing more intense by the day. Patriotism never quite did it for you, I know. But consider this an official request.'

Head of counter-espionage at Vauxhall Cross. Mole-hunter in chief. The mission he had always wanted to complete ever since being turfed out unfairly and condemned to wander the earth. Now welcomed back to do what had to be done. But Vine felt that old impatience rise again. He wasn't interested in positions. The present, not the future. 'And what about Emma Lockwood?' he said. 'I was told a diplomatic flight left yesterday evening?'

It was Norris's turn again. 'Yes. Last night, Russian officials flew two planes out carrying numerous urgent items classified as part of the diplomatic bag. They included a large black plywood box supposedly for a music speaker. Thanks to the Vienna Convention, we were legally unable to interfere.'

'Big enough to hide someone inside,' said Vine. 'To risk that, the order must have come from the very highest levels. The top of the Kremlin.'

'Indeed.' Norris opened up a file in front of him and took out a briefing paper, sliding it across the table. 'In fact, more analysis has been worked up in the last few hours by GCHQ and other intelligence teams on Emma Lockwood's air-gapped private computers. We've also had teams going through her record as National Security Adviser and her recruitment history. This is only the first result. But, as you'll see, it provides a convincing lead.'

Vine picked up the briefing paper and began flicking through. 'You've found something more?'

Norris nodded. 'According to the Rosenholz Files, as you know, Lockwood was recruited and run out of East Germany in the late eighties. The KGB used the Stasi as cover. As the files show, such a scalp wasn't run from the East Berlin office, as would be expected, but from

Dresden. More private, more secure.' Norris paused, as if gathering his thoughts. 'At this point, we have particular interest in one individual from that period. The Stasi liaison officer for the KGB in Dresden in '88. We believe he was Lockwood's first handler. A graduate of Leningrad University and the Red Banner academy who ran sleepers at the time.' Norris paused again, as if nervous of articulating it. 'The name will no doubt be familiar to you.'

Vine didn't follow at first. The riddle and the hint. Norris pushed across two other documents. Now, though, the last piece of the puzzle finally slotted into place. Vine glanced down at the papers and saw the name and the photo. A face so infamous, then so ordinary. A minor player in a grand geopolitical war. The first document showed the photo of a Stasi identity card. At the top it read: 'Ministerrat der Deutschen Demokratischen Republik'. Beneath that was 'DRESDEN' and a signature. Vine turned to the next document. It was dated 8 February 1988 and was an order from Erich Mielke, then chief of the Stasi, conferring an honour on one of his men: 'BRONZE MEDAL OF MERIT OF THE NATIONAL PEOPLE'S ARMY'. Vine looked at the anonymous photo on the first page and then back again at the name that ran like granite across the second. Still trying to take it all in.

The Stasi liaison officer for the KGB. Nineteen eighty-eight. Dresden.

The man who cultivated and ran the PHOENIX asset. The thin cheeks and sallow complexion; the beady, calculating eyes and pouty lips. He was weightier now, puffed up by the grandeur of office.

Emma Lockwood's first handler.

ARTHUR himself.

Vine read the name out loud. 'Major Vladimir Vladimirovich Putin,' he said. His last questions disappeared. Everything now made horrible, visceral sense. The scale, the ambition, the exfil, the flight using diplomatic protocols. It all fit with this one last piece of secret history.

'Putin was Lockwood's first handler,' said Norris now. 'He was the Stasi liaison officer who ran her out of Dresden. He knew her from the very beginning.'

Vine was still churning through it. 'You're sure this is real? Not another fake from Department 2?'

'As sure as we can be,' said Norris. 'Added to that, we believe that Lockwood was only the tip of the iceberg. According to what we've discovered so far, she could have been part of a much larger ARTHUR network operating in the West. Long-term penetration agents planted during the dying days of the Cold War by Line N of the First Chief Directorate. Putin's secret weapons. Still run to this day from the highest ranks of the Kremlin.'

Vine suddenly felt stifled by the room. He needed air. Some space away from this. He choked out the words: 'If that's correct, what would my new assignment be?'

Sutherland took charge again. 'If you agree to return to the Service, you'll head up the counter-espionage efforts to roll up the rest of the ARTHUR network,' she said. 'That will be your specific and only assignment. That means targeting every sleeper planted within British intelligence no matter how high up and no matter how far back. A full reckoning. You might be our only shot at cleaning the stables and putting your old Service back together again.' She paused, staring at him frankly. 'We need you, Solomon. Now more than ever.'

68

Vine was escorted to the car and asked the driver to head to Chelsea. At Wellington Square, he checked the house was still intact and then showered and ate properly for the first time in too long. He brewed gallons of strong black coffee and toured the house again, glad to be back where he belonged. Everything was dancing before him: Lockwood lying there, the ambulance, the agony of the impact on the road. The photo on that piece of paper, ARTHUR. The scale of it all. His body ached and his legs were numb and he longed more than anything to retire to his library and shut the rest of the world out entirely.

The hours ticked by, but Vine seemed oblivious. As the deadline loomed, he felt the decision clarify in his mind. Emma Lockwood could be in Moscow soon. Housed, praised, decked with medals. Living out her days under a different sky. Like Kim Philby before her, a curio to be paraded and exhibited to the Centre's new recruits, a lesson for both sides.

His reverie was broken as the alarm sounded and Vine knew, reluctantly, that his time was up. He found another burner and dialled the secure number. It was answered on the third ring.

'So?' the voice said. Norris, now, the new boss. The Whitehall ruler. 'Do you have an answer?'

One last chance for freedom. This, still, was the moment he could turn away. Vine thought of that brief dream again at Hanslope, the small flat in the countryside somewhere, counting down his days in peace. Putting all of this behind him.

'I want a new role,' he said, at last. 'My own team outside official channels. Beyond Five, Six, Cheltenham and the MoD, beyond them all. I want a dedicated unit to hunt down the ARTHUR network. I get to pick the people. It would have no outside interference and be completely free from political control.'

Silence, then: 'That's your final decision?'

Run, Vine told himself, run and never look back. 'Yes,' he said.

He heard the rest without properly listening. The congratulations, the next steps, the system clicking into place with its smooth official glide. After five minutes, the call ended and Solomon Vine stood by the window and looked out over Wellington Square. This neat hideaway, this quiet idyll. There was peace for a moment. The world seemed to stop and the details intruded. The grass, the silence, the anonymous figures going about their day.

Twenty minutes later, he saw a car pull in from the King's Road down below. Official, waiting in readiness for his answer, like an echo of the one before. An envoy calling him back to the only life he'd ever known.

The next operation had already begun.

Acknowledgements

My thanks, as always, to all my family: my father, John, my siblings, Peter and Sarah, and to Mary. A particularly special thank you to my mother, Ruth, who inspired me through her own extraordinary gift for storytelling and has acted with tireless dedication as researcher, proofreader, editor and chief of morale. No one has suffered through more of my writing over the last two decades than she has. For such a feat of lifetime endurance, my eternal and never-ending love and thanks. And to my wider family and friends – from all corners of the UK – whose support has meant so much.

Huge thanks to my agent Euan Thorneycroft at A. M. Heath, Richenda Todd for such immaculate copy-editing, and Ruth Atkins, Ariel Pakier, Nick Lowndes, Laura Nicol and Rowland White at Penguin for getting this book on to the shelves. Thanks also to Helen Piper for advice on forensics, Stuart Gibbon for help with police procedure, and to Conrad Williams and Louisa Minghella at Blake Friedmann for their incredible work and support on the screenwriting side. And to George, Fiona and all the team for being such great colleagues and friends. It's a pleasure working with you.

Interweaving fact and fiction is one of the great joys of writing thrillers. For more on the real-life Rosenholz

Files see: 'End the secrecy about British Stasi spies' by Ben Macintyre in *The Times* (23 March 2019). For more on Putin and his KGB posting in Dresden see: *Putin's People* by Catherine Belton, *Russians Among Us* by Gordon Corera and *From Russia with Blood* by Heidi Blake.

A final thanks to those who supported and championed *My Name is Nobody.* The list is too long to name everyone. But an honourable mention must go to Tim Shipman and Nick Quantrill for so generously supporting the book on Twitter, Fiona Sharp for hosting a signing session at Waterstones Durham, Ian at Rother Books in Battle, East Sussex, for promoting the book, Bob McDevitt for inviting me to the Bloody Scotland festival, and to the exciting new writing talent and future thriller bestseller Matthew Thomas. To them and to so many other kind and wonderful souls – thank you!

He just wanted a decent book to read ...

Not too much to ask, is it? It was in 1935 when Allen Lane, Managing Director of Bodley Head Publishers, stood on a platform at Exeter railway station looking for something good to read on his journey back to London. His choice was limited to popular magazines and poor-quality paperbacks – the same choice faced every day by the vast majority of readers, few of whom could afford hardbacks. Lane's disappointment and subsequent anger at the range of books generally available led him to found a company – and change the world.

'We believed in the existence in this country of a vast reading public for intelligent books at a low price, and staked everything on it'
Sir Allen Lane, 1902–1970, founder of Penguin Books

The quality paperback had arrived – and not just in bookshops. Lane was adamant that his Penguins should appear in chain stores and tobacconists, and should cost no more than a packet of cigarettes.

Reading habits (and cigarette prices) have changed since 1935, but Penguin still believes in publishing the best books for everybody to enjoy. We still believe that good design costs no more than bad design, and we still believe that quality books published passionately and responsibly make the world a better place.

So wherever you see the little bird – whether it's on a piece of prize-winning literary fiction or a celebrity autobiography, political tour de force or historical masterpiece, a serial-killer thriller, reference book, world classic or a piece of pure escapism – you can bet that it represents the very best that the genre has to offer.

Whatever you like to read – trust Penguin.